Five Pillars

A Journey Through the Modern Muslim World

By Ali Nazar

ISBN: 0692225919
ISBN 13: 9780692225912

Speak

Speak, for your two lips are free;
Speak, your tongue is still your own;
This straight body still is yours –
Speak, your life is still your own.

See how in the blacksmith's forge
Flames leap high and steel grows red,
Padlocks opening wide their jaws,
Every chain's embrace outspread!

Time enough is this brief hour
Until body and tongue lie dead;
Speak, for truth is living yet –
Speak whatever must be said.

Faiz Ahmed Faiz

Introduction

Sufis say that there are two truths - one with a big 'T' and many with a little 't', and that all the little truths are but different roads leading to the one big Truth. I believe this, and believe that there are as many of these roads as there are humans that have ever existed because of one simple fact: every human is unique.

Maybe that's why he came to me. Now that I think about it, he's always been there - shadowing my dreams, lurking in his green nooks and crannies. Crouched behind Oscar's garbage can in my Sesame Street versus Fragglerock third grade daydreams. Or in that tidal wave nightmare that plagued my high school years, the one where San Francisco's skyscrapers are swallowed by a gigantic tsunami that blows through the Golden Gate, I'm pretty sure he was the person I always ran to, towards the redwood grove at the base of the Transamerica building. It would be just like him – close but not too close. Helping but not telling.

The man I speak of has many names, but in Arabic his name is *Al-Khizr*, which means the Green Ancient. His mission from God is to help his fellow humans – to make sure we don't lose sight. He is a living saint - a dynamic dervish who has seen it all and presses on, hoping to ease suffering and spread knowledge in his personal quest that is destined to play out until the end of days.

He's at every conflict, subtly working his angles in an unending bid to ease suffering. That's what he hates most I think – suffering. If I could be so bold as to guess, I think that our grief is what ultimately drives him. He knows the Truth behind this world, and I think it kills him that we consistently stray. Suffering is so unnecessary, so uneducated, he must think. The right path is often the easiest, he might say.

He has lived a long time. Too long, in fact. Longer than any other man. Khizr, you see, is the only man to have drunk from the Fountain of Youth. It's true. This privilege (if you can call it that) was bestowed upon him in the time of the Greeks, when Alexander's hubris drove him to find the one thing that eluded his all-powerful grasp.

Immortality.

But Alexander failed in this quest. He became too cocky – too greedy. Khizr was his confidante, his *consigliore* if you will, and instead of Alexander, it was he who stumbled upon the mythical stream. And Khizr tasted it, not knowing that it would relegate him to a lifetime of earthly eternity, roaming this world as a go-between for man and God.

So now he has lived for multiple millennia. During his travels he has learned the secrets of the world - of Mother Nature's unrivaled perfection and of man's tortured soul. I'm sure he could talk at great length about his knowledge, but that's not his style. He chooses to appear in the mundane, helping people who don't know they need help. To press the smallest of history's levers so that he may ease man's suffering, if only a little at a time.

Maybe he puzzles with trivial matters so that he can have some small victories in the face of growing losses. Or maybe it's more than just style – perhaps that is the nature of his agreement with Above. Maybe he isn't allowed to write a book or make a movie. It would certainly be easier for him, I think, to teach people that way.

Instead, he came to me.

Chapter 1

My American Dream

The T.V. talking heads were at it again, postulating about the hearts and minds of the Muslim world.

"We must understand the man on the street's viewpoint," said the liberal bald white guy in a grey suit. "This is a battle for hearts and minds."

"Of course," said the conservative old white guy with saggy shoulders in the dark suit. "But we already are winning their hearts – in fact, it is only a small portion of the Muslims who are the terrorists. This small minority is intent on hating us and our freedoms. The rest of them love us – I know this for a fact. The Saudis– they drive American cars and buy American products, just like everyone else in the world. They want to be just like us."

I sat on my couch watching, wondering if that dope knew how it felt to be anything but a big bag of hot air. My annoyance grew, but my masochistic side prevented me from changing the channel.

The Washington insider shows had long ago become more numbing than informative for me, but I couldn't help but watch. I would tune out their voices, only looking at their faces and gauging the earnestness with which they plied their points. Most of the liberals seemed genuine, if ill informed, but every once in a while some Fox News type guy would have the slightest of smirks as he talked about the day's battlefield news, the we're-really-kicking-some-A-rab-ass kind of smirk, and it would get me riled up.

I changed the channel and found another one, discussing the virtues of invading Iran with a caller from Mississippi. This'll be choice, I thought, but as I turned up the volume to prepare for a classic redneck rant, I heard my name called.

"Mo!"

I was startled and turned my head to see Odessa, clad in only a towel and a look of exasperation.

"Mo! I've been calling you for five minutes now. You're such a space cadet!" she exclaimed with an annoyed laugh. "I just wanted to tell you that I'm almost outta here – my shift starts in an hour. I've got to jump in the shower unless you want to, uh, you know…" She smiled and waited for me to get up, but I just sat there, staring right through her. The T.V., which was at high volume, was in rare form.

"Well, you know sir, I just think that the way to solve all these problems is to really kick some ass with the Marines. I mean, let the bastards see us up close in an armored Humvee – I bet those I-raneians would think twice about attacking us then!"

As the realization that I was ignoring her advance set in, Odessa spun and exited the room in one quick motion, leaving me back to my caller from Mississippi and the tail end of an attack that had now devolved into an assault on Hilary Clinton. I clicked away, surfing around aimlessly on a Sunday morning.

My inner voice, the one shaped from growing up in the heart of San Francisco, began to scold me. A few years ago, it said, you would never have turned someone like Odessa down. In high school, it said, you would have thought your life today to be the pinnacle of existence.

I had money. Growing up in the Bay Area during the end of the 20th century was a good thing – people were making money at crazy levels, everywhere. Major in computer science, and you were guaranteed to be making six figures within a few years of graduating. I had made that plus much more in my six years of work – an IPO had gotten me two million dollars at my first job out of school. At twenty-seven years old I had bought a house in San Francisco for myself and a Cadillac for my parents, and I felt as though I could never want for anything for the rest of my life.

My house was a beautiful two bedroom right above the south end of Dolores Park - with a sparkling view of the Mission, downtown, the Bay Bridge, and Oakland, shimmering across the bay. It was an old Victorian with sculpted moldings and gargoyles on the corners – the kind of house that made me think of Dirty Harry and Joe Montana and all things San Francisco. I rode a vintage Triumph 450 all over the city, zipping from activity to activity with a girl on the back and a plan to wreck havoc in the works. Almost every close friend in my life lived close by, and my social schedule was packed to the brim with parties and trips and dinners and games.

And I had time. At twenty-eight, I found myself jobless, my department being among the first to be outsourced to India after the bust. At first, I was ecstatic – ever since I had made the big money, I hadn't felt the passion for work that I had felt before. My whole life had been the one of an immigrant's son, obligated to validate your parent's move to America by making good on the opportunities given to you. I had not stopped, through school, college and work, achieving at a high level, always afraid that I would let my parents down in the end, if I didn't turn out to be something big.

But, after the ups and the downs and the eventual payout, I had a clear schedule for the first time since kindergarten, and I resolved to take some time and indulge. For six straight months I had lived completely according to my whims - I surfed, took road trips, played in a punk band, and read everything I could about Islam, the war, and politics. It had been a good six months, but the incongruence of my lifestyle began to wear on me, and Odessa had become the symbol of this unhappiness.

She was the curvy-hipped blonde waitress at a hip sushi joint on Valencia Street. I had come in a few months back, high rolling with some friends from out of town, and had somehow gotten her to party with us after she got off. We'd been dating ever since – I liked the fact that she didn't want a serious relationship and she liked the fact that I lived right up the hill from her work, so she didn't have to worry about getting back to Oakland after work anymore.

But, we both knew our relationship was a sham, and just as a new talk show was starting in about Russia's problems with the Chechnyans, Odessa came storming back into the room, fully dressed and with her backpack on. She came between me and the T.V., and I could see the chip on her shoulder and the fire in her eyes. Her cheeks were a little flushed from the shower she had just taken, and her hotness made me consider what an idiot I was to have pissed this one away so quick.

"Mo - we need to talk. You and I – well, this isn't really working out, is it? I mean, who are we kidding, huh?"

I felt that I should at least offer some defense. "Oh, come on, O. Don't get so pissed – I'm sorry, ok? You know I love the Sunday morning shows – I was just kinda zoned out."

She rejected my lame excuse. "Forget it Mo – you and I have avoided talking about our relationship because we both knew that the minute we talked about it we would kill it. So, here I am, officially killing it. You and I worked as long as it stayed fun – you know, Mo and O, O and Mo and all that crap. It was cute, but lately it hasn't been. I've had a good time with you Mo, but it's over. Later dude."

I was so impressed with her decisiveness that I easily relented, taking her peck on the forehead with eyes closed and then watching her hourglass figure swing down my hallway, one last time. In her wake, I realized that I had not left the couch during the entire breakup, and I began to wonder just what kind of person I was becoming.

I turned to my laptop for distraction. Ever since I had stopped working, computers had begun to feel toxic to me, but email is a chore that can't be put off for too long. This session immediately rewarded me – I had a letter from my favorite uncle, Yousuf Mamu, whom my brothers and I called YuMa for short.

YuMa was my Dad's younger brother. While most of my parents' siblings had followed my parents' lead and established home bases outside of Pakistan, YuMa had been the only one to return to Pakistan. His emails to me had become more frequent and deep in the years since the towers had fallen in New York.

YuMa had left Pakistan in the sixties and gotten a medical degree in London. Through the seventies he had built a successful practice, one that enabled him to buy a house in England and a house in Karachi's exclusive Defence neighborhood. His wealth grew, but he often told me he had never felt at home in the West, where he said that 'everyone had so much wealth but such little faith.' All told, I think he spent twelve years in the West, never marrying and saving up a small fortune.

When the war broke out on Pakistan's western border, between Afghanistan and the U.S.S.R. in 1979, YuMa's idealism got the better of him, and he chucked his Paddington medical practice to go straight to the battlefield. He served as a doctor in Afghanistan's pan-Islamic resistance to the Soviets, the *Mujahideen*. I was a little kid then, and I remember my Dad would always sound worried when he talked long distance with his brothers and sisters on Sundays, complaining about the infrequency of YuMa's calls from the front.

But I had always found him to be the coolest - his stories had always been the stuff of cloak and dagger to me. Fighting from mountaintops, double agents and double crosses, of bringing down state-of-the-art Commie-bastard-helicopters with nothing more than a machine gun and praise for Allah. It was a source of pride for me – growing up in the Cold War, it was my duty as an American to despise the Soviets. I used to tell my friends in grade school about my valiant uncle, on the front line, fighting the good fight in a united Muslim/American war for goodness and decency against the Godless Ruskie heathens. Those were the days to be an American Muslim.

YuMa had stayed until 1987, near the end of the war, rejoicing with his comrades in Kabul at the imminent defeat of the Soviet empire. But, as the victorious Mujahideen descended into civil war between warlords and factions, my uncle quickly became disillusioned and moved back to Pakistan and settled in Karachi. He started a clinic, where he provided basic healthcare to the poor and underprivileged of the city. His investments in the West sustained his good deeds in the East, and for the last fifteen years he had expanded his clinic to be one of the largest charity organizations in the city, delivering food and medicine to thousands of people in need.

YuMa had never married, the worry of a wife and children much too cumbersome for his idealistic pursuits. He lived his life in study and service, his revolutionary heart keeping him true to the cause and to the religion he served. In recent years YuMa's mother, my Dadi-jaan, had moved in with him, after years of house surfing the globe from one child's house to the next. She too had tired of living in the West, and as she neared her own end preferred to be back in her own country. Together, YuMa and Dadi-jaan lived as they chose, firmly in the homeland, both protecting their values in their own ways.

His letters to me had always come regularly – first in long hand, every six months or so in the 80s and early 90s. He loved to tell stories, and he loved to write. Sometimes, you could tell that the letters weren't just to you – they just needed to be written, for YuMa's sake. With the advent of email and my arrival into adulthood, his messages came more frequently, every month or so. Recently, they had begun to focus more on religion, though, as it seemed he was trying to engage me on a deeper level.

His email began as he always did:

Dearest Nephew,

Salaams! I hope this letter finds you well - your spirits up and your mind occupied.

I haven't heard from you in a while, and I can't help but wonder what it means. I can only hope that you are busy plotting and planning to take advantage of this fine opportunity you have in front of you. You are young, you have time, and there's much to be done - the sky's your limit, really. *Subhan'allah*!

Back in your homeland of Pakistan, things are getting better. We are actually starting to see the benefits of Musharraf selling our souls to the U.S. - buildings are going up, and so is the stock market. I am seeing improvement for even the lowest strata of society - there is more food and less need for medicine, even for the beggars.

The political situation is not so good, but I ask you, when has it ever been? We still have the Wahabbis to deal with. There are still bombings and violence – the *Sip-e-Sehaba* are still running their ruinous operations. There was a bombing two weeks ago, not four blocks from my office! The bastards just won't quit – I fear that their will is stronger than ours, and if we don't fight, they will win.

It is not the West that can save Islam, my young Nephew, it is clearly the Muslims' own duty. The tyranny of the Wahabbis must be met with an even stronger thrust of love and compassion, coming from the true Muslims, the ones who do not judge but who are humble and forgiving. These Muslims are the true followers of the *din*, not these crazed suicide bombers that will blow up schools and mosques out of pure hatred.

But, you know that, of course, because you are my Nephew. My wonderful brother's son, the one who is my favorite. I miss you, Mohammed-jaan – you should come here for a visit. You can do so much good here, so much more than ever could be done back in your Babylon.

Come home to Pakistan – Dadi-jaan and I are waiting for you. If you can't do that, you should at least write, don't you think?

Love,
YuMa

I started to reply but got stuck after 'Dearest YuMa'. There was so much I wanted to say to him, but it was so much easier to go silent – to just forget about it all and to get drowned in the day-to-day distractions of my charmed American life. I knew I should be doing something, anything, but with no plans of any consequence I felt anything I would or could say to YuMa would either be a lie or a disappointment, so I sat there, writing nothing.

I was granted a reprieve when the phone rang.

Chapter 2

Ballgame

'I knew you'd still be at home," said the voice, which I did not recognize as Toby's until he qualified this first statement with, "you idiot."

"Crap," I said, "what time is it?"

"It's 12:45, dude – get your ass down here." Toby was mildly annoyed that I had forgotten about the Giants game. "I just parked at South Park – it's 75 and sunny. Perfect weather to kick some Dodger ass, don't you agree?"

"Sorry man – I'm out the door. See you at the Seal in fifteen minutes." I threw my glove, hat, and jacket in my bag, fired up the Triumph and raced out into a warm San Francisco day. I sped along the city streets, splitting lanes and tempting fate at every traffic jam and intersection. I glided by the 500 Club, where I had met and broke up with Amy, the one long term girlfriend of my life. I gunned it around the detour at Kelly's Mission Rock, where I had danced away my early twenties with E and Charlie. By the time I arrived at the Lefty O'Doul Bridge, I had passed the last eight years of my wonderful, San Francisco life, and I was feeling pretty good.

I parked the bike at 2nd and King and walked around back to McCovey Cove, where the bronze seal statue (built to commemorate the San Francisco Seals of the 40s and 50s) on the east end of the cove had been my crew's official meeting place since the park opened, in 2000. Toby was leaning on a railing a ways back from the statue, looking out over the bay towards Oakland and smoking a cigarette. He looked like he always did – tall and lanky, with his kneecap spiderweb tattoos showing beneath his torn jeans and his trademark Carhart sweatshirt unzipped and flapping in the breeze.

We had all adhered to a pre-cursor of his look, back in the late 80s, when Toby and I and all of our friends were playing punk rock shows during our teens. But, while most of us had left that lifestyle behind, Toby had perfected it. He had become a full time musician, singing in three different bands in the last ten years and getting a record contract with his latest gig, a swing band. He still lived the life of a rock star – mostly nocturnal, fast, furious, and full of benders.

But, no matter how divergent our lives were, we had always had baseball to keep us close – Toby and I had been on the same little league team when we were seven. I caught his attention, slapped him five, and we went in through the back gate, up the stairs and in to the left field bleachers, ten rows behind Barry Bonds.

The game progressed quickly – both teams had their aces going, and they threw matching zeros for the first five innings. Toby and I managed to keep up with the pace of the action, drinking a beer per inning and getting sauced pretty quickly in the hot bleacher sun. Between plays we caught up, mostly talking about his band and their touring exploits. They had just been in Europe, and Toby's main story centered around two girls he had met in a tulip field in Holland.

The crowd all around us was in fine form – everyone was in shades and shorts, on a high from the weather and the game. The Dodger's left fielder was being ridiculed and cursed in every possible manner, including the old SF favorite where one man screams:

"What's a matter with (insert name or uniform number here, in this case it was Finley)?"

While the rest of the crowd yells, "HE'S A BUM!"

We were into it, and in the bottom of the 5th the Giants busted through, batting around, plating seven runs and touching off a big party in our section. The next inning Barry hit a grand slam and everyone went nuts. When we settled down, we suddenly realized that we were hungry, out of beer, and watching an 11-0 yawner. We decided to get some Cha Cha bowls at Orlando's BBQ in centerfield and sit behind the scoreboard, away from the sun, so that we could replenish our energy with some jerk chicken, beans, rice and Red Stripe.

"So," said Toby, as he loaded up on three different kinds of BBQ Sauce, all approved by the Baby Bull himself, "Uh, Mo, um – I've been meaning to talk to you. About Islam and terrorism and all that shit – I just can't get my head around it."

"Yeah – whaddya wanna know?" I loved where this was going, and as we sat down to eat I plunged into the chicken, trying to eat a lot upfront so that I was free to extemporize at length later.

"Well," began Toby, his lack of confidence in the subject matter oddly amusing to me, "you know that bombing last week, where all those innocent people died – what's up with that, man? I knew someone who died – I was in a band with him a while back and we had stayed in touch. It's messed up man. I don't get it." He took a bite of rice and beans from the bowl before continuing. "And every time one of these things happen, you hear the same thing over and over again – Qu'ranic verses found, tape from Al Qaeda, Abu so and so left a paper trail or some shit like that. I don't want to be hating on your people, bro – but how can a religion sanction such heinous carnage? You are the only Muslim I know, so I figured you could enlighten me, you know?"

Toby's expression was sincere – his look searching. It wasn't the first time I had been given the 'you're the only Muslim I know' line, and Toby was an old friend whose opinion I truly valued. I wanted to set him straight.

"Well," I said, "I'm sorry about your friend – I really am. This war is senseless – terrible. People are dying, people are getting rich, people are suffering – I really can't say anything that can make all that better. But I can tell you that Islam has many faces, and unfortunately one of those is this terror you talk about. It is ruthless – they have killed many innocent people and have been doing it for years, since long before September 11th."

There was a big roar from the crowd, and we paused to catch the T.V. replaying the Giants turning a double play to get out of the top of the 7th with the shutout intact.

"Nice! A shutout will do wonders for our pitching staff's morale – they've been sucking it up recently." I said, between swigs of the Red Stripe.

"Yup yup," said Toby, "So anyway – getting back, what are you saying about before September 11th? Are you talking about that bombing Al Qaeda did of the U.S. embassies in Africa in the 90s?" Toby was obviously intent on pressing the conversation back to Islam. "You mean the one where Clinton volleyed a bunch of missiles into Afghanistan in retaliation for, but then ended up just pissing them off that much more?"

"Right – that was another battle too," I said, gaining momentum slowly. "But that was still a battle in *this* war, the one between the West and the fanatics. These crazies have been after other people before – for practically the whole 90s they reaped terror throughout Pakistan against other Muslims. Shias – which is what my family is. The Shia, or Shi'ite as they are sometimes referred to, are the largest minority sect of Islam, while the majority sect is Sunni." I took a bite to allow Toby to process. The Cha Cha bowls were sobering us up a bit, and as he gave an understanding nod I continued.

"These nuts are a fanatical subset of Sunni Muslims, relatively new to the game in terms of history. Islam is almost 1500 years old, but they've only been around for maybe 200 years. These guys are evil, and they have a name." A pitching change was being announced over the loudspeaker, and as the crowd quieted down, I lowered my voice to a more conspiratorial tone. "They are called Wahabbis."

Toby smiled. "Kind of like wasabi, huh? Whaaaaahhhhaaaaaabbiiiii!"

"Yeah – but with an H instead of an S." I said, killing any chance of the conversation taking on a lighter tone. At that moment, once you got me rolling on the 'Ills of the World' topic, there was no getting me off my soap box.

"And these Wahabbi Muslims hate Shia Muslims maybe even more than regular ol' Americans. We are worse to them because we are blasphemers, while Americans are just your run of the mill infidels. But, Wahabbis have plenty of hate to go around, so it really doesn't matter. If you aren't with them, you're against them - end of story. And they have a special fondness for oppressing women – the Taliban, who basically banned women from any sort of public life, were Wahabbis. And so are Al Qaeda – they are Wahabbis. That's why Mullah Omar, who is an Afghan, and Osama, who is an Arab, get along so well, even though there are big differences between Afghan and Arab culture (the least of which is the language barrier) – they're both Wahabbis. They even married each other's daughter or some crap like that."

The din of the crowd began to rise, and we stopped to watch the Giants set-up man go into his stretch. The bases were loaded with Dodgers, no outs, and the score was 12-0. The game was in hand, but there is no mercy when it comes to beating L.A., and the crowd wanted a shutout in the worst way. His first pitch was a strike on the outside, followed by another on the inside corner before his third pitch, a nasty split-fingered number, broke towards the hands of the hitter at the last second and jammed him, inducing a weak pop to first base and a nice round of applause.

"Anyway," I continued, plugging the gap in time as the next hitter came in from the on deck circle, "the Wahabbis have an armed wing in Pakistan called *Sib-e-Sehaba*. These guys are nuts – they ride two guys to a motorcycle, one guy driving and one on the back with a machine gun, and spray bullets into Shia mosques during the Friday prayers. Sometimes they mix in a grenade or two for maximum carnage. They also targeted Shia doctors, lawyers, prominent businessmen – anybody who is a contributing member to Shia society is a target for professional style hits – they'd just be driving to work or at a restaurant and get filled full of lead by masked bikers."

"Wow, man – that is crazy. And where is the government during all this?" Toby rightly inquired. "I mean – it sounds like gang warfare kinda – why don't the police do more?"

"That's what's so screwed up. The Wahabbis aren't only living in caves. They don't only come by with masks and on motorcycles. They also happen to occupy some of the most important land in the world – Saudi Arabia. In fact, it was only called 'Arabia' before, with tribes and clans controlling different parts of the peninsula, before the Wahabbis joined forces with the Saudi family to unite the kingdom under one king and one sect. Before then, Wahabbis occupied only a small part of the Arabian peninsula and nowhere else."

My speech was stalled again by a gasp from the crowd. The hitter had stroked one – a huge blast destined for the water behind the right field fence. The whole crowd held its breath until the final moment, as the ball took a hard curve towards foul ground, and then let out a relaxed cheer.

I filled in immediately. "I mean – the Muslim world is huge. It goes from Morocco to Egypt in North Africa, then through the Middle East with Iraq, Saudi and all the gulf countries, up into Iran and then Afghanistan and Central Asia, all throughout South Asia and finally into Southeast Asia. It covers a huge swath of lands, peoples, cultures and sects. And before oil was found in Arabia, the Wahabbis had only a tiny following in one part."

"How long ago was this?" asked Toby.

"I think about 200 years ago. Anyway, the Saudi/Wahabbi dynasty was born in Arabia well before black gold was discovered there. I mean – can you imagine? The message of Wahabbism is that any interpretation of the Qu'ran in a modern way is wrong. They believe that it must be interpreted and acted upon exactly as it was in the time of the Prophet, almost 1500 years back. To them, the Taliban were a model regime – the way things ought to be run. Public stonings, beheadings – these were commonplace in almost every society in 600 A.D. And to these people, people bound by their faith to hate all things modern, was given the greatest oil fortune the world has ever seen. I mean – it is like some big joke really – like God is trying to make things as hard as possible. These Wahabbis, they control the world's oil, but they are no better than the Nazis."

I played the Nazi card specifically for Toby – he had been raised Jewish, and I wanted to impart to him the depth of my hatred for Wahabbis. He didn't get a chance to respond right off, as a big roar from the crowd had us running back to the bleacher railings. The Giants had gotten a double play, and the Dodgers had failed to score.

"It's the ninth," I said, "wanna go catch the end in some better seats?"

"Sure," said Toby, "I think I see some good ones over there – behind third base." As we made our way around the park Toby picked up the thread. "So, let me get this straight. You are comparing the Wahabbis to the Nazis because they want to kill doctors in Pakistan?"

"Well – it's not that simple. Wait a sec." We pushed passed through the crowded bathroom line and entered the lower box seating area, walking straight to two seats halfway down the arcade. Toby and I were old pros at sneaking in to better seats at the ballgame – we had been doing it together for almost twenty years. It is all about acting like you belong – it's your right to sit in those seats. After we sat down and made sure no ushers saw us, I continued.

"The Saudis have actively promoted Wahabbism throughout the Muslim world. Wahabbi schools have sprung up by the thousands in places like Indonesia, Pakistan and Afghanistan over the last twenty-five years. Where do you think the Taliban got all the mindless drones to carry out their backward policies? These boys are young and poor, and they get free room and board from the schools in return for their minds. They are not taught geography, they are not taught mathematics. They are taught to memorize the Qu'ran in Arabic, a language they don't even know, and to adhere to the strict tenants of Wahabbism – that's it. They are taught to hate anyone who is not like them."

The crowd around us suddenly became excited, and we knew that the buzz in the air could only mean one thing – Barry Bonds was at bat. The slugger, long ridiculed for being a jerk and a cheater, was a hero in San Francisco – he had wowed the crowd with so many superhuman at-bats over the years that we didn't care if he used plutonium to do it, as long as he kept killing the ball. Everyone in our section stood and started chanting his name, hoping that he would put one out and give us the cherry on top of a perfect San Francisco baseball afternoon.

We were disappointed – he flied out to the warning track, and as the game was all but over, the crowd started to leave in droves. Toby and I moved down another ten rows before I continued.

"And so, these Wahabbis, when they graduate from their schools of hate, they look for somewhere to place their venom. On America, for being two-faced and godless. On Israel, for being Jewish and superior. Or the Shias, for believing in a different kind of Islam. On anyone, really. So, the *Sib-e-Sehaba*, the guys who shot into mosques in Pakistan, are a manifestation of this hatred, as was September 11th, as was last week's bombings. But like I said – Islam has many faces, and this is but one. The Wahabbis are by no means a majority, even within the Sunnis. But they do have tons of money, and they continue to open schools and mosques all around the world. In fact, they have opened tons of mosques right here in the good ol' US of A."

"That's scary man," Toby sighed. "And we are super down with the Saudis aren't we – that's so messed up."

"Not only are we down, but we promoted all this Wahabbi bullshit. When the Russians invaded Afghanistan in '79, we, the Saudis and the Pakis all recruited these nuts from all over the Muslim world and dumped them into the resistance against the Commies."

"Yeah – that's right. Osama was on the payroll, Saddam was on the payroll – everyone's been on the payroll at one time or another. Listen - thanks for the info bro – you certainly have learned a lot about this stuff. To be honest with you, it's a little much to take in right now, especially since I'm still kinda ripped. Let's get out of here, huh? This chick I know is having a bonfire tonight at the beach – whaddya say? Shall we get a twelver and hop the N-Judah?"

I could see that Toby's brief yearning for Islamic knowledge had come to an end, and although there was more I wanted to say, I left it at that. We left Pac Bell and took the N-Judah train out to the beach, swillin' brews and recalling different hijinks from our adolescent years with much embellishment and nostalgia. After a heated debate concerning the craziest party of our senior year, we decided that it had to be the Johnny Depp party, where three bands had taken over some poor kid's house while his parents were away (he had mistakenly given Toby that information) and completely trashed it, throwing a blow-out, all-night rager and plastering Johnny Depp posters on every inch of wall space in the house (someone worked at Videola and had brought hundreds of promotional posters for 'Cry Baby' to the party).

When we finally made it to the beach, it was just past sunset. The sky was hued to perfection, every shade from a purple and orange palette being played out over the long horizon. As we came over the little hill that separates Ocean Beach from the Great Highway, I was dazzled by the site of the Pacific. It glistened in the dim dusk light, gently lapping at the shore with its massive tides.

It was an exceptional San Francisco evening – warm enough to be in short sleeves, and with clear visibility as far as the eye could see. There was only a gentle breeze to caress a pale crescent moon hanging high in the darkening sky. I have always loved the crescent moon – it provides you with the beautiful luminescence of the moon, but in a more modest way, with less light to obscure the other heavenly bodies in the sky the way a full one does. I had always felt it to be the perfect symbol of Islam, as a complement to the heavenly bodies around it.

We found the party, at the southern end of the beach – they had stolen fifteen palettes from a nearby Safeway and had a huge bonfire going, at some points twenty feet high in the air. We sat around the fire for hours, passing whiskey, smoking spliffs and singing songs. Toby and I traded off playing old Johnny Cash tunes and getting the girls to sing with us. I drank myself into a steady oblivion, and at some point passed out, alone, somewhere further up the beach. The next morning I woke up to a dog licking my face and a hangover – I had spent the whole night on the sand, and I couldn't remember a thing from the later stages of the night.

I do, however, remember what I dreamed that night. Vividly, in fact, despite my sorry state. Perhaps, because for the first time in a long time, something in my life spoke the truth.

Chapter 3

Khizr's Challenge

In my dream, I am sitting at the beach, enjoying a warm autumn day. I am unhappy as I smell the sea's fishy scent – vaguely upset over something. It is sunset, and as the sun disappears over the horizon I see a green flash.

There is a presence behind me. I turn and see an old man, maybe 5'3", with a flowing white mane and beard. I think I see a faint smile on his face. He is wearing a green hooded cape, drawn over his forehead so as to leave his features in shadows. But, from beneath the hood one thing is unmistakable - his emerald green eyes. They bore into me, benevolently surveying my confused face.

"What's up Mo? You and I need to talk, my friend. Don't you know who I am?"

"What are you?" I stammer. "Where'd you come from?"

"From across the ocean, man – I'm from everywhere and nowhere, you might say. Ha Ha Ha!" cries the old man, slapping my hand and doing a little jig in the sand.

"How do you know my name?"

"I've been keeping tabs on you since you were born, my friend. It's my job." With this he stops, putting his hands on his hips and smiling into my face with love.

"What do you mean? I've never seen you before."

"I can watch from many places, far and near, undetected. I'm pretty bad-ass, if I do say so myself – at least as far as these terrestrial concerns go!"

"So, what are you, some kind of supernatural stalker troll or something?" I still cannot get a read on this crazy blue-hair with the green robe.

"Ha – that's good Mo. Umm - I guess that's one way of describing me. Let's just say that I've been interested in you for a while."

"Why?"

"You are Syed Mohammed Khan? Born on May 6, 1974 in Kaiser Permanente Hospital on Geary Street of San Francisco, California U.S.A?"

He asks his questions with rhetorical clarity.

"Uh – yeah."

"Well, there are three reasons right there. Number One: Your first name is Syed, which means you are of direct lineage to the Prophet Mohammed and therefore possessing of significant spiritual ability. Number Two: You were born on my birthday, so I like you. And Number Three: You were born in San Francisco, the Western-most city in the Empire of the West, and this makes it easier for you to come full circle."

I am confused and pause before speaking. "Well, I don't know about the Syed thing – I never use it except as an initial. And I don't know about the Western-most city thing - what about Honolulu?"

The old man smiles. When he speaks again, he has dropped the slang and become more dignified. "You are correct geographically, young Mohammed, but not spiritually. San Francisco represents a spiritual center of a movement that has been afoot since the time of Dante. It is the culmination of the advancements in individual liberties, democracy, and secularism that have pushed the West to what it has become today. It is a place where there are no rights, no wrongs, no rules. As long as you don't hurt anyone else, you're okay, right? It embodies Western belief. Since you are a child of this city, you know what the true freedom of Western civilization means. It is holders of such truth that I seek now, and you are a special such one."

He now speaks with a certainty that makes him impervious to debate. He watches me process his words with an air of expectancy, as if he is in a hurry and needs to make this quick.

After a pause I continue my interrogation. "Are you with the Agency or something? How can you have watched me so closely and I've never even seen you before?"

"It was not through my own eyes that I witnessed your progress. I have many ways of obtaining the information I seek – via the wind, the moon, the animals. There is no greater spy than Mother Nature herself – she is everywhere and sees everything. You just have to know how to talk to her." At this he smiles.

"And, who exactly are you?" I ask.

"Well, I have many names, but you can call me G – I think that sounds cool. Short for the translation of my name into English – the Green Ancient. You know – I'm hip to the times – I get BET at my pad."

I freeze. YuMa had once told me about a Muslim saint who was said to have drunk from the Fountain of Youth in the time of Alexander the Great. He had become immortal, and wandered the Earth, helping those in distress and acting as a go-between for God and man. I had forgotten the story, and his name, until now.

"You are Al-Khizr, the Green Ancient! No way, I don't believe it. You are real?"

"Oh, yes yes – I am very real. Too real, in fact. I am three thousand years old, give or take a few centuries here or there, and I have come to know this world all too well. I can tell you I know the truth behind this world's reality more than any other human alive today. I'm sure the Big Guy would agree with that."

"The truth behind this world's reality? What does that mean?"

"You want the answer before I ask the question. It is not so easy, young Mohammed. First, you must do something for me, and then I can provide you with this greatest of knowledge."

"You, the all-knowing Khizr, have a request for me? Why would you come for me? I'm no traveler or Sufi mystic. I'm not even a real Muslim." The last two words hurt my own ears, as they always did.

"Ah, but you are. You are a traveler. And a Sufi. And a mystic. We all are these things – they are inherent in the human spirit. They just need nurturing. You are all these things and more. I am here to tell you this, that you must follow your heart if you are to help those that need you most." As he speaks this last bit he withdraws his hood, and the twilight illuminates his windswept face like a planet reflects light. "Because," he says serenely, "things have been going very wrong recently. The Most High doesn't like to meddle too much in the affairs of Free Will, but he is not above intervening when things get out of hand."

Khizr takes my hand into his. I am taken aback at the strength and vibrancy beneath his leathery touch.

"See these lines that crisscross your palm?" he asks. "They represent lines of your destinies that may or may not be fulfilled. Your Creator has endowed you with the power of choice and it is ultimately you who chooses your path in this life. The choices are rigged, of course – those who choose rightly are rewarded, and those who choose wrongly are not. It was decided that I would contact you in hopes of encouraging the right path. It is an honor, for most people do not get the advice I am offering. In the end, though, you will be held solely responsible for your actions, as are all men and women when their time comes."

"Why would the most powerful entity in the universe need my help?"

"It is simple. God loves us. He wants only the best for us. But, He has a problem – it is hard for Him to communicate with us. His essence is too huge – too big for us to deal with. It is difficult for Him to overcome the power, greed, and usury that seem to propel many of the same humans in which He also instilled love, compassion and humility. Such is the perfection of human creation – we have so much freedom that not even our Creator knows what we'll do next!"

I eye him quietly, not sure what to do or think.

"He has tried many times to give us the way to Paradise – there were Prophets like Moses, like Abraham, like Jesus, like Mohammed – peace be upon them all – like so many. Prophets for every type of people – Zoraster, Confucious, Buddha. He's sent angels, books, miracles – but He hasn't found a way to provide humanity with a foolproof way to what He wants for them – happiness."

"So I'm the new prophet, huh? Sweeeeet."

"No way dude – not even close. The time for Prophets is over, and even if it weren't you wouldn't be the first choice – trust me. Anyway - humans have all the rules already, all the info we're going to get in this existence. We just need to refine it a bit, get back to the true meanings. Time is marching on, and there isn't enough sand left in the old hourglass to start over."

"So what is it? What is your request?"

"The choice is to either seek true knowledge, your own knowledge, or to stay under your veil of half-truths and assumption. You are a

Western Muslim. You straddle a divide that pits two of His children's greatest civilizations apart, and while they vilify and terrify you do nothing but add to the flames. You spread knowledge that is half-cocked and deceitful. You do more harm than you know, because there are so few of you available to us that each of your words means exponentially more. You are no better than the talking heads on T.V. that you so despise."

"Hey – I try to spread nothing but love and understanding. I do not hate anyone."

"Do you include Jews in 'anyone'?"

"Yes. My buddy Toby is a Jew, and I love him."

"Do you include Wahabbis in 'anyone'?"

"Um, well, I don't know." G's question is a tough one, so I change the subject. "But, why me? Why would I receive this honor?"

"You are not the only one we are working with – the fate of the world does not rest on your shoulders. What we request is that you embark on a journey of discovery. Of observation. Travel to the Muslims, learn about your religion and its people. Take time to look into their eyes and know what they know. Follow your heart and discover their truths. Just learn. This is all we ask. Try to see their truths like the truth you see in San Francisco. We ask that you give us three months. When you are done, you can reassume your place in your society, but from then on when you speak you will know you are right – you will speak from experience. Because, at the end of this trip you will receive a treasure – the greatest treasure on this Earth, in fact. And this treasure will give you the knowledge that you truly seek."

"Why me, why am I so special?"

"We are all special, we are a special creation of the Most High. Your makeup, your heritage – it just makes you more relevant for the time in which you live. Believe me – 50 years ago I wasn't giving quests out to too many Muslims. Back then it was all Jews and Christians – anyone working against those crazy Nazis."

"How do you expect me to do this? I'm a nobody. I like my sinful life, with my wine and my women. Why would I abandon all that in favor of some altruistic quest, a quest with no discernible goal? Why would I leave San Francisco? And why should I believe that you really are Al-Khizr? Is this some kind of dream?"

The old man's gaze falls from my face and settles on the waves beyond me.

"Too many questions. I am too old to satisfy your cynicism. You must do what you feel is right - that is your own conversation with Free Will. All I can tell you is that you have been selected for a special path. If you accept, give your prayers at the Kairouine Mosque next Friday and you will be on your way to great reward. I have confidence in you."

The old man pulls his hood over his head and lets out an ear-piercing screech. Two dolphin heads appear beyond us in the ocean. Each dolphin holds a rein in its smiling mouth, and first one, then the other flips their rein into the old man's outstretched palm. He mounts them, one foot on each fin, shakes the reins, and is off. Against the purple-orange backdrop of the last remnants of sunset, I watch his green shadow disappear over the Pacific horizon.

Chapter 4

Fez

The line of discontent that had formed in my subconscious, the one drawn by being a Muslim American after 9/11, had finally been crossed with Khizr's arrival. So I took his challenge and bought a ticket to Morocco leaving in three days. It was an email exchange with YuMa that convinced me – he approved and suggested that I pack light and leave my affairs in order. He never once doubted my dream encounter, for at YuMa's heart he was a Sufi, and by definition a mystic.

When I left San Francisco all I had was a backpack of clothes, a camera, a passport, and an ATM card. YuMa had also taken care of my reading materials for me – attached to his email had been various stories, essays and poems on Islam that he had thought would be of value on my journey. I had printed and binded them into a small, ninety-three page book at Kinkos at four in the morning, the night of my going away bash, in a farewell nod to my unbalanced life.

Four days after my dream I sat in a window seat of a Royal Air Maroc flight, slowly descending into Casablanca's Mohammed V Airport, a continent and an ocean away. I was surprised to see plot after plot of agricultural land, bursting out of the ground with bright greens and reds and beiges. I had always imagined North Africa to be barren, like the dull desert brown of southern Pakistan - the only Muslim country I had ever been to, for a few boring summers of my youth. But the African Atlantic looked more like the lush coastal zone of the Pacific, between San Francisco and Santa Cruz, than the barren shore of the Arabian Sea.

We touched down and parked on the tarmac. It was mid-morning, and the sun gently warmed us as we descended the stairs onto the tarmac and boarded buses for the short ride to the terminal. I sailed through immigration and customs with ease, received a thirty-day visitor visa, and walked into the arrivals lobby. All signs were in Arabic and French, but Madame Murphy's eighth grade French class was enough to get me down to the train station, which was located directly underneath the arrivals terminal of the Casablanca airport, find the counter, and buy a ticket for Fez. It would be a five hour ride – first I was to go through the capital city, Rabat, and then switch trains for Fez, which Google had informed me was the home to the Kairouine Mosque.

The train arrived and we rolled out of the airport and into a ghetto – shanties, lean-tos and trash lining both sides of the tracks as we slowly built up speed on the northbound track. A few people milled about the slum – a woman walking hand in hand with her child, a few men sitting around having a smoke, a boy staring intently into the train. His look was neither malicious nor pitiful – he just looked bored.

The Moroccans surrounding me in the first class cabin were all dressed in Western clothes. There were three other guys besides me – two older men in slacks and blazers and a teenager in soccer sweats. There were also three twenty-something women, all dressed in tight jeans and lots of makeup. The cabin was big, and the men spread to all four corners while the women sat in the middle and chatted. From my window seat, I dialed up some Black Sabbath on the iPod and enjoyed the ride, my adrenaline overcoming any effects of the sixteen hours I had been on the road.

We left the ghetto and, after a couple of stops, started chugging through the countryside, whipping past the fertile coast of the Atlantic I had spied not thirty minutes before from the air. In Rabat, I started seeing some traditional dresses, Moroccan *jellabas* and Islamic *hijabs*, in the bustling crowd of the station, and when I boarded the train for Fez the crowd was decidedly more mixed.

It was a three-and-a-half hour ride from Rabat to Fez. I was nodding off in my second-class carriage when the conductor poked me.

"*Werqa*," he said.

"Um – you speak English?" I answered groggily.

"Yes, little. Ticket – see ticket."

"Oh yeah – sure. Here." The conductor punched it and moved on to the man next to me, who got his punched and then turned to me and smiled brightly.

He was fair skinned, with salt and pepper hair and bushy black eyebrows. There was a hint of girth, but if it was there it was camouflaged under his loose green *jellaba*. He fumbled in his pockets and produced a bag of nuts, which he offered to me and I declined. He smiled and put them away without having one himself before turning back to me and smiling again.

"I hear you speak English," he said. "Where you from?"

"America – San Francisco."

"Oh that's nice. I like America. It's so big – I like it. But you look like Moroccan. Your family is from America?"

"My family is from Pakistan."

"Oh – yes, yes – you are Muslim?

"Yes."

"*Assalaam Alaikum,*" he said quickly.

"*Wa'alaikum Salaam.*" I replied. There are a few binding things between all Muslims, and that greeting is one of them. It is an exchange of pleasantries – peace, and to you peace – in Arabic, but surprisingly devoid of divinity. Everything else in Islam is about God, but the standard greeting isn't – it is a testament to the Arabness of the religion.

"Where are you going?" my new companion asked.

"Fez, to the Kairouine," I said.

"You should do that," he said, becoming excited at the subject, "it is a great place. One of the holiest places in all of Morocco. I love it there. I am from Fez." He said this proudly, as one does Manhattan. "Fez is a holy city."

"I don't know much about it." I said.

"For centuries our city has been one for learning, for art. The Kairouine is a mosque and also is a university – many many famous teachers and students from all over the Muslim world for the last thousand years has studied there. It is a great place – you wish to be a student there?"

"No – I just want to give my Friday prayers there today. I am a traveler, and have heard much about the place."

"This is good – you should do this. Where will you stay?"

"I don't know – somewhere near the train station, in the ville nouvelle, I think."

He shook his head and gave a magnanimous smile. "No no – this is not good. If you come to Fez you must go to the *medina*. You must stay there – the ville nouvelle is 100 years old, built by the French. You must go to the medina – it is 1000 years old, and built by the Moroccans!" He laughed and gave me a friendly slap on the back. "It is the best part of our city. What is your name?"

"Mohammed."

"Mohammed, today you have luck because you meet me. I will get you hotel and guide for the medina – the best in Fez. My friend is guide – he knows good English. He is a body builder, you know?"

This guy was starting to make plans for me to hang out with Moroccan body builders, and I wasn't sure I liked it.

"Well – I don't know," I said. "Um – what is your name?"

"Ali," he said.

"Ali, yes, well I don't know Ali. I don't think I need a guide. I am just going to give my prayers and then walk around a little by myself."

Ali sensed my reservations and addressed me a bit more forcefully, looking straight into my eyes and saying, "Mohammed – I am Muslim, you are Muslim. You are in my home country and I will help you, as you would do for me, ok? You are like my brother - hold on one moment please."

He dug out his cell phone from his robe and called someone. I watched him closely for signs of mischief, but his animated conversation in what I guessed was Arabic seemed pleasant in tone, and after a five-minute chat, he hung up the phone and laughed again.

"Mohammed, it is all settled. Your guide, his name is Abdullah, he will be waiting for you at the train station and will take you to the hotel."

"Listen – Ali. Thanks for helping, but I don't want a guide."

"It's okay – trust me. The medina is big – there are over 9,400 alleys in it. No joke! You get lost easily, and people don't speak English, like me. I am a travel agent – I can speak seven languages. The people here – they speak two, maybe three languages – Arabic, French, and Berber – maybe a little Spanish. But, not so many English. The Kairouine Mosque is right in the middle – you need help for the first day, then maybe you go by yourself, okay?"

His smile was persistent, and I knew there was already a guy coming to get me, so I decided it better to surrender to Ali's apparent hospitality than to cause any bad feelings.

"Okay," I said. "Thanks Ali."

"It is no problem – it is my pleasure to welcome travelers to my city."

"So," I said, figuring I might as well keep chatting with him now that he had co-opted my plans, "tell me more about Fez. Why is it so holy?"

"Oh, well, it is because we have strong Islam there – good Maliki Islam there, for many, many years. Fez was the capital of many empires - Islamic empires that went from Spain to Senegal. And then when the great artists of *Al-Andalus* - you know, when Muslims owned Spain, and they built the most beautiful castles and mosques - when they all left from Spain because of the Christian, what do they call it?"

"Uh, I'm not sure. Maybe the Crusades?"

"No."

"Inquisition?"

"Yes!" he exclaimed, "many of them came here, to Fez, to escape the In-qui-si-tion," he said, sounding out the new word perfectly. "These were very smart cultures, back then, you know. This was 1,000 years ago. Their achievements in art and science were big and plentiful. And you should see the buildings they made– the Alhambra in Granada is beautiful!"

"Oh, where is that again?"

"It is in Granada, in Spain," he said quickly, happy at my interest in the greatness of his hometown. "It still there, the Alhambra. But, all its artists came here, to Fez. It is our *zellij*, our tiles, that make our city so beautiful. We have for years been the home for the world's greatest *zellij* artists. Fez is famous for this art – it is everywhere. For a time Fez was such a big and powerful empire that all the best artists from all over always came to work here, to gain work at the Sultan's court."

Ali's English was fair, and his knowledge sounded real, so I decided to ask more questions. "How old is the city?"

"Moulay Idriss came here, I think, in about the year 200 in the Muslim calendar, I think 800 on the Western calendar. He was the founder of Morocco – he was a great man. Before he came, there was nothing here – just some wandering tribes and people like that. But Moulay Idriss – he was a great man. He came here from Arabia and started Morocco."

As he said this he moved to the window seat, motioning to the landscape whipping by outside as he spoke of his country. We had moved away from the coast and into a hilly region – the train was starting to climb a slow incline, and the land was becoming more and more rugged.

"So, is that when Islam came, with him from Arabia?" I asked.

"Yes. They brought with them their Islam. They forced none of the original tribes of Morocco to convert, but the people, especially the Berbers, liked Islam very much, right from the beginning. They formed an army, went and conquered Europe, you know? From then on Morocco has been important. We are the closest to Europe, right? We are right across the Straits of Gibraltar. Don't you know what that means? Gibraltar?"

"What?" I asked.

"Gibraltar. I love this one, Mohammed, you know. I love to learn language, and I always like when words go from one to another, and people don't know how. Gibraltar, this is from Spanish, but it is actually coming from Arabic. It was what the rock was called by the Muslims, after the captain of the first ship to sail from Morocco and begin to conquer the Christians in Spain – his name was Tariq. They called it *Jabal Tariq* – it means mountain of Tariq. You see – Gibraltar, *Jabal Tariq*, they sound the same, no?"

He laughed again at this, taking out a pack of smokes and excusing himself to the hallway.

After a few minutes he came back and struck up an animated conversation (in either Arabic or Berber, I wasn't sure) with another gentleman next to him. I drifted off to sleep with the gentle jostle of the train, and awoke to Ali shaking my shoulder.

"Mohammed – we are here! Time to go. Your guide will receive you outside our train car. His name is Abdullah. See you later, and enjoy my Fez!"

He smiled and left the train in a rush. As I gathered my stuff I saw him outside the train speaking to a shorter bald man, dressed in denim from head to toe, but by the time I had gathered my gear and disembarked, Ali had hurried off. The denim man he had left behind looked at me and then turned and ran down the platform. A couple of minutes later he ran back, straight to me, and stopped.

"You are Mohammed from America?"

"Yup – that's me."

"I am Abdullah – I am your guide. Nice to meet you."

He grabbed my hand and shook vigorously. He was in obvious good shape – he was maybe forty and built solid, like a linebacker.

"We have a car waiting – the owner of the hotel has come with me to get you. Please come."

He grabbed one of my bags and sprinted out in front. I followed and we went through the station and found an old Mercedes in the parking lot outside. Abdullah introduced the driver as Hasan, and said he owned the Hotel Dalilah, where I would be staying.

"First time in Morocco?" Abdullah asked as we pulled into traffic. He seemed always in a hurry, and even after we were driving in the car his first question had been delivered with urgency.

"Yes." I said.

"What do you want to see in Fez?" said Abdullah, cutting to the chase. "I am your guide – you tell me what you want."

"Wow – thanks Abdullah," I said, trying to catch my breath. "I would like to give my prayers at the Kairouine today, that is number one. And see the architecture, I guess. I would like to meet some people here – talk to regular people from Fez, and get to know them, you know?"

"I know many people – I will introduce you. But, you cannot go to the Kairouine if you are not Muslim," said Abdullah sternly. "Are you Muslim?"

"Yes."

"Assalaam Alaikum, brother."

"Wa'alaikum Salaam," I said. It was becoming a pattern in Morocco, this vetting of my Muslimness, and it was the first time in my life where

Five Pillars

I wore it proudly on my sleeve, like a badge of honor instead of a scarlet letter.

"Okay – I'll find you people to talk with," he said. "And today, we will take a tour of the medina, and then tomorrow I will take you for prayers at the Kairouine, okay?"

"No – I must give my prayers today. I want to give the Friday prayer."

"Why, why must you do this?"

I didn't feel much up to explaining myself, not that I knew what I would say anyway. "It is a promise I have made, to give prayers today. We still have time, yes?"

"Yes – the main prayer starts at one – we have time if we go straight there."

"Then let's do that." I said.

Abdullah grunted his approval and began to relay our conversation in Arabic to Hasan, who took it in, threw me a quizzical look, and then stepped on the gas. All of it sudden it dawned on me that I had been very trusting, and at that moment I was speeding in a car down a side street in Africa with two strange Arabs I knew nothing about.

"Um, Abdullah – this is very nice, you know, you picking me up and all. But I told Ali on the train that I'm not sure I need a guide. Just a nice hotel, and I think I'll be fine."

Abdullah cracked a smile – the first since I had met him. He nodded his head and put his hand on my shoulder. "Brother, do not worry. Everyone who comes here has a guide – you can trust me. Times are bad here – not many tourists, you know? This is our main business, and so many have stopped coming since the terrorists started. We have an empty hotel, you know? We'll take care of you, so you'll tell your friends to come, okay?"

His meager attempt at hospitality coupled with my limited options convinced me. "Okay, I will trust you. But, how much does a guide cost? Ali told me nothing."

"Brother – please do not discuss this. You give me whatever you want when we part, okay?"

31

This was very against my contract-oriented American sense of business. "No – I'd rather have an agreement – please. How much do you normally get?"

"Please – I don't know. You pay me whatever you want."

I shrugged my shoulders and we drove the rest of the way in silence, skirting the walls of the old city for a while before turning right into an open lot filled with cars. We pulled up in front of a big pink building with the words 'Hotel Dalila' painted in white across the front.

"This is it," said Abdullah, proudly pointing to the pink hotel. "We are here. This neighborhood is called Ouedzhouer, it is on the north wall of the medina. From here, the mosque is close. Come."

We got out of the car, and Abdullah and Hasan grabbed my bags and went into the café in the bottom of the hotel. Though it was still under construction, it was beautiful – there were low lying benches with brightly colored cushions lining the walls, and painted wooden coffee tables with ottomans scattered around. The bottom half of the walls were covered in an intricate geometry of tile work – circles and triangles and sine curves woven in blues and greens and gold. The whole front of the building was open air, and the sides had stained glass windows letting blue and red light into the seating area.

We went through the café, past by the eight or so men seated there, and then proceeded up two flights of stairs. The whole hotel – the hallways, the stairs, and the reception area – was decorated with beautiful paintings and rugs – it felt like something straight out of *Arabian Nights*. We came to my room and I was even further impressed – behind a beautifully carved door were more rugs and tile work, a ring of Arabic writing carved in a ceiling-wide rectangle in the plaster above, and a big bed piled high with colorful wool blankets. A small green stained glass window opened onto the lot below and the Middle Atlas Mountains a short way off in the distance.

"Here – your room. You like it?" Abdullah asked.

"Yes – very much. It is beautiful. How much is it per night?"

"Hasan says 150 dirhams, okay? Special price for Muslim brother, okay?"

I said yes and Abdullah asked me to pre-pay for the first night. I produced the money and he was off, coming back a few minutes later with a receipt in hand.

"The *azan* is about to start – if you want to go we must go. I do not attend the Kairouine Friday prayer – I take my son to another mosque. But I have spoken with a man – he is a neighbor here, a leader of the medina. He said he will take you, but he speaks no English, only French, so it will be hard for you to talk. But, he will take you if we go right now."

We went out the door of the hotel and went up ten steps around the back and into an alleyway of the medina, which felt like a giant mud labyrinth. The brown walls on either side of every winding turn contained storefronts, homes, restaurants, and hotels - some structures two and three stories high. The maze of streets came in all shapes, sizes, and angles. We took a couple of lefts, then some rights, went underneath a giant earthen archway, and then into a tunnel that for a few seconds worth of walking was pitch black. Abdullah looked back at me on the other side and laughed.

"I don't usually take tourists that way, but we are in a hurry, and you are a Muslim brother, so I know you trust me, right?" He was obviously enjoying my bewilderment at our crazy route.

We made a right down another side alley before coming to an opening where men were milling about outside of a café. Abdullah bee-lined it to a tall man in his 60s, who greeted him and then beckoned me to follow him. I came over and Abdullah introduced me to Ahmed, explaining that Ahmed would bring me back to the café after the prayer. Abdullah was to meet me back there, and would then be at my service for the rest of the afternoon.

"Ahmed will take care of you – just stick by him so you don't get lost," said Abdullah, before disappearing back into the dark tunnel we had just come from.

At that moment, the azan started, stirring the crowd into motion. I have always loved the Muslim call to prayer – its poetic melody has rung true in my heart from the first time I heard it as a four year old boy visiting Pakistan and listening to it from my grandfather's bedroom. It is the ultimate in community – you always know you are in a Muslim country because there is no getting around the azan, calling all the believers together five times a day to remember and worship God.

Allahu Akbar, Allahu Akbar!
(God is most Great, God is most Great)

Allahu Akbar, Allahu Akbar!
(God is most Great, God is most Great)

Ahmed and I set off down a different alley from the one Abdullah had brought me, this one growing narrower as we progressed, with more crowds of men joining us from all directions as we inched further and further into the old city.

Ash-hadu Allah Ilaha Il-Allah!
(I bear witness that there is no other object of worship except God)

Ash-hadu Allah Ilaha Il-Allah!
(I bear witness that there is no other object of worship except God)

The Kairouine is said to hold over 25,000 people, and the Friday prayer is the most attended weekly event. The small cobbled streets leading up to the great mosque were packed with men heading to listen to the weekly sermon and offer their prayers, and as I was swept along with them down the cobblestone alleys, dodging donkeys and stalls, it felt as though this could have been any other Friday of the last thousand years.

Ash-hadu Anna Muhammad-ar-Rasoolullah!
(I bear witness that Muhammad is the Messenger of God)

Ash-hadu Anna Muhammad-ar-Rasoolullah!
(I bear witness that Muhammad is the Messenger of God)

Ahmed looked at me and smiled. "Allez, allez" he said, before pressing ahead through the crowd. French was his western language, not English, and I wondered how I was to communicate with this man in the bowels of the ancient city.

Hayya Alass Salah!
(Come to Prayer)

Hayya Alass Salah!
(Come to Prayer)

Abdullah was a big man and that was helpful – standing at about 6'3"
he was a head taller than the crowd and I could easily find him if we got
momentarily separated. He maneuvered us to a huge wooden door off
the main alleyway, where we took off our shoes and walked into a giant
courtyard.

Hayya Alal Falah!
(Come to Success)

Hayya Allal Falah!
(Come to Success)

The juxtaposition of the giant mosque just inside the walls of
the tiny alleys of the labyrinth outside is powerful. The Kairouine's
courtyard welcomes you in from the claustrophobia of the medina, its
huge open space covered with tile work and lined with white archways
on all sides. Two large, beautiful fountains, covered by freestanding,
intricately carved gazebos, stand at either end for washing, and smaller
fountains line the middle area, open to the heavens above. The floor tiles
are blue and white, while the rooftops and gazebos are painted in green,
the traditional color of Islam.

Allahu Akbar, Allahu Akbar!
(God is most Great, God is most Great)

La-illaha Il-Allah
(There is no other object of worship except God)

The main area of the mosque is archways as far as the eye can see –
white twenty foot high archways with red straw mats wrapped around
the bottom of each pillar. The floor was also covered in straw mats.

People were filing in, shoes in hand, and taking places all around us, and Ahmed motioned to me that we must perform ablutions and get ready quickly – the azan was over.

We edged our way along the mats to one of the fountains in the courtyard. Ahmed put down his shoes, rolled up his pant legs and sleeves, and started to perform *wuzu* alongside a dozen other men. I had long ago forgotten how to do this, so I watched him and did as he did a few seconds later. Ahmed caught me watching but said nothing.

The ritual ablutions, or wuzu are performed before every prayer, five times a day. As with most Islamic traditions, there is a precise method in which to perform the ablutions, one which all Muslims must adhere to. You must wash your mouth first, three times, and then your hands, arms, neck, face and feet, first right and then left, before you proclaim yourself ready to offer prayer and can proceed.

Once we were done, Ahmed led me to the front of the main prayer hall. He got us close to the *qibla,* which orients the flock towards Mecca, and then sat down and motioned for me to do the same. After a few minutes the *imam* stood up at the head of the congregation and started giving a sermon in Arabic. The numbers inside the mosque were swelling rapidly – we were surrounded by dozens of lines of men, sitting down and listening to the imam's sermon, letting out an *Allahu Akbar* (God is Great) every once in a while in the same way a Hallelujah! might be heard in a Baptist church.

Not being able to understand the sermon, I realized I had overlooked a small detail that might prevent me from fulfilling Khizr's first request – I hadn't prayed in fifteen years. I learned my prayers from my grandfather, Dada. He came from Pakistan and stayed with us for a year in 1984. Our family was young and busy then – there was always a soccer practice or a band rehearsal or something going on. But Dada had fit right in – I think he loved America and the better life it was providing for his son's family. He loved the Price is Right, Cadillacs, and the lottery– all things that exemplified the exotic capitalism of America he found so different from the middle class life he had lived in Pakistan. He loved to take it all in, but he also wanted to make sure his American grandchildren knew something of their religion.

He sat me down for thirty minutes every day that year and taught me my prayers in Arabic. The proper Muslim prayer must be done the way the Prophet did it, so it must be done in Arabic. I once asked my grandfather why – wouldn't it be better to say them in English so that I could understand the words? No, he had answered, this is just one of the things you must do if you are Muslim. If you really want to know what you are saying, he'd said, then learn Arabic.

He taught me that prayer is obligatory in Islam. It is meant to be a five-times-a-day reminder of your submission to God, to be a daily expression of your love to Him and your humility before Him. And it is especially encouraged in a congregation – to submit with your brothers all at once carries more merit, especially on Friday (the Muslim Sabbath) or on holy days. Of course, I had concocted my own special rules for my prayer obligation – I had excused myself of it, long ago, content to believe that the Golden Rule was all I needed to find my way into heaven. Do unto others as you would have them do to you – that had been my justification for my lackadaisical spiritual existence.

But, as the imam transitioned from sermon to the start of the prayer, I recognized the Arabic from Dada's lessons and knew it was time to stand up and begin. Lines formed, with people moving up and filling the line in front of him until everyone stood shoulder-to-shoulder, facing the qibla and east. As the imam started to lead the congregation, I started to feel anxious, and I couldn't remember the first lines of the first prayer.

The Muslim prayer is broken down into *rakats*. A *rakat* is one circuit of the four positions of the prayer – standing, bowing, prostrate, sitting and back to standing again. In each position you either recite Qu'ranic verses or other Arabic phrases glorifying God, transitioning from one position to the other by saying *Allahu Abkar*. Muslims are required to give two *rakats* for *Fajr* (morning prayer), four *rakats* for *Zuhr* and *Asr* (early and late afternoon prayers), three at *Maghrib* (sunset) and four at *Isha* (night).

I stumbled through the *rakats*, mixing up the order of positions and drawing a blank for long stretches when I should have been reciting verse. Surrounded by all these worshippers in their country's most sacred and beautiful mosque, unable to properly pray, I felt like an idiot – like a poser. Khizr's words started coming back to me - hadn't he told me that I was fake, nothing but a talking head like the rest of them?

To be pretending in a place Dada could never have dreamed of going to – what kind of Muslim was I? In the prostrate position I forgot the words but caught the eye of the boy next to me, who smiled and winked, like he too was just going through the motions.

Putting on our shoes as we left Ahmed said something to me in French that I didn't understand. His look for me had changed – it was a mix of suspicion and pity, I think. He led me back to the café and the waiting Abdullah, saying a few words to him before turning and walking back towards the Kairouine.

Abdullah eyed me slowly. "You gave your prayers, you are happy?"

"Yes – thank you for arranging that. I'm hungry now – can we eat?"

"Yes, of course. I will take you to a nice restaurant. And then later, Ahmed has invited you to come have tea with him and his friend. He says now that you have prayed together, that he would like to meet you again."

Khizr had told me to meet as many people as possible, so I said sure, and after eating and resting a bit we returned to the café that evening to find Ahmed playing gin rummy with a young white man.

"Eric, this is Mohammed. He is from America too." Abdullah introduced me to Ahmed's friend as he ushered me in to a seat by the table.

Eric looked up from his game and surveyed me. "Where from?" he asked.

"I'm from San Francisco. And you?"

"Dallas – I'm from Dallas."

"Texas huh? What brings you here?"

"I'm studying Arabic in Rabat – I've just finished, actually. Ahmed here is a friend – I'm here to say goodbye. And you?"

"Just passing through. I'm on a world tour – traded the job for a backpack and that whole thing."

"Cool – that sounds like fun." He said it with such little conviction that I felt a bit patronized. He went back to his card game, and Abdullah ordered some mint tea for us as we settled and watched a few plays.

Ahmed shot me a couple of looks between cards and said something to Abdullah, who said, "Ahmed would like to ask you if you enjoyed the Kairouine today."

"Yes, of course I did. Tell him thanks for taking me, and for inviting me here."

"I told him that you would like to meet people here, and Ahmed is an important man – he represents our section of the medina. So, he said he would talk with you. What would you like to ask Ahmed, Mohammed?"

"Um, well, Ahmed," I said, not sure of what to ask, "you are a politician of some kind? You represent the medina?"

Abdullah, with the help of Eric, translated my question to Ahmed and back came an answer in Arabic. Eric and Ahmed had a few exchanges, making me think that they were doing more than just translating.

Abdullah relayed to me, "He is a farmer, a simple farmer. But he has lived here for a very long time, and his family has been here in Fez for a very long time. So the people trust him, and he speaks on their behalf to the city government officials in the ville nouvelle. He represents them."

"So is it an elected position?" I asked.

"No – it is not. He has it because of his family and because of who he is."

"Are there elections for any other kinds of positions?"

Ahmed considered the question, conferred with Eric again, and then responded, saying he could not say – the king runs the country and he is the one who makes the decisions.

"And what do you think of the king's decisions?" The course of the conversation had naturally turned to this question, in my mind, and I thought nothing of asking him what he thought of his leader.

I was wrong. Eric quickly translated what I said and Ahmed became animated in his response, looking at me and pointing at Abdullah as his voice rose a bit. Some of the other men at other tables threw glances our way, and Abdullah shifted nervously in his seat as he took Ahmed's abuse. He finally stood up and motioned to me to do the same.

I lowered my voice and addressed Abdullah only. "Is there something wrong Abdullah? I am sorry if I have offended someone – this is not what I intended."

"We should just go – it is okay." He said something to Ahmed, who angrily waved us away.

Abdullah hustled me out from under the harsh glare of Ahmed. We made it outside the café and plunged back into the medina, down a couple of dark alleys and into a secluded nook before Abdullah stopped and confronted me.

"Who do you work for?" he demanded.

"What do you mean?" I asked innocently.

"Do you work for the CIA?" It had become dark out, and I felt the situation leaving my comfort zone in a hurry.

"Are you crazy? No – I don't. I told you, I am just a traveler – I'm here to learn, and to give my prayers like I did today."

"But Ahmed told me – you don't even know how to give your prayers. He saw you. So you were lying – you are not a Muslim. Why would you do that?"

"I know – he is right. I did not know my prayers. I am a Muslim, just not a very good one. I have forgotten much about my religion, and I was ashamed today. That is one reason I am here – I want to learn."

"And what about the questions about elections and the king? You cannot ask a Moroccan such questions, it is dangerous. Who do you work for?"

I could see the bodybuilder in Abdullah coming out, even in the advancing night. The veins on his neck were beginning to bulge, and he caught my arm in a vise grip, firing his questions in a hushed, urgent manner.

"I don't work for anyone, "I said. "I swear to God. I am just a traveler."

"Have you been followed?" He asked. I could not tell if he was demented or if there really was something to fear, but I knew the situation needed defusing quickly.

"No – I don't think so. I came to the Hotel Dalila because your friend Ali told me to. I didn't even know where I was going. Please, Abdullah. Let me go – I mean you no harm."

His vise grip loosened. I could see my feeble logic helping the situation a bit, so I pressed on.

"Abdullah – you don't understand. I am sorry. I didn't know to not ask questions about the king. You are my guide – you should tell me these things. I am here to learn, in peace. I trust you will tell me what is right and what is wrong. I don't even care what he thinks of the king – I just asked him out of curiosity."

Abdullah released my arm and started pacing in front of me.

"Mohammed, I am sorry. I get a little excited. You're right, I am your guide, and I should tell you. I will. But, there are many strange things that happen here and I am always nervous. People think any American here might work for the CIA. There are stories."

He looked around conspiratorially before continuing.

"There was this one time when this American, he came to Fez. He had no money, so he made friends with one of my friends – he lives not far from Hotel Dalila, in Ouedzhouer. He stayed with him for a month. Every day he would leave the house and talk to people and ask questions, and every night he would just sit and write and write, at my friend's house. After a month, the police came and took them both away. I don't know what happened to the American, but my friend slept on the floor of the jail for two weeks before he came home. He has not worked with foreigners since."

He stopped and watched for my reaction. After making sure that I was sufficiently shocked, he continued.

"This happens all the time," continued Abdullah. "You can trust almost no one. Just a few weeks ago, two Pakistani men were here asking strange questions in the medina. My friend was their guide, and he went and told the police that the Pakistanis were acting strange. The police told him that they were already being watched, and that my friend would have been in trouble if he hadn't gone to them himself."

Adbullah's voice had dropped to a whisper, and the way he told his stories of governmental suppression showed a genuine fear that I had not felt among Moroccans until that point. He motioned to me that we should start walking again, and we started weaving through the medina, my sense of direction completely lost.

"I get very nervous," he said. "I have five kids, you know that? Five kids. And no job. There are no jobs in this country. So I guide tourists, I help at the hotel, I do whatever I can to make money. I provide a home and food for my children. They are the most important thing in my life, them and my wife. But here in Morocco – it is dangerous, it is not like where you are from. We can't say whatever we want. We can't say we hate Bush, you know? There are people listening everywhere. It is not as bad as before, before with King Hassan II, but it is still dangerous. People talk, and then I get the trouble because I'm with you."

"Abdullah – don't worry, I'm not in the CIA. I'm only here to visit, okay? I don't want any trouble – believe me."

"Okay – I trust you. But no more political questions, okay?"

"Deal."

He finally smiled and stopped – we were back at the hotel. After a strong shake, he promised to take me around the city the next day before hurrying away into the night, up an embankment and into the darkness of the medina.

Sufficiently drained, I went upstairs and threw myself on the bed. My mind was alive, processing images and events and feelings, but my body was tiring and I drifted off to sleep.

There are times in life, usually after some kind of momentous event, when you wake up after an exhaustive sleep and wonder if yesterday was real. You ask yourself - did it really happen? Has your life really been given these new and strange parameters? Like the day after a loved one dies, or the day after a big break up.

For me, the morning after I was accused of being with the 'Agency' held this feeling. It had jarred the very core of my non-conformist being. By getting on a plane and flying fifteen hours, I had gone from liberal leftist Californian to suspicious agent of the Empire in the eyes of those around me, and as I got ready for the day my wonderment slowly disappeared and was replaced by a pragmatic new reality – I am an American traveling abroad, and I had better watch myself closer if I want to keep safe on my little journey.

I came downstairs and had a smoke on the steps of the hotel. A storm had moved in during the night, and the ground of the medina had turned into a muddy mess. I watched as two men tried to push a taxi out of a tough mud spot, the small car's back left wheel barely budging from the sinkhole around it.

As I watched the men struggle with their car, Abdullah came trudging through the rain, dressed in a snappy nylon sweatsuit. Behind him was a young boy, maybe ten, getting wet and muddy in his father's wake.

"Whew – is wet, you know? So sorry for this bad weather, Mohammed." Abdullah extended his hand and caught me in a vice grip handshake. "Are you ready to see the Medina?"

"Yes – let's go. And who is this?"

"This is my son Jaffar. He wants to come with us today – he has no school. Okay?"

"No problem – let's go."

We entered the medina in the same way we had the night before. In the light of day, the medina was less daunting but more exotic. As we snaked through the cramped confines we had to negotiate donkeys, goats, and children coming at us from every angle, just within the first few gullies.

Getting my bearings a little more, I recognized that we were following an alley that was somewhat of a main artery – the street was a little bigger than the others and the shops a little better established. Abdullah saw me scoping the surroundings and launched into his tour guide spiel.

"Fez is an ancient city. It was founded by Moulay Idriss II over 1200 years ago. He built this city to be like the Muslim cities in Arabia where he was from. At the center of the city is its greatest mosque – the Kairouine, where you gave prayer yesterday. It is a center for learning, for knowledge. The *souks* near the center are for learning and worship – you can buy books and prayer beads and such things there. As you move from the mosque out to the medina walls, you get the *souks* for clothing, then for the artisans – the wood workers, the jewelers, the tile workers. Then comes the fruits and vegetables, the spice *souk*, the henna *souk*, and then further away, on the outskirts, you get the leather workers and the butchers. Their work stinks – it smells. This is why they are at the edge."

We continued through the medina and progressed through the rows of shops. Abdullah stopped at a fountain where an old woman was filling up a bucket with water. The fountain was beautiful – it had the classic Muslim-style carved archway, with two semicircles converging to a single point at the top. The back and insides were lined with small colored tiles arrayed in an intricate pattern – dozens and dozens of blue, white, black and green squares arranged to make a larger pattern of eight circles surrounding one large circle.

"Fountains like these were built 1000 years ago by the great rulers of Fez. The medina has more than sixty of the big ones – they bring the water from the mountains to the city so the people can wash and drink and cook. They are very important – very beautiful. In the old times the princes and rich men would give different fountains to the city as presents, each one being more and more beautiful. Do you see the beautiful *zellij* work on this one? I love it – you know, sometimes, at night, I can tell where I am in the medina just by listening to the way the water runs through the canals under the city."

"Really? I was wondering how you find your way around."

"Well – it is really only difficult in the medina at night, in the places with no light. Then you can use the water, or the tilt of the street. But, in the day it is easy – you should know where you are by the shops you are near. If you get lost, find a major street and walk for a while – you'll make it out eventually."

At this he again turned and hurried away into the maze, which was growing muddier and muddier with the constant rain. After a few minutes we stopped at a large carved wooden door.

"This is the Medersa el-Attarine. A great example of our architecture here in Fez. Go in and see – I'll be back in ten minutes. Jaffar will wait with you."

After paying a ten dirham fee I entered the building. The inside was a courtyard, with covered two-story hallways running along the outer edge. Every inch of the main courtyard was covered in art – the floors and bottom three feet of the walls in *zellij* and everything else in intricately carved wood or plaster. Running along one wall was a horizontal strip of blue, green and white *zellij* that contained Qu'ranic verses in black calligraphy. The patterns and carvings that were not Arabic letters were of all kinds of geometry – squares and diamonds and various polygons stretched in repeating patterns everywhere.

In the middle of the courtyard was a fountain, gurgling up water into a shallow basin. It must be for saying wuzu, I thought. I had known what a medersa was from the crash course in political Islam I had given myself post 9/11 – they were Islamic theological schools. But, in my knowledge they served solely as a tool for the Saudis to brainwash legions of young unsuspecting third-worlders into a life of fundamentalism. As I stood in this exquisitely designed place, I wondered what medersas used to be like, or were like in other parts of the Muslim world. Surely a religion that creates such an inspiring place to study religious thought cannot advocate the ideology of hatred, I thought.

After about thirty pictures I left and found Jaffar waiting outside, looking at me shyly.

"Hi Jaffar," I said. "Do you speak English?"

He nodded his head yes but said nothing.

"You learned it in school?"

He hesitated, looking first away and then at my chest. "Yes, little."

"Do you like it here in Fez?"

"Yes."

"Do you like school?"

"Yes."

"Do you like futbol?"

I found the right question. His face lit up and he grinned, nodding his head vigorously at the mere mention of his passion.

"Yes – yes. I like. I watch."

"Who do you like? Who do you watch?"

"Manchester United. Nistelroy – he is good!"

Abdullah had walked up and butted in. "Yes, yes, every chance he gets he comes to café and watch Premier league. Jaffar will play there, in England, some day – yes Jaffar?"

Jaffar became shy again and looked away, down the street. The Premier league is to the poor Moroccans as the NBA is to the poor Americans, I thought.

"Mr. Mohammed," he said, slowly, "I have been wanting to say something to you. I have bad feeling for last night, you know? When I just left you right now I went to see Ahmed. I told to him that you are okay – that you are good Muslim and just here to see Fez."

"Well, thank you Abdullah. I hope he was satisfied with your explanation?"

"Yes, I think so. He says to tell you he is sorry, that he would like to have tea with you again tonight. He say he have present for you, yeah?" Abdullah smiled at me, looking like a man expecting gratitude.

"Wow – this is good news," I said, playing along. "Thank you Abdullah, I would be happy to see Ahmed again."

"Ok good, it is settled. So, now we finish our tour, and then later we go see Ahmed, okay? Let's us go eat, okay?"

After lunch and some more tourist places in the medina, including a pottery factory and a jewelry store, Abdullah finally decided it was time for me to go get my present, from Ahmed. He beckoned me to follow him back into the medina, through a separate alley entrance to the back right of the hotel's lot. He moved quickly, and I had to half jog to keep up with him as we twisted and turned our way through the blackness. The medina took on a different aura at night – it was much more sinister, and the claustrophobia much more oppressive.

After a hairpin turn I could see light at the other end of the alley. As we came upon it I recognized the same tea shop that we had been to the night before. There were men everywhere inside, sipping tea or coffee in groups of two or three. Almost every table was occupied by an intense card game, and the room rolled with the shouts and moans of winning and losing. Abdullah grabbed my wrist and led me to a smaller room to the side where we found Ahmed sitting with another older Moroccan man.

We greeted each other and Ahmed bade me sit down. He began speaking in French, and his friend immediately began translating.

"Mr. Mohammed, I am Wajid, and I am a good friend of Mr. Ahmed here. He has asked me to translate for him. First, he would like to give you a present."

Ahmed reached for a book on the table and handed it to me. It was thin – more of a pamphlet than a book. On the green cover was a picture of a sun rising over a mythical looking minaret, and in purple letters above the scene were written the words "*Salat*", the Arabic for 'prayer'.

"I own a book shop in the ville nouvelle," said Wajid, "and Ahmed asked me to bring this over for him – you can't get any books in English here in the medina. This is a book to teach you how to say your prayers. Ahmed wanted to give it to you as a present – he said, if you will excuse

his forwardness, he felt bad to see a man who claims to be Muslim not
be able to say his own prayers properly. He asked you to learn them
with this book, and he has offered that you come pray with him at the
Kairouine and practice until you have it right."

"Tell him I am not offended, but that I accept his generosity," I
said. I was anxious to deal with my ignorance, so I accepted on the spot.
Ahmed smiled widely, and said something in French.

"Okay – meet here at sun-up tomorrow for your morning prayers.
You can say all five prayers every day with Ahmed, if you like, until you
learn."

I figured, if this trip was about learning about the Muslims, that
spending a few days praying with Ahmed was about as good a way
as any to spend my time. I accepted, and we all had a glass of tea and
chatted for a while before Abdullah, who had been rather silent the
whole time, cleared his throat and looked at me.

"Okay, now maybe we go?"

He looked anxious, so I said okay and promised to meet Ahmed first
thing in the morning. Abdullah showed me some markers on our dark
walk home that would lead me back to the tea shop in the morning, and
at the door of the hotel I paid him the 200 dirham I had set aside for him
and said goodbye. He seemed happy with the amount (which we had
never negotiated), called me his brother again, and left.

I got through the first three pages of the book before falling asleep.
When I awoke for the morning prayer, I resolved myself to learning it
backwards and forwards.

The next three days I prayed fifteen times with Ahmed, between
each prayer reading and memorizing the Arabic in my book and after
each prayer sitting with Ahmed in the grand old mosque and practicing
my Arabic pronunciation (even though we could not speak each other's
languages, he proved adept at teaching me Arabic pronunciation through
imitation). My memory revived quickly, and I soon could give my prayers
in a solid, respectable manner. Ahmed took great joy in this, and after
the third day's Isha prayers he brought me back to the tea house, where
Wajid was involved in a game of cards with many onlookers.

"U-hem," said Ahmed, getting Wajid's attention before spilling a
torrent of French.

Wajid smiled and looked at me. "Ahmed says you are done – he is going away on business tomorrow, but you have learned your prayers already, so you two are done."

I silently rejoiced. "Well, please tell Ahmed that I thank him from the bottom of my heart, that I will always be indebted to him for his time and kindness."

Wajid translated and Ahmed smiled before responding. "He says that you do not need to thank him – he was doing God's work, and God will thank him when He sees him. He says he is old, and needs all the help he can get." Ahmed let out a laugh and embraced me before we parted.

Back at the hotel, I felt good. Calm, relaxed - at peace with myself and the world around me. Three days of praying had had an amazing meditative effect - my body and mind felt in complete rhythm, operating at the top of their games, ready for anything.

Chapter 5

Welcome to the World

Khizr comes to me that night not as he has before, with flashing green lights and pet dolphins, but subtly, in a more regular setting. We are sitting at a table, like two old friends, having a cup of tea. We are in Fez, in the medina – our table overlooking a small square with a fountain in the middle.

"Hey Mo – welcome to the world. Glad you could make it my friend," he says as he reclines and crosses his legs.

"Make it where – to Morocco? To get embarrassed at the Kairouine?" I say. My tone is accusatorial, even though I don't mean it.

"Yes – to get embarrassed. Being judged a fake is harsh for the ego, but it's the right kind of medicine. It exposes reality, if you will." He laughs and strokes his beard.

"What reality? That my reality is that I've only ever given prayers a half dozen times at family functions, and that I don't know them very well?"

"And why is that?" asks Khizr. "Why don't you know them very well?"

"I dunno. Habit, I guess. Nobody I interact with in my daily life would ever think of saying their prayers, so I don't. I mean – my friends and me, we're a bunch of wiseasses, you know? The peanut gallery is our place of worship, I think."

Khizr gives me a poker face, sips his coffee and sighs. "Yes, yes. Reveling in the minutia of Seinfeld trivia doesn't leave a lot of time for remembering your Creator. It's kinda the point, what you are saying, the point of why Islam requires the people to pray so much. Because, if you pray five times a day, you won't forget the big things, you know? You won't forget God, and the moral code that comes with this belief. Prayer is discipline – it is the most direct connection you have with the truth. This is the Islamic perspective on this – remember that."

"So, what is this? You've brought me here just to lecture me to say my prayers?"

He pauses, crinkles his nose and shakes his head. "No, not at all Mo. I'm here to help you see what the truth is. And the truth is that Islam asks you to pray five times a day, and that there is a certain way that it must be done. It must be done in Arabic. It must be done in the right sequence. It must be done at the right times of the day. All this is prescribed, but it isn't a major concern for you right now. I wanted to ask you – what do you think of Morocco?"

"Well, I think it is many, many things at once, I guess. I'm surprised at how old school the medina is. It is like stepping into medieval times, you know? And I'm surprised by the people - I'm surprised at the amount of tension here. I was fingered as a CIA agent for crying out loud! Once I won them over it was okay, but there is a hesitance to some of them – especially the older ones."

Khizr takes a long draw off his tea while he listens to my observations. When I finish he brings a hand-held mirror out from a pouch in his cloak and gives it to me.

"Look into this, look at yourself. What do you see?"

"I see me."

"Yes, yes, of course. It is you. But what else? Tell me."

"I see a brown face – a South Asian face. I see a man who has no idea why he is here. I see a man who is embarrassed by his ignorance. I see a man whose beard is too long. What else do you want me to say?"

"You have forgotten the most important part. You should also see a man who has accepted a quest from me, one that has only just begun. And you should see that your knowledge is already growing, that you have already matured. You should see a man who's gaining strength, gaining knowledge, in a world that desperately needs more people to do so. And so, you are here – you have made it to the Kairouine and given your prayers. I thank you, and now I give you another challenge. You must perform a pilgrimage for me."

"To Mecca?" I ask expectantly, "Straight into the Wahabbi nest, huh? Confront thine enemy and all that?"

"No," says Khizr forcefully, "I am not requesting that you go there. You are not ready – the pilgrimage to Mecca must only be done when one has fulfilled all his other duties to the Creator. This is Islamic law. No – I want you to perform another kind of pilgrimage, to the tomb of one of Islam's greatest men, to the Mevlana."

"Who is the Mevlana?"

"Go to Turkey and ask – you will find him. Go to see the Mevlana and learn from him – his way was one of our favorite ways, and you should learn from it. And remember - the trail you have embarked on will teach you – remember to listen and learn, all the way through. We have faith in you."

Khizr gulps the last of his tea, looks lovingly into my face, raises his green hood, and sweeps out of the room in one smooth motion.

Chapter 6

The Straits of Jabal Tariq

A few calls and internet searches the next day landed me a plane ticket, leaving from Madrid to Istanbul, for three days later. I said my goodbyes in Fez and made my way north to Tangiers, where I spent a night in the Hotel Ibn Battuta. I thought it was romantic, to stay in a hotel named after the greatest Muslim traveler of all time, but the romance was cut short when I walked through a wall of kif smoke to get to my dingy room and was greeted by stained sheets and a huge roach on my bed.

The next morning I got passage on a ship crossing the Straits of Gibraltar. It was named the S.S. Bismillah, and was one of the huge ferry lines that ply cars, people, and cargo back and forth between European Spain and African Morocco. Ferries leave on the hour from Tangier to the main port on the Spanish side, Algeciras, and I made the noon ferry, negotiating through hordes of young Moroccan hustlers waiting at the ferry docks for the next unsuspecting group of day trippers from the Continent.

The ride was two and a half hours – Africa on one side, Europe on the other. I chatted with a Portuguese student on the top deck for a while, but soon became bored and brought out the book I had made from YuMa's suggested reading. The first article was by YuMa himself – he had written it, he said, to provide 'easy access to the Prophet's story.' It had first been published by a newspaper in England as part of a Sunday series on Islam in the late 80s.

> *From Arabia to Andalucia – the Spread of Islam*
> *By Yousuf Khan, March, 1988*
> *The first three hundred years of Islam were witness to an*
> *explosion of conquest and culture the likes of which the world*
> *has rarely seen. Believers like to say that the reason for the*

early success of the religion was that its light was so pure and true – a divine message so easily accessible that it easily won converts from across the world. Another reason for the success of the religion can be seen historically, with the triumphant emergence of Islam arriving at the same time two ancient empires of the East, the Byzantine and the Sassanian, were failing.

The Prophet Mohammed was born in 570 AD. The Arabia of that time was a nomadic land, where tribal law ruled. The society was one where tribal loyalty was the highest virtue, and independence fiercely guarded. The tribes would move from various settlements and oases to the Red Sea, trading or selling or raiding other caravans from other clans.

The Prophet was born to a powerful merchant tribe in the city of Mecca, the Quraysh. It was a good time for the city – peace was reigning after years of warfare and more and more tribes were giving up desert life to move to the city and find better options. Business was booming. Pagan tribes from all over Arabia would come to visit the city, known by all since the days of Abraham as an ancient pilgrimage site. The Quraysh, pagans themselves, had become guardians of the shrines of the city and had adorned the main one, the Shrine of the Ka'bah (Abraham's House of God), with 360 statues of their various gods.

The Prophet was orphaned at a young age and landed in the care of his uncle, Abu Talib, at around the age of eight. He grew up a trustworthy member of the family business, participating in long trade voyages and in tribal excursions and battles. He was a shy and thoughtful young man, and honest in his dealings to the point where he earned the nickname of al-Ameen, meaning 'honest' and 'reliable.'

His reputation earned him an invitation for marriage from a wealthy widow named Khadija, which he accepted. The Prophet and Khadija enjoyed a happy marriage and he continued to work as a trader, but slowly he became increasingly introspective. He would retire for long periods of meditation to a cave in the mountains around Mecca called Hira, and it is here at the age of forty that he received his first revelation from the Angel Gabriel, explaining to him that he was God's last prophet and with him would go the final message of Islam to humanity. The revelations were to come and go for the next twenty-three years, and after each one the Prophet would memorize the verses and recite them to a growing number of followers as the words of God. The accumulation of all these revelations is the holy book, the Qu'ran, which Muslims take as the word of God as revealed to His last prophet, Mohammed.

The mission of Islam is to establish that there is only one God. Islam is monotheism. It sees itself as the culmination of many transmissions from God to humanity that explain the existence of one and only one true God, and prescribes details for worship of Him. Many of the transmissions came via men – it is said in the Qu'ran that God sent man 124,000 prophets to spread His word. Jesus, Moses, Noah, Abraham, and many Old and New Testament figures feature prominently in the Qu'ran as great prophets of the past, and their books, including the Bible and the Torah, are considered to be sacred books by Islam. The Prophet referred to those followers of the older traditions, the Christians and the Jews, as 'the People of the Book', and recognized them as legitimate worshippers of his same God.

The monotheism Mohammed began to preach in Mecca offended the ruling elite, and in particular threatened the pagan pilgrimages on which the city made big profits. At first he was ignored, with only a small band of close supporters (including Khadija, his cousin Ali, and his friend Abu Bakr) believing in his new religion. But as his flock grew, the Meccan authorities began to suppress the fledgling group, arresting and torturing or even murdering the most feeble and unconnected. Mohammed's message of equality and justice began to resonate louder and with more and more people, and as he challenged the old social order he was finally convinced that his own life was in jeopardy and left Mecca, along with seventy or so of his followers, and moved to Yathrib, an oasis city 300 miles away that had offered him asylum. This migration from Mecca to Yathrib, which occurred in 622 AD, is known as the Hijrah (migration) and marks the start of the Islamic calendar.

The Prophet almost immediately became the spiritual and civic leader of the community in Yathrib, which was renamed Medinat al-Nabi (city of the prophet), or Medina for short. The majority of the inhabitants of the city converted to Islam and the next few years were spent establishing a living model of Islam. The Qu'ranic verses the Prophet received while in Medina were much more concerned with governance of the community, while his earlier transmissions in Mecca dealt with man's relationship to God. There remained a minority of Jews in the city as well, who entered into an alliance with the Muslims without accepting Mohammed as a prophet of their God.

The Meccans pursued the Prophet, and the next few years saw clashes between the armies of Mecca and Medina. His own tribe, the Quraysh, were leaders of some of the raids and considered Mohammed to have committed the worst possible sin, the sin of going against one's tribe. In these battles it is said that the Jews aligned themselves with both sides, betraying the Prophet in one critical battle and henceforth sowing the seeds of hostility between the two faiths that still flame today.

The Prophet eventually won the battles with the Meccans – within ten years of the Hijrah, Islam had won 200,000 converts, from Syria to Yemen to Persia. The Prophet rode this tidal wave of momentum back to the city of his birth and took over peacefully, granting immunity to all those who had opposed him before. The Quraysh were included in this generous offer and converted to the very faith they had been trying to destroy for a decade. Within two generations it would be they who would assume the reigns of the new Islamic empire.

After his conquest of Mecca, the Prophet performed the pilgrimage that is the duty of all Muslims, the hajj, as prescribed in the Qu'ran. The manner in which he performed the hajj to Mecca in 632 AD – from the dress to the prayers to the rituals – is still emulated today and is one of the requirements every Muslim, if able, must fulfill in their lifetime.

The Prophet died after performing the hajj and the empire he had built was left without a leader. Unlike Jesus or Moses, Mohammed had enjoyed military and social acceptance in his day – he left a large and expanding kingdom that needed the guidance of a ruler. The closest companions of the Prophet elected Abu Bakr to be the next Caliph, or leader of the faithful.

It was during the election of the first successors to the Prophet that splits emerged between different factions within the Muslims. The two main sects of Islam today, the Sunni and the Shia, were born from these wars of succession. The Shia believe that the Prophet's cousin and son-in-law, Ali, had been legitimately dubbed the heir to the throne by the Prophet and that his line of descendants should have ruled the Muslim empire. The Sunni believe that the first four Caliphs - Abu Bakr, Umar, Uthman and Ali - had been chosen legitimately by the people. Both sides recognized the fifth caliph, Mu'awiya, as a usurper who strayed from the piety of the first four caliphs and embraced a dynastic form of despotism.

The time of the Prophet and the first four Caliphs is regarded as the golden age of Islam for the purity of those who were leading the faithful. Islam was practiced in the exact manner as it was prescribed. It was after this time, when Empire became more important than religion, that Islam lost some of its purity.

In contrast to the burgeoning Muslim power in Arabia, two older empires to the north were faltering. Byzantium, which ruled most of Christianity from its seat of power in Constantinople, had occupied the border lands of Palestine, Syria and Egypt, while the Sassanian Persian empire, which practiced the ancient fire and nature religion of Zoroaster, occupied much of present day Iraq and Iran. Under the direction of the Caliphs Umar and Uthman the Muslim armies advanced from Arabia at a torrid pace, using quick hitting tactics against the larger and slower armies of the older empires to score quick victories. The Muslims also began to swell their ranks with more and more Bedouin converts turned soldiers. Within twenty years of the Prophet's death, the banner of Islam had taken such ancient places as Damascus, Jerusalem, Alexandria, Persia, and Libya, and was en route to the farthest corners of the known world.

Mu'awiya moved the center of power from Medina to Damascus and established the first Muslim dynasty, the Umayyads. They ruled the ever-expanding Muslim empire for over a hundred years and adopted many of the mechanisms of government employed by the Byzantines and the Sassanians before them. The Umayyads allowed all conquered people to retain their religious beliefs and a certain amount of autonomy, and it was through these pragmatic measures that they were able to keep control of the huge empire they were creating, which had at this point taken virtually all of the Middle East and most of North Africa.

In the summer of 710 AD, a substantial Muslim force crossed the Straits of Gibraltar from Morocco. Under the command of Tariq ibn Zayad, they had instructions from the caliph in Damascus to take as much land north of the Straits as he could. After he landed on the Iberian peninsula, ibn Zayad symbolically burned his ships – he was not going back.

Within a matter of weeks he had taken Cordoba and Toledo from the Vandals, who ruled southern Spain at the time. The Muslim force, swelling in ranks with more Berbers from North Africa, pushed past the Pyrenees before finally being defeated by the Byzantines at the Battle of Poiters in 711 AD. There are some who believe, had the Umayyad empire desired, they could have sent more armies from their power base in Damascus and taken Paris and London. But they did not, and were content to retreat to the area they named Jazirat al-Andalus, meaning 'Land of the Vandals.'

The Muslims set to work reaping the riches of the Andalusian soil. Berbers who came from Morocco brought with them terrace cultivation skills that worked well in the hills – many of the terraces they made are still used to grow crops in southern Spain today. Agrarian technologies such as canals, crop rotations, and waterwheels were imported from places like Iran and Syria.

Abdur Rahman I was an Umayyad noble who fell out of favor with the elite in Damascus. His exile led him to Morocco and then Andalusia in 756 AD, where he united the various Muslim armies who had staked out claims to different cities in Spain under one kingdom. He proclaimed himself the true Caliph, made his capital Cordova, and set about construction of the Great Mosque of Cordova, which stands today as one of the most beautiful works of Islamic architecture in the world. The mosque was built to be the finest, and the king imported materials and artisans from all over the Muslim empire to create it. Besides setting a standard of excellence and refinement in Muslim Spanish architecture, the mosque became a center of Islamic thought, producing the Maliki school of jurisprudence and various theological luminaries of the Islamic world.

The Umayyad rule was to last 300 years in Andalusia, but Muslims were to rule there for a total of 700 years. Separate Muslim kingdoms arose with capitals in Cordova, Seville, and Granada, but competition between the various Muslim kingdoms eventually weakened them all, and the rising tide of Christianity could not be stemmed. In 1492 the last Muslim kingdom in Spain, Granada, was surrendered, to King Ferdinand and Queen Isabella, right as they sent Christopher Columbus westward to find the New World. For Islam it was a bitter new world, as the balance of power that had so clearly begun to shift to the West signaled the waning of Islam's moon, and the end of its original glory days.

I finished YuMa's article and went to the ship's rail to see if I could make out the rock of Gibraltar. I could see nothing but the Spanish coastline, and when I asked a fellow passenger they said this ship veered north before passing it. To think – 1000 years ago the Muslims were so strong they launched an all out attack on a Western European country and took it with ease. Now, the Muslim world seems split between Uncle Toms in the West or barbarians in the East, fighting with cell phones from caves and hell bent on violence-incited anarchy.

As the ship settled into port, my mind kept wandering. How different would it have been today if the Muslims had pushed through to Paris, or Rome, or even London? Would the Renaissance have happened? Could Reason, Democracy, Liberty and the rest come into such fashion and spawn something like the American Constitution? Had there been Muslims on the first boats to America, what might it have ended up like? Playing the shoulda-woulda-coulda game is a luxury for a dreamer, but then, that's what travel affords you - the ability to be transient, and to dream idle thoughts usually buried by rigmarole and responsibility.

Chapter 7

Turning Point

After a three hour bus ride, I checked in to a hostel in Granada and slept like a rock. In the morning, I decided to check out the grand old Muslim castle on the hill, the Alhambra. The irony of one of the greatest accomplishments of Muslim architecture being used as a major tourist attraction for a Catholic country was just too much for me to ignore.

The Alhambra receives two million visitors per year – it is the largest tourist attraction in Spain – and crowd controls are strictly enforced. Ten minutes into my wait in the ticket line a voice over a loudspeaker announced first in Spanish, then in English that the morning tickets had been sold out but that we could buy tickets for the afternoon session, starting around 2pm. I waited in the midst of a busload of Germans, listening to Spearhead on my headphones, and after twenty minutes purchased my eight euro ticket for the afternoon session and found a cafe to have some lunch at.

At 2pm I was back in line, entering the hallowed grounds. The place is laid out like a mini Moroccan city. The kasbah of the Alhambra, the Alcazaba, is on the border that looks over the river valley, while the medina area where the king had reception halls and lavish palaces is spread out going up the hill. The whole complex sat on the lower hills of the Sierra Nevada mountains of Spain, lording over the city of Granada below and framed by the snow-capped peaks above it. With walls on one side and mountains behind it, the Alhambra was an almost impenetrable city unto itself, with palaces, houses, schools, barracks, and gardens all once being housed on its grounds.

Up the hill from the Alhambra is the Generalife, whose name comes from 'gennat alarif' (garden of the architect). This complex has terraces and promenades with views of the Alhambra and Granada below. Between the areas of the Alhambra and the Generalife is the convent of San Francisco, an addition by the Christians after they took over that now serves as a high-end hotel.

I hooked up with a guided tour and followed a young, pony-tailed Spaniard as he led a hodgepodge group of tourists through the grounds.

"After the completion in the late 1200s," he said in a thick Andalucian accent, "the Alhambra began to take a quality which the Moors called 'Paradise on Earth.' The common people down below in Granada would have gossip about Alhambra's magical gardens and vast riches. Inside the walls of the fortress the best poets, musicians, and artists played for the King's pleasure, and the highest quality of life was lived."

We were walking through a beautiful garden, with impeccably manicured shrubs forming classic Muslim archways that looked out over the city below. As we walked, the pace quickened as the first drops started to fall from an ominous cloud cover that had come in overhead.

Our guide continued. "But many wars weakened the Moors, and eventually King Ferdinand and Queen Isabella came to take this place. Many Moors in Granada wanted to fight – they had pride in their city. Many thought the Alhambra could never be taken, and that they could fight to the death in the streets below. But, they did not get a chance to fight. Boadbil, the last Moorish king in Spain, surrendered the fortress to King Ferdinand in 1492 because he was promised safety for him and the people of Granada. Of course, within a year of the surrender, Boadbil, along with most of his Muslim and Jewish subjects, ran to Morocco to escape the Inquisition, and they lost everything anyway. But, because he surrendered peacefully, the Alhambra was spared a major battle, and she stands here today for you, to enjoy. Here, everyone, please – come quick to the Palace."

The rain was pouring down now, and he led us into a large foyer of one of the main buildings on the grounds. As the crowd shook off the rain, he continued.

"King Ferdinand and Queen Isabella loved the Alhambra and made it their home until they died. It is here where Columbus came, with his report on the discovery of America. Eventually, the monarchy moved and the Alhambra fell into a state of disrepair, being inhabited by bums and stray dogs for much of the 17th and 18th centuries, before Napoleon's army took up residence in 1812 and almost destroyed the place. In 1832, the American historian and traveler Washington Irving spent several months living on the grounds, and his subsequent book, *Tales of the Alhambra*, revived much interest in both the fortress and its legends. Now, it is one of Spain's biggest attractions. You are now in the Palace of the Nazarenes – the center point of the ground."

Large parts of the palace were open-air courtyards, and the rain was slamming through, a wet wind whistling in that felt like it came straight from the snowy mountain tops above. Groups of cold tourists moved from room to room, taking in and sheltering under the exquisite architecture all around. Beautiful Arabic tile work and geometric stucco carvings, grander and more intricate than what I'd seen in Fez, adorned every hallway and curved arch. I came into the main court, the Court of Myrtle, and huddled on a corner bench for a while. The large pool in the middle was overflowing from the rain's wrath – I wished that my teeth would stop chattering so that I could enjoy the moment a bit more. Sitting wasn't working, I decided, so I ran into the next room, the Hall of the Ambassadors, and then the next, which was the Court of Lions, going into speed tourism mode.

Delicate marble columns, not even a foot in diameter, lined both sides of the outer hallway around the courtyard. In the center of the courtyard was a fountain surrounded by twelve stone lions. Each column morphed into a large carved box before finally merging to form the border of one of the archways covering the walkways. The archway architecture, while sticking to the traditional shape of the Islamic arches I'd seen in Fez, was more ornate – almost Gothic in its grandeur. The slim intricacies of the carvings were breathtaking, and I found it unimaginable how these beautiful works of art survived the earthquakes, storms, and neglect they had seen in the last 700 years.

"This is the Court of the Lions," boomed the Spanish guide, who suddenly appeared next to me, his breath clouding the air around him. "It is maybe the most intact of all the monuments in Alhambra. These twelve lions in the middle are said to be each sign of the Zodiac, because the Moors were very much concerned with astrology in their daily affairs. The four streams running out from the fountain are to be the four corners of the earth, and I like to think that now, after all this time, people from all four corners have come here and seen the streams."

The guide led us through the remaining halls of the Palace of the Nazarenes while telling us a long Washington Irving tale about the presence of magic on the grounds. Through the narration of the story the guide led the group through the palace, for some photo ops on top of the turrets of the Alcazaba, and then back through the gardens of the Alhambra. The rain had slowed to a drizzle, and as he finished the story he brought us to the Gate of Justice – the main entrance to the Alhambra.

Satisfied but drenched, I tipped the guide and found my way to a bus headed for the next hill over. I wanted to get a view of the Alhambra from a short distance – I felt as though being on its grounds didn't give the full effect. Inside there had been rooms and terraces that had looked down on the hill next door, across the Darro River, and I had seen on my map that it was the old Muslim neighborhood of Granada, called the Albaicin.

The bus snaked down the Alhambra's hill and then up the next and into the old neighborhood. The streets were steep and narrow, paved with cobblestone and slick from the rain. The white walls on either side of us, like the walls of a medina, hemmed us in at every turn. The district looked up and coming – mixed in with tiny old homes were larger, newer villas. I asked the bus driver to drop me in the center of the neighborhood, and he kindly did, pointing towards a small road next to the bus stop.

"Photo," he said as he smiled and pulled away.

I took the road up a small hill and emerged at some stairs that climbed onto a plaza named Mirador de San Nicolas, which stood in front of a church with the same name. The view from the plaza was breathtaking – rising above the river below, with reddish brown ramparts and turrets, the vast Alhambra complex jealously guarded its treasures within. Around the citadel the hills and trees were all shades of autumn browns and reds. Behind the fortress lay the snow capped peaks of the Sierra Nevada mountains, completing the postcard perfectly.

As I snapped pictures I heard an unlikely sound – the azan. For a second I thought it was false – I was in Spain, not Morocco, right? The only Muslims I'd seen in town had been North African shopkeepers, and I doubted they had the kind of money to maintain a mosque in this neighborhood. I looked around for the muezzin and finally spotted him, in a small tower next to the plaza. His familiar song drew me to him.

Inside the main gate of the mosque was a courtyard that had an equally breathtaking view of the Alhambra as that of Mirador de San Nicolas. The mosque itself stood facing the old palace, with windows from the main prayer hall looking out onto the gardens between it and the river valley below. I went to the main entrance to the mosque and saw a solitary man standing under an umbrella.

"Hello," I said. "You speak English?"

"No."

The man looked at me for a second, and then drew my attention to a bookshelf just inside the entrance. On it were pamphlets that gave the basic fundamentals and history of Islam. From the variety of languages they were provided in, I realized that he thought I was a tourist and was showing me the tourist zone of the mosque. Just beyond the bookshelf was a desk, and then beyond that another inner courtyard, partway fenced off with a 'No Tourist' sign posted on the barrier.

"No, no," I reassured. "I Muslim, I Muslim. Salaam Alaikum."

His face brightened immediately.

"Wailaikum Salaam," he answered before taking my hand and leading me through the inner chamber and into the prayer hall. Immediately inside were cubbyholes for shoes and he pointed at my muddy boots as he took his own off and stowed them away. He waited for me and then signaled to his watch – we had to hurry to make the prayer. We went downstairs and came into a large bathroom, with gleaming white tiles and a large trough with running water. Everything in the place seemed brand new, and of the highest quality. We hurriedly performed our *wuzu* and rejoined the congregation in the prayer hall. There were nine men, standing in a line behind the imam, of all different backgrounds. The imam started the prayer and we were off, performing the four rakats of the late afternoon prayer, I stood in the line between the man who had brought me in and a thirty-something white guy with a peach fuzz beard and said my prayers, trying not to feel too prideful that now, thanks to Fez, I was no longer a poser in the Muslim prayer room.

The prayer ended and the men dispersed quickly. I spotted the imam, who took off his black robe to reveal slacks and a tailored shirt underneath, putting on his raincoat and readying himself to go back outside.

"Excuse me – Salaam Alaikum."

"*Wailaikum Salaam Vo Rham A Tullahai Vo Berakato*" he said.

"Do you speak English?" I asked.

"Only little."

"This mosque is beautiful – how old is it?"

The imam shook his head and shrugged. "I no speak good. Daoud – he speak English. Come."

The imam led me outside the mosque and around the wall, down a little stairwell and then into the mosque's bottom floor. Kids were running around, and women in hijab were chatting, drinking tea, and directing child traffic. A passing snippet of the conversation sounded like English, but the kids were yelling at each other in Spanish.

We knocked on a door and after a few moments a young white man answered. His smallish stature and neat appearance made him look like a bookworm – an accountant or lawyer of some kind, I thought. As the imam spoke to him in Spanish he looked over at me with a quiet confidence, nodding his head and bidding the imam adios.

"Daoud – he speak with you. I go," said the imam, reaching out to shake my hand.

I thanked the imam and he left the two of us alone in Daoud's office. He invited me to sit down in an impeccable British accent, and then resumed a phone conversation, in Arabic, that I seemed to have interrupted. After a few minutes, he hung up, let out a deep breath and turned to me.

"Salaam Alaikum, brother - what can I do for you?" he asked.

"Walaikum Salaam," I said back. "Um, well, I'm not sure Daoud. I think there's been a misunderstanding. I just prayed at the mosque and wanted to ask the imam about it – it is such a beautiful place."

"Yes, yes it is. *SubhanAllah*. We are glad to have you." He dropped Arabic terms in with his English effortlessly, making it sound natural and routine.

"Hey – it's okay." I said. "Look – I didn't want to interrupt – you are obviously busy, so I'll let you go. Thanks so much Daoud – you have a great facility here."

"You are always welcome here – it is no interruption. I love speaking with travelers coming through – I am assuming you are a traveler?"

"Yes – from California, but my family is from Pakistan."

His cell phone rang, and he excused himself for a few more minutes before hanging up and apologizing for the interruption.

"I am so sorry – things are rather hectic around here today. So – you are from Pakistan? I thought so – I definitely thought of the Subcontinent when I saw you. We usually don't get Muslim travelers – usually it is Europeans and East Asians, taking pictures from our courtyard or peeking in when we say our salat. We welcome a fellow brother to our prayer – I saw you in the *masjid*. I have plenty of time now – let us talk. What is your name?"

"Syed Mohammed Khan."

"What a fabulous name. So, Syed..." he began.

"I go by Mo." I said.

"Oh right, well Mo, then – what do you think of Granada?"

"I think it is lovely – I just wish I had more time to see it. This is really my only day, and it's been pouring rain since morning."

"Oh, I am so sorry. You should really come back in spring – it is lovely then. And what brought you to our mosque?"

"Well – I came to get some pictures from Albaicin of the Alhambra – I took the tour of the palace today. I was standing in the plaza when I heard the azan and I was surprised, so I followed it and here I am. I didn't think there was an active Muslim community in Granada – how did this mosque come about?"

He paused for a second and glanced at the computer screen on his desk. "It's a long story – I will tell it to you, but there may be some interruptions, as I am expecting a phone call soon, okay?" he said.

"Yes – of course," I said. "Thank you so much for your time. My trip is very much about learning, so I have all the time in the world – you tell me when you have to finish and I'll take off."

He seemed to like that comment – his eyes glistened and he resettled in his chair, shifting his weight and shuffling some papers, before beginning.

"Well, there wasn't really a great deal of Islam in Spain say forty years ago. There were a great deal of immigrant workers from North Africa, and they were the modern Muslim presence in southern Spain until now. Most of them were Algerian and Moroccan, and most of them had come here illegally or quasi-legally, for migrant worker type jobs. They lived in small areas, they had a small prayer room where they might congregate, and if they were lucky, they could bring their families over and live life on the bottom of society over here. Then thirty years ago a movement started taking place. There was a man in Scotland named Sheikh Abdul Khadr, and he embraced Islam. Specifically, he embraced it in North Africa. He embraced Islam forty years ago, and basically he was given the task to take the *Deen* of Islam to the Westerners, and that's exactly what he did."

"The *Deen* of Islam? What is that?" I asked.

"The Arabic word '*Deen*' doesn't have an English equivalent. The closest English word would be religion, but there is also an element of obedience to *Deen*. It is like your contract with God. Anyway, after learning everything he could, the Sheikh went to London and he started a *zawi*, or place of learning, and started teaching. In those days, and I'm talking about the 50s and 60s, London was a booming place, and there were people from all over the world coming and going, searching for answers and truth in all sorts of places. His following started to grow – he is Sufi and was teaching from a certain mystical viewpoint. And then, four Spaniards came, listened to his teachings, became Muslim, and then carried, like a torch if you like, the *Deen* back to Spain. Not the religion as learned by the Moroccans who had settled in Spain, which is more of a belief based in tradition and roots. This was a rekindling of the true spirit of Islam, and of the true meaning of the *Deen*. It was an intellectual, cultural and spiritual transformation for the religion in this country. These men were intelligent, normal European-stock Spaniards who had come to this conclusion after searching for light and truth in what they regarded as an age of confusion and darkness."

I could see where he was going with this. "So you are saying that these kind of men wouldn't have embraced Islam without doing a thorough intellectual examination of it?"

"Exactly," said Daoud. As he prepared to go on, the glint in his eye grew stronger. Daoud's eloquence was simple and certain – he reminded me very much of some of the Sufis I had met in my uncle's crew in Pakistan. His British accent and his spiritual subject matter made him come off as a professor, as an expert in what he was saying.

"It's not something that happened by accident – these people wanted the *Deen*, and were ready to hear God's will. But they also found that the Muslim people themselves, the ones they would go out and meet in the world and whose families had been living with Islam for generations, were in darkness and disarray. These new Muslims took care to follow their own path in acceptance of the *Deen*." He emphasized this point by raising his voice a little, as if this was central to the story of the mosque.

"So, these Spaniards came back with this new thing they had discovered, so fresh and so beautiful, and they came and settled in Granada. And they started telling their friends, and then their friend's friends. And slowly people started to convert, and that was the beginnings of the community you see here. And as the Spanish Muslim community began to grow, it began to interact and work with the North African Muslim community and to absorb parts of its Islamic practices, as the people of the Maghrib are the closest link to the practices in the times of Al-Andalus, which is the heritage of this area. So, that tradition came and replanted itself, you could say."

"Wow – that's amazing," I said, knowing full well that the Islam that most of Europe faces today is one of immigrant ghettos. "So, it is a new generation of converts? I'm sure the Catholic community was none too pleased – don't want to dredge up any old wounds here, huh?"

"Yes – that comes with the story," he said, somewhat impatiently. "Conflict is a part of our world today, but it is really beside the point. What happened here – this community of Muslims and what they built – that is the important thing. So as the community began to grow, they realized they were lacking certain instruments that were crucial to their lives, including a mosque. There were certain Muslim pockets around town but none condensed strongly enough in one area to build a mosque. Of course, the Albaicin still had its fair share of Muslims, as it always has, and twenty-two years ago land was very cheap around here. It was a pretty run down neighborhood. So, these people banded together and bought this big plot of land for a relatively small sum of money."

"They got it for cheap, even with that stunning view of the Alhambra?" I inquired.

"Yes, well, twenty-two years ago there wasn't that much tourism going on in this country. Spain didn't have the...," Daoud paused for a second to find the right word, "*banking* to really get things on the move like they can nowadays – it was more of a closed economy. There were less people coming from abroad and buying properties. Now, with the EU rules, French, German, English, and even American buyers come here and drive the property values up by overpaying. Less and less do you see the locals buying property here, but that is another story. Twenty years ago this wasn't the case, and we were able to get the land and start the process of building a mosque. But we have had long delays – it seemed like the local authorities and the Catholic Church were pulling every trick out to sabotage us. First we had to do proposals and then this was too big and that was too small and then we had to build a scaffold and model tower for environmental study – so many things that no other building has to go through to get built here. They did not want a new mosque in Granada. I found it odd – here were a bunch of modern people, intelligent, peace loving Europeans who wanted to have a place together for praying in their community. And it was so hard to do. All we wanted was a place of worship! Did you know that the church in Spain doesn't pay taxes, but we do?"

"Wow. So, there is no separation of Church and State here? Catholicism is the state religion in Spain?" My American constitutional superiority peaked out before I could beat it back in.

"No – no it isn't, but it exerts much power. Well, certainly in the time of Franco it had enormous power, and it still does today. There was an old church, not far from here but not in use. It was derelict. And it had originally been a mosque – almost all the churches you see in this neighborhood were once mosques. We wanted to buy - the construction time on this mosque was taking so long – but as soon as the Church heard they fixed it up and performed one marriage a month in it or whatever the minimum was for upkeep. They didn't use it, really, and we went without."

He managed to deliver his speech without bitterness, stating his case matter-of-factly and with little emotion. "They couldn't accept a beautiful new mosque being built here – the Vatican would never accept a Muslim rebirth in Catholic Spain. They've been subjugating the Muslims to their control for years here. It's one thing to have a slave class of North Africans to do your dirty work for you, it's another that they stand up and begin to practice their faith openly and with pride. They fear this. We think it is wrong – they have nothing to fear at all, really."

"Well, do you think that it's because the Church has a long memory? Maybe they remember the wars of 800 years ago?" I asked.

"Well, I think both the Muslims and the Christians have long memories, don't they? Of course they do. In fact, most people just have a fear of the unknown. Not understanding something makes you not like it, it makes you worry about it. That's always been a problem between East and West – there's been a complete lacking in understanding, with no one really wanting to know the other."

"But maybe that's easier for the rulers – it helps them to rule," I said, coming from Bush land. "Fear keeps them in power."

"Well, either you empower yourselves by making your population fear something, or you empower your population through education and morality. We empowered ourselves with lawyers and finally, in July 2003, we were able to open our new mosque. Sheikh Sultan came and did the inauguration – he is from Sharja in the United Arab Emirates, and he was the one who finished the mosque. He provided the funding in the end."

"So, most of the funds were raised from abroad?"

"Well, the funding came from several sources actually. The Malaysians put up funding for several parts, and the Libyan government actually gave the money for the initial purchase of the land."

"Really? Qadaffi?"

"Yes, of course. We went all around the world, shopping this cause. Some leaders gave freely, some didn't. Qadaffi said 'Here's the money and good luck to you', and that was it."

"But I didn't think that Qadaffi was such a religious guy. Isn't he a colonel or something?"

"Well – he is what he is, but he gave us funding. And we took it from him. The fact is, many governments wanted to give. We went to the Saudi government and they said sure – they'll build the whole thing. And then they'll put their imam in it, and then they'll put all their books in it, and then they'll run it. And we said no thank you. We are Spanish Muslims, we told them, and we are making our own Islam here. We do not need another Saudi embassy in the West, because that's what they do. They take over a mosque when they come in with their fundamentalist interpretations, and they ruin it. They make it inaccessible and isolated from the local population, and this is their worst mistake. It is our responsibility to take the *Deen* to the non-Muslims. We can't put up more barriers, more walls preventing them from what we have."

I loved the Wahabbi bashing but backed off the path of conversation, as I wanted to keep the conversation more about this place. "So, what has been the reception from the community around you? I mean, it's a beautiful facility."

"Well – yes. There have been fourteen converts already. And the gardens are open – people are always in them, tourists and locals alike. We maintain them free, for the public. And you see how we have built it – people can see us offering our prayers. We do not want to hide behind closed doors and make people wonder about us. We love the *Deen* of Islam – we are proud of our submission to God. It is important to be open and to not become isolated – it is important to mix and learn from each other. This is how Islam spread – the Muslims were traders, knowledge seekers. They spread out and integrated, learning from the cultures they met and teaching Islam. They took the courtesy and the *Deen* of Islam, and it spread. This was the tradition of the Islam of Al-Andalus, and this is what we are re-establishing here in Granada."

Daoud was interrupted by a flurry of office activity – a phone call urgently demanded he send an email. He excused himself and I went to the drinking fountain for some water. I couldn't help but be impressed by him – he spoke at least three languages fluently, he was well traveled and spoken, and he had conviction in his beliefs. I sat back down and he finished up his work, sat back and cleared his throat. Before he could start on his train of thought again, I posed a quick question.

"So, Daoud, thank you for taking the time to speak with me. I'd like to know – what brought you to Islam? How does an Englishman become a Muslim?"

"Well, I was one of the more fortunate people in the world to come to Islam, I think. I came from a part of the world – a small town on the east coast of England, in a particular region and in a particular county which is known for its conservatism. There weren't any Blacks, maybe a few Chinese, but Muslims? I don't think there was one where I grew up. So, Islam wasn't in any way, shape or form present in my world. I think – you know most people, at around age fourteen or fifteen, the intellect kicks in and they start to think, to become more aware. And then you are in your teenage crisis – your adolescence. I tried to get answers – I started to question everything around me. I started to find out that my parents didn't have all the answers. In fact, they were wrong a lot."

"And when I thought about myself, I wondered. What was this path I was on, that I and everyone around me took for granted? What were we studying in school, while there was famine and civil wars going on all over the globe? I mean, after so many years of civilization, after so many wars, you think hang on a minute. Have we not learned anything? Have we not reached the pinnacle of human civilization yet, with everything we're capable of? And then I realized that the pinnacle, the height, of a human being's life in our times was to be employable, preferably by a big corporation. That was it – that was what we were studying for. The equation was employability equals job equals wealth. And then, do what you want. If you think about it, while you watch all the fish swim upstream in the developed world, all those people are just battling to be employable, to get their money. And then I thought – why should I be employable? Why should I join an organization whose sole motives were for profit – what were their morals? What kind of people were they? And the more I went down this road of understanding the society around me the more I began to think it was mad. It was all mad, or, that is the way it's supposed to be – this is as good as it gets and the problem is that I'm mad. But I only had me to rely on, and in the betting world I guess you'd say I bet on myself. I bet that I wasn't mad and that there was something else out there, beyond what I had seen, that would make sense. This was really my first exercise, really, in thinking for myself, and it was quite shocking. The more I confronted the modern world the more disillusioned I became, and the more I searched for answers in spirituality. Since I was a child I'd always believed in the Creator – I had always understood the beauty and perfection of the Creation itself."

"Your family were Christians?" I asked.

"They were Methodists, but um, they did the normal thing, you know – church once a week. I don't know how much they believed in it – I always got the feeling they were doing it more for us than for them, and that they thought it helped to keep us on the straight and narrow path or something. But, through this I kind of knew about the Old Testament and Jesus and the other Prophets, and I believed that this story was true – that it was all pretty much the case. But I never did believe in the Trinity – I could never swallow that. And I could see corruption – even in the Church. It is just as corrupt as any other political body in the world really – it's all just a way of controlling people again, and it does not give to people what they truly deserve. It just could not be, in my mind, that God sent that to us – God, who made the world and humans so perfectly, couldn't send us hypocrites to dispense His religion. Surely He had provided a path for us to follow Him on and to show our love for Him properly."

He paused to take a sip of water and then continued. "So I started researching – I looked at many old tribes and how people existed before modern times. It seems that they all had more contact with nature – there was more of oneness between them and their elements. And I decided that I must find something that gives me that same oneness – that explains to me my relationship with my fellow beings in this modern world. I believed in the prophetic tradition and the divine messages, so I looked into all the major religions, going deeper into Christianity than I'd ever been, and submerging myself in theology. And then there was a friend of a friend who was thinking about becoming a Muslim. It was through the thinnest of threads, really, because I had no idea about Islam until then. I just knew it was from the Far East – that was it. I mean, in my school growing up, they don't teach you anything about Islam – you just learn that they are foreigners."

"Same thing in California."

"Yes – you see? So, I started to pull that thread to Islam, and slowly I learned more, and slowly I began to see more and more truth. What I realized was that the message can't die – as long as there is a world and as long as there are people in it, there has to be some kind of message. And the message must contain justice, equality, and some kind of reasonable way of living together. And while I could not see the message in the West, I began to learn about the Prophet Mohammed, Peace Be Upon Him. I began to learn how he had lived, and how well documented it had been. What he said and what he did for all aspects of life were there for reading, ready to learn from. And the more I learned about the man and his influences on those around him – I mean, anyone can go into a cave and live on their own and be in perfect harmony with himself – they harm no one and no one harms them. But it is all about society – people and civilizations grow and interact – they need rules to succeed, they need values. And the Prophet had left a footprint – a documented footprint on how to create a true and just society."

"Unfortunately, as I grew to love Islam more I began to study the Muslims of today, and in particular the Arab Muslims from the Arab countries. I was appalled – the rulers had betrayed their religion and were using it, just as the Church had, to create borders and frontiers. It was being manipulated. But even with this realization, I knew inside of me that Islam held the truth – that it was the only thing left, really, that a human being could touch, that had a divine message."

"So I began traveling – looking for a teacher who could enlighten me. I was only eighteen. I spent a whole year, going up and down the coast of Britain, searching for a man of light and knowledge who could show me the way – I had realized I knew nothing. But, most of the Muslims I met were immigrants, and they could not relate to me – I was a white boy who didn't speak their language. And they didn't come from the same spiritual angle I came from – they were traditionalists, performing the rituals their families had performed for generations. There wasn't the philosophical discourse I was looking for. I spent time with them all – mostly Pakistanis and Bangladeshis, and they taught me all the basics. They were great people – very friendly, but I kept searching for that higher ground. I couldn't help feeling that some of them were like the Christians I knew – you have a Christian name and go to church on Sundays and that's it, you know? I knew there was more – Islam has to have a transformative effect. If it doesn't, then it's not Islam."

"What do you mean? It must transform the person?"

"It must transform the person and it must transform the society. It must confront them. It has to be moving, it has to be expanding. If it is not expanding then it's contracting. If it's not in growth, it's dying. If it is not measuring out justice, it is allowing injustice."

"So, if it has to be expanding, does that mean that the world we live in today is doomed? If Islam must continue to expand, then isn't it headed with an all out confrontation with the West, who rules today?"

He smiled at my foray into politics and paused. "No, I wouldn't say doomed – you can't really pose a question like that. It is a complex situation. Muslim countries and the so-called Muslim leaders are very strong in their belief with an amazing lack of knowledge – they don't truly understand their own religion. They fall easy prey to the seductions of the material world – for example, one of the things that is forbidden to all, Muslims, Christians and Jews alike, is *riba*." He said this word with a flourish – a roll of the 'r' that lit up his face with excitement. We had obviously come to one of his pet peeves.

"Riba is usury - the practice of charging interest. It's very straightforward – everyone knows it is a sin. The reason it is forbidden is that it allows one human being who has means to take advantage of another human being who has needs. A richer man makes profit from a poorer man." He paused for dramatic effect, before declaring, "the entire modern world, everything that has happened in the last 200 years, has taken place because riba was permitted."

"What do you mean?"

"Oliver Cromwell is what I mean – he started this. Oliver Cromwell conquered Britain, got rid of the King and established a government that we consider today as modern Britain. What few people know is that his armies were raised and paid for by the Rothschild family, who at that time were finding it hard to perform their usurious banking transactions in France. They were being blamed for ripping people off and were running on the wrong side of the church – they needed fresh ground. So, they paid for Cromwell to sweep aside the King, and one of the first laws enacted by the Cromwell government was the legalization of usurious banking practice. Before that it was forbidden. Kings would privately go to outside sources for capital, but the practice of banking as we know it, with interest and credit and the like, was illegal. But then everything changed – you can look at that as a major – maybe the major turning point in modern civilization. I mean – look what the British did after that. Look where they went, and look at the influence they had. It is ironic – Cromwell is regarded as a hero of the common man in Britain – he did away with the aristocrats, away with the monarchy. But what he really did was enslave his whole country, his entire nation, by allowing the Rothschild family to get away with what they got away with. And they were a banking family – I'm not even going to mention what religion they were. I don't need to. They were a banking family – that was their religion. If they couldn't practice it in France, they were going to practice it in England, and they had the monetary means to make it happen."

"I didn't know Christianity forbid usury." I said.

"Yes, yes of course," he said impatiently, his hatred of the modern banking system bubbling up to the surface. "Since the beginning of time – the beginning of the prophetic teachings. Riba, usury, is *haram*, or forbidden. There are *hadith* (sayings of the Prophet Mohammed) that say it. The practice of riba is worse than having sex with your mother 80 times in the Ka'aba in Mecca." This last line he said was the first real sign of emotion he had given me, waving his hand in the air in the general direction of Saudi Arabia.

Shocked at this suddenly horrific image, I was silent for a second before recovering lamely. "Really? Wow. That's pretty bad."

"It is the worst sin. It is the entire reason we find ourselves in the situation we are in today. The Ottoman Empire fell because of riba. The financing of the armies, the mass production of weapons all took place because of riba. The major corporations – riba. Futures, stocks – all riba. The entire financial bubble of the world economy, which is worth something like twenty-eight times real world production, is riba."

"So, does that mean it is a sin to have a credit card?"

"Yes – technically it is. But, if you live in a world where you can't get by without it – say you have one shop and you need food and they only take credit cards, then it is okay. Islam is flexible like this, but its flexibility has been abused. Many Muslim societies have accepted riba as a necessity of keeping up with the Western world, but it's a joke. They don't need it. Have you heard of Islamic banking? It might as well be called an Islamic whorehouse, the way they twist the meanings of Islam to fit the West's usurious practices. Look – I can probably go to Iran right now and find a law that will allow me to contract a woman for one night, pay her a dowry, do what I want and then leave her in the morning. There would actually be a law for it, so I can easily put the words 'Islam' and 'whorehouse' on the same line. But there wasn't even a word in Arabic for 'banking' until very recently – it doesn't even belong near the word Islam. It is forbidden."

"Well," I ventured, "an American might say that you have a very radical viewpoint about all of this. Our world is run off credit."

"Well, I could tell them that they are the one that have the radical viewpoint. Any quantity of non-Americans must die so that you can sit on your nice chair and watch T.V. all day? I find that incredibly radical. If you think about the amount of deaths that the rest of the world has endured to ensure that the average American Joe can sit in his recliner chair and enjoy his bourbon and coke – now that to me is radical."

"The Muslims, who have been given an alternative to this madness, a system based on equilibrium and justice, are simply not doing their job. They have been told again and again that their way is primitive, so they have dropped it and grabbed the reigns of this new, sleek imperialist vehicle. They've left behind the very thing that they need – they need to bring the Truth to the West in order for us all to be saved. The mosque and the marketplace – that is what society should be. Everyone should be able to worship what they want and sell what they want, without restriction and on an equal playing field. Why not?"

"But it seems as though the Muslim world is at its lowest point on every front now – we seem to be doing nothing."

"Well, things transform – things rise and fall. Islam is down now, but I think it is waking up right now to some very hard realities."

"So do you think people such as yourself, Western Muslims, are the ones to bring back the faith?"

"When you see a tree with some dead leaves, you may be able to pluck them out, but there may still be a problem with the tree. Only when you get to the root, to the soil do you find out what the problem is. Maybe there's a drainage problem. Maybe there's a fungus. I mean, we can take studies of what the West has done to our religion over the years, but it is not useful. It is only when you take the pure religion and shine the light at the root, which is here in the West, that we may see real change. If we don't do it then we will only see more skirmishes and misery for the Muslim countries, all of them stemming from the darkness and misunderstanding in the West. We have to take our religion to them – we have to teach them, we need to show them. We cannot become them – we have to show them that there is another, better way. It is our duty as Muslims. We have to stand for what Allah has taught us. We have to continue to study, to grow. We have to get better – we have to establish Islam in the new era, in the new place and with new people. We cannot become them, even thought that is what they want. We must not take off our headscarves, we must not shave off our beards. We have absolutely every right to practice and share our religion – to give them the message."

At that point a class of children let out into the hallway and we were flooded with little kids, screaming and chasing one another. A little girl ran up to Daoud and hugged him – she was maybe three and looked Arab. He kissed her before looking up to his wife, who followed her daughter out of the class. She wore a hijab, a long skirt and a flowing top – she was stylish in her modesty. She could've been Moroccan. They spoke in Spanish, and then Daoud quickly introduced me to them both before they hurried out the door.

"Listen brother Mo – it has been a pleasure speaking with you, but duty calls, and I have to go now. I've got about an hour more of work to do before closing up for the day, and my wife says I am not allowed to stay late today." Daoud laughed at this last line and extended his hand to me.

"No problem – thanks for the conversation," I said, shaking his hand. "It was enlightening, to say the least. What do you do around here anyway?"

"Well – a bit of everything really. My job title is technical director, and I make sure everything in the building is working, run the web site, schedule the conferences and talks and such. I take the garbage out if need be – whatever. I speak to people like yourself who want to know more about the mosque – I do anything that needs to be done."

"Well – thanks so much – and good luck with the mosque. *Mubarak* – it is beautiful."

I left Daoud's office and I wandered back upstairs and into the garden. The rain had stopped, and two huge rainbows hung over the Alhambra, one of them ending up right inside its courtyards. I took some pictures and thought of how lucky I was to be in that moment in time. An overwhelming freedom from responsibility and openness to ideas enveloped me, and I began calculating in my head exactly how long I could travel for before my funds ran out. Four years living the high life, six on a budget, I thought.

I remember thinking that, in a time of so many contradictions, perhaps the best action one can do is to pursue the intellectual indulgences that travel tends to offer. Daoud was right – the main problems between East and West could be blamed on a lack of understanding, and Khizr's challenge to me had forced me out of my own cocoon of ignorance and in to the world at large. The only thing that could be better, I thought, is if I was standing in this spot 800 years ago. I would have loved to see the height of Islam's Golden Age, instead of the dark ages my religion faces today.

Chapter 9

Euro Islam

I was one of the first in the Madrid airport to check into the plane for Istanbul and was rewarded with the first seat in economy class. As it was a long international trip, the plane was big, and I had plenty of room to spread my feet in front of me – biz class feel at budget prices. I was on the aisle, with an empty seat next to me and another young guy at the window filling out our three-man-sled.

After takeoff I passed out almost immediately. I hadn't slept on the overnight bus from Granada to Madrid and had sleepwalked through the Madrid transit system, finding my way from the bus to the trains and finally to the plane. I slept for about half of the six hour flight before waking up when the Air Turkey attendants started serving lunch.

Over coffee I busted out the Turkey guidebook I had bought in the Madrid Airport. I was leafing through the Istanbul section, checking for hotels and whatnot, when my neighbor from the window leaned over and pointed at a page detailing a street named Istiklal Caddesi.

"You must go dere, is wonderful," he said in a strong accent. "Is great place – they close off street, you know? No cars allowed – there is only street car that goes up and down. And street is very long, with shops and bars and people all over – it is great fun."

"Ok, thanks – I'll check it out. You are from Turkey?"

"Yes, I am from Turkey," he said, leaning back and looking dreamily off in the distance. "I love Turkey – I am excited to be going back! These last three months I have traveled, this way and that, and now it is time to be home."

"Where have you been?" I asked.

"Well, I spent most of my time in India. There I study Indian medicine – it is called Ayurvedic, you know? I study in Kerala, in south. But, then my friend in Morocco – he became sick, and I came to help him."

"Wow – that's pretty far to go, India to Morocco. He must be a great friend."

"Yes – he is. He is like brother. But, this my off-season now, so I have time. I work at tourist resort on the Turkish Mediterranean – here, let me show you." He held out his hands for the guidebook and I gave it to him. As he went through the pages he would laugh to himself at each new section, delighted to be seeing pictures or reading about places he apparently knew.

Finally he found a full-page map of Turkey and pointed out a town on the southwest coast named Akyaka.

"This is where I work – I am doctor. I am doctor for resort, but we only open from April to October."

"Oh – too bad I won't be here then, I'd love to see it. Is your friend okay now?"

"Yes – he is, thank you." He said, grabbing my hand and shaking it as he spoke.

"So, you are a doctor of Ayurvedic medicine?" I asked.

"No, no – I went to school in Istanbul – I am proper doctor. I have Western degree. But, I love learn medicine of all kinds – from many countries. Right now I am very interested in Indian medicine – you are Indian? You look like."

"No – not really. My family is from Pakistan, but I was born and raised in California."

"Ahhhhh – California!" He said this as if it were the answer to one of life's oldest riddles. "California. Yes – is good there, no? Very beautiful?"

"Yes – it is." I brought out my laptop and showed him some random pictures from SF – shots of the freaks running the Bay to Breakers and surfing off Noriega Street on Ocean Beach. The doctor nodded in approval at each one, delighted both at the images as well as the PowerBook, which he oohed and ahhhed over repeatedly. After our slide show was done, he went back to his book for a while before putting it down again and addressing me.

"So, what will you do in my country?" he asked, seemingly unable to control his interest in my travel plans.

"I am going to see the Mevlana," I said, feeling stupid that I had no idea who he was. I had not had Internet access since Khizr's direction, and the guide book I bought for Turkey had not yet produced a Mevlana definition for me.

"Ahhhh – Mevlana. Yes – you should see the Mevlana. He is wonderful."

"Really?" I hadn't thought he would be so famous. "Do you know where I can find him?"

"Well, of course – he is in Konya. That is where his shrine is, at the Mevlana Museum. Here – let me show you."

The doctor grabbed my book and flipped through it before finding the right page and eagerly pointing at it. The chapter was on South Central Anatolia, and the page was on Konya, the biggest city in the region. I flipped through until coming to an inset talking about the Mevlana, which I found was only a name given to a man who had lived 800 years before. Mevlana means 'Our Guide', and the man's name was Jelaleddin Rumi.

I had read some of Rumi's work before – my parents had English copy translations of his work in our house growing up – and I knew him to be one of the most beautiful poets I had ever come across. His works all spoke of love, and I particularly remembered trying to cite one of Rumi's poems in an argument with my mother when trying to justify drinking alcohol to her. Rumi often spoke of his love of wine, but my grasping for justification had been quickly shot down when my mom explained that Rumi had used wine as a metaphor and nothing more.

I started looking up more Rumi facts in the book, but before I could learn more, the doctor started up again.

"My name is Bugra, but everyone call me doctor, so you do too. And what is your name?"

"My name is Mohammed, but everyone calls me Mo."

He grinned and grabbed my hand.

"Ok Mo from California – excite to meet you. But, I wonder – why you go to see Mevlana in Konya? You know, it will be very cold there – very cold."

"Yes – but I want to learn about the Mevlana. I am not so much a tourist – I want to learn about the Turkish people and the Islam there."

At this the Turkish lady behind us, who had been listening to our conversation and responding with clucks of approval or disapproval, could no longer restrain herself. She popped her head over the middle seat and chimed in.

"You should not go to Konya – it is boring. This is your first visit to Turkey?"

"Yes." I said, craning around to see her.

"Well – you should not go there. You should go to Istanbul, and Troy, and Izmer – there are so many places better than Konya! The people there are old – they live in old times."

I turned and popped over the top of the seat to face her more fully, but the gaudy jewelry she wore almost blinded me so I sat back down and craned back around.

"Well – like I said. I am not so much a tourist, you see. I want to learn about the Mevlana."

She did not accept this and said something to Bugra in Turkish that made him look at me and wink. She then clucked and said, "Turkey is a great place – the best in the Muslim world. We are not like those other backwards countries – we are from Europe. We are a democracy. You should see those things – Konya is our past. The people of Turkey don't think like that anymore. You should go to Istiklal Cadessi like your friend here says. My daughter goes to school in New York, but when she visits that is where her and her friends go – almost every night!"

After mentioning her daughter's hipness, the woman sat back down into her seat, apparently content to have made her point. She picked up a Vogue magazine and started flipping the pages.

Bugra turned to me and lowered his voice a bit.

"She says true – Konya is old way. But that ok – we may still love those things. We can still know what Mevlana teach us – Islam is fine in Turkey, with democracy too."

"So, do you consider yourself a Muslim?" I asked.

"Yes – of course. It is my religion. But in Turkey, we are modern – people have fun. They party, you know? Just like you in those pictures you showed me from San Francisco. It isn't just all seriousness all the time. We are modern Muslims, just like maybe people are modern Christians in America. But you, you are Muslim?"

"Well, yes. But not really practicing I guess. I do not pray five times a day."

"See – you are modern Muslim, like me. I mean, you have interest – you are coming to see Mevlana Rumi. But, you drink, you have fun, you live life."

"Yeah – I guess so."

"Perhaps you should come with me tonight. My friends will pick me up from the airport, and we will go out tonight. Where will you stay?"

"I was thinking of staying in old Istanbul – Sultanahmet."

"You have reservation?"

"No."

"Then you should stay at Hotel Keban. My friend's hotel. Not in old part of Istanbul – new part. More lively – more fun. It is in Taksim - much more action. We take you there tonight!" He almost shouted his invitation, apparently so overjoyed to have stumbled on to me that including me in his homecoming after three months was a foregone conclusion.

"Wow – Bugra, that's so nice. I really don't know anyone here. But, don't you already have plans?"

He waved off my feeble protest and grabbed my guide book again. He pointed out the area of the city he was recommending to me – a place called Taksim Square, at the top of Istiklal Cadessi. His attention back with the guidebook, he started leafing through the Istanbul entertainment and restaurant guide, underlining options for me and writing menu notes in the margins. I could see he was enjoying these places in his mind as he recommended them – kind of like how I loved sending out-of-towners to sit on Zeitgeist's back patio on a warm San Francisco evening.

We chatted for a while longer before settling back and reading on our own for the rest of the flight. We landed and disembarked, Bugra making me promise to meet him at the baggage pickup after we cleared our respective immigration. As he hurried to the Turkish nationality line, I consulted the sign posted at the foreigner line, giving the visa prices (in American dollars). My jaw dropped – UK - $10, Australia

- $20, Canada - $40, USA - $100! And hard currency only – no credit cards allowed. Luckily, I had a couple of Benjamins stowed away in case of emergency, and I grudgingly handed one over to the immigration clerk before getting a three month stamp on my passport.

Bugra and I arrived at the baggage claim at the same time, collected our bags and then hit the duty free, where Bugra bought booze and cigarettes for friends and family, all the while taking orders over his cell phone. Outside, a short stocky man in a heavy wool overcoat embraced Bugra in a bear hug before shaking my hand and leading us to a parking garage, arm and arm with Bugra, animated in conversation the whole way. Bugra explained to me that this was one of his best friends – his name was Dinar and he and Bugra had known each other for fifteen years, since their college days.

Five minutes from the airport Dinar received an urgent phone call which changed their plans for the evening – they were going to have to go to Uskudar, on the Asia side of the city, and could not party tonight. Pulling up to a side street, Dinar handed me a 10 Million Lira note, and Bugra apologized for them both, saying that this was enough to take a taxi from the stand they were dropping me off at.

"Go check in to the Keban Hotel – I will call you tomorrow and we will go out then. Nice to meet you, Mo from California!"

I shook both their hands and watched them drive off. As I surveyed the scene around me, I found myself in a residential neighborhood, with small mom-and-pop-looking shops scattered about and a neglected looking basketball court directly across from me. It was cold – everyone was bundled up. After a few minutes I asked a passerby if any taxis were coming, but he didn't speak English.

Finally a van rolled up that had a 'Taksi' sign on the front and a 'Taksim' card in the front window. I got in – there was only one seat left and my baggage crammed everyone considerably. The van started up again, and I could see the driver looking back at me in his rear view mirror, saying something in Turkish. I passed up my 10 million and received 7.5 mil back as he sped away into the city.

The first impression of Istanbul, if you are one who loves history and beauty as I do, is one of awe. Our taxi rose up a hill and then through a column of stone archways towering above the road. They looked ancient – straight from Roman times. Coming over another hill I caught my first glimpse of the skyline of old Istanbul – various low-lying hilltops studded with domes and needle-tipped minarets, as far as the eye could see. We moved through the city and took a bridge over the Golden Horne, the inlet from the Boshporous Straits that separates old and new Istanbul in Europe. Rising up another hill I could see across the Straits, wide as the Hudson and East Rivers together, over to Asia and the other side of Istanbul. Istanbul is the meeting of the world, where Asia and Europe both exist within the city limits.

The taxi dropped me off in bustling Taksim Square, a huge plaza flanked with hotels, restaurants and a bus depot. I walked towards the hotels and saw the sign for Hotel Keban, rising out of the morass of people and shops. The weather had cooled considerably – the sun was setting and people were hurrying back and forth, trying to get to where they were going before the real cold set in.

The hotel had vacancies – a single for $70 US. I pre-paid for the night, was led upstairs and took a long, hot shower. The room offered complementary tea, so I brewed some up and turned on the T.V., hoping for a little CNN or anything else in English.

Unfortunately, there was nothing in my language, so I settled for a Turkish drama that seemed to be set during Ottoman times. Belly dancers and low-production values seemed the norm, and I watched with detached amusement before a T.V. commercial came on and Chevy Chase appeared, selling TurkCola. The premise was that Chevy was a normal American guy, coming home from work, when he greets his wife, but freaks out because she is speaking Turkish. Then, they have a dinner party and all the guests take a swig of TurkCola and burst out into what sounds like a Turkish drinking tune. Finally, Chevy himself takes a sip and he too joins the Turkish chorus. The final scene shows the dinner guests leaving and Chevy waving to them, turning around to reveal a handsome, bushy Turkish moustache.

As I contemplated Ty Webb's new low, the azan burst forth from some loudspeakers on a mosque right around the corner from the hotel. Its singsong call to prayer reminded me that, although it seemed very European, this was still a Muslim country. I decided to get out and explore, wrapping myself in the warmest clothes I had and venturing out into the night.

It was Thursday at about 9pm, and the streets were packed. I passed various kebab stands – all with meat rotating on sticks and men in chef's outfits singing their sales pitches to the passing crowds. I followed the flow of people onto Istiklal Caddessi, where it split into two sides with railway tracks down the middle. There were no cars on the cobblestone streets, and the people were walking in groups, laughing and window shopping like at Union Square back home. Fashions were of the highest level, and I couldn't help but be shocked that this was the capital of the last great Muslim dynasty, the Ottomans. There was not a hijab in sight, and every block on the street had its own bar. As I wandered, I began to wonder if Istanbul might be the perfect place for me – the crossroads between my two worlds.

The next morning I decided to see the sites of Sultanahmet, the old part of town. I took a taxi to the heart of it, which is where the Aya Sofia sits – the church turned mosque turned museum that embodies the history of the city.

Istanbul is over 3000 years old. It has seen it all – from a small fishing village to the capital of the world. When the Emperor Constantine pursued his last rival from Rome to its shores and beat him in 324 AD, he proclaimed it the 'New Rome,' laid out an imperial city to befit an empire's capital, and established the Byzantine Empire, otherwise known as the Christian empire of the East. It was to be this way until 1453 AD – a millennia later, it would fall to Mehmet the Conquerer, a young Turkish sultan who established the Ottoman Empire.

This empire would last another 400 plus years, making Istanbul an imperial city for more than 1500 years and well into the 20th century. Cities like Rome, Cairo, Baghdad, and Jerusalem were all at one point under its jurisdiction, and for many centuries each great King or Sultan would build a new monument to the city's greatness.

The Aya Sofia started out as the Sancta Sofia, built by the Byzantine Emperor Justinian in 537 AD. From its huge dome filled with millions of colored tiles to its sacred walls filled with mosaics to its towering marble columns, it is a true work of art, and it reigned as Christendom's greatest church until it's conversion to a mosque under Mehmet. The young Sultan saw himself as an emperor in the line of Constantine, and he ordered the city rebuilt, adding more support to the Aya Sofia's dome and adding carvings in Kufic script praising God or Prophet Mohammed.

The mosque survived as a place of worship until 1935, when modern Turkey's father, General Kemal Attaturk, made the place a museum. It was one of many changes that Attaturk implemented to fulfill his vision of a modern, secular Muslim country, and it is hard to argue with his results – it can be argued that Turkey is the strongest democracy in the Muslim world.

Outside the museum was more history – the beautiful Blue Mosque, with its six spiked minarets framing its multiple domes loomed in front, located just behind Sultanahmet Park and the Hippodrome, the sight of endless chariot races and human riots. I took it all in, headphones on and falling more and more in awe. It was the first time I had ever felt pride in the accomplishments of a living Muslim city.

My whole life I had felt different – I did not know one other Muslim kid growing up. All I knew was that we didn't get Christmas, and the stuff that we did get was always harder and different. Praying when you were twelve in Arabic sucked. Not listening to music ten days out of the year for Muharram sucked. Fasting for a month during Ramadan sucked. It always seemed Muslims, and me, had it harder, and we were more about denying ourselves then celebrating any joy or beauty.

And then 9/11 happened, and then the split – going from an anonymous ethnic group in America's cultural cocktail to being profiled as a mass murderer in the airports of my home country. Making apologies for Muslims when I didn't know anything about it. The inherent contradiction, and shame, from identifying myself as a Muslim American. But, somehow the magnificence of Istanbul began to change this perception in me. For the first time I began to feel proud – it was the first living, breathing Muslim city I had seen that I could want to live in, and just the knowledge that it existed gave me a sense of relief – that I and my kind were not completely alone in the world.

Back at the hotel Doctor Bugra was waiting for me, dressed in tight jeans, a half-length leather jacket and a wide grin.

"Mohammed! We are beginning to think you not come home!"

He grabbed me in a bear hug. He was seated at a booth at the bar inside the Hotel Kebaan with three other people – his friend Dinar, a guy who looked just like Dinar, and a petite blond. They were all dressed for a night out, and Bugra implored me to do the same, as time was wasting and they wanted to see their friends' band play down the street. I changed quickly and the five of us strode out, down Istiklal Caddesi as a sprinkling of snow started to fall on the cobblestone street.

As we walked I was introduced to Dinar's brother and his girlfriend, both of whom spoke not a word of English and smiled before going on with their own heated conversation. Bugra and Dinar were boisterous, belly-laughing their way through the throngs on the street. Once in a while Bugra would shoot me a line in English – something like "hey Mohammed – welcome to Istanbul!" and fall laughing again – I guessed that they had been drinking for a while before I showed up.

We hit a side street off the main drag and pulled into a narrow long bar, with low lying booths on both walls and a stage set up at the back. The place was lit dimly and whitewashed – everything, from the furniture to the bar to the walls, were white, and it seemed every bit a cosmopolitan waterhole as any bar in SF or NY.

My crew apparently knew the manager, as he came over and greeted everyone before seating us at a booth near the stage. A waiter immediately brought out snacks – chips, peanuts, cucumbers, olives, carrots, and bread. Another waiter brought over a bottle of scotch, a bucket of ice, and five glasses.

Dinar's brother's girlfriend ordered a beer as Dinar poured us all a scotch on the rocks. After a couple of drinks Bugra started in on an interrogation of my day.

"So – what have you done today?"

"I went to the Aya Sofia – it was beautiful."

Bugra smiled, topping off my drink and signaling to the waiter for more chips. Another young hip couple joined us at the table, and Bugra launched into a long Turkish monologue that seemed to be about his recent Indian travels, laughing loudly at his own punch lines and obviously enjoying being home.

After another drink the couple we were seated with got up and went to the stage, where they proceeded to belt out Turkish pop tunes for the next hour and a half, backed up by guitar and keyboards. The crowd was loving it – the bar filled up and people started dancing in whatever open space was left. Our table grew more and more raucous, feeding off of Bugra's stories and belly laughs. He sang, he drank, he joked – all to a continuously changing lineup of seemingly endless old friends. He ordered another bottle and jumped to his feet, singing along to his favorite songs and toasting everyone around him.

Around 4am Bugra's singing friends had finished their third set and the place started to thin out. Bugra held his liquor well – his audience smaller, he became less boisterous and more conversational, turning to me and asking me about Americanness.

"So – why is it America so fucked up, huh? You tell me, Mo, you from there. I never go – I been so many places in this world – South America, Europe, India. And everywhere – people don't like the U.S."

"Well," I said, trying to think through my clouded mind of a reason that would satisfy him. "People don't usually like the person who's number one. You know, America is number one, and everyone wants to be like us, so it doesn't matter what we do. Everyone will eventually hate us anyway."

"So what? So fucking what if you're number one? Does that make you more of human than me?" He said this with a completely non-threatening, shit-eating grin on his face, so I did not at all worry that I was at risk.

"No. I mean – there are many reasons why America is fucked up. But I'm just saying that any country in America's position would be hated – what if Turkey was in America's position? The only superpower in the world? Do you think everyone would love Turkey?"

Bugra liked my answer and slapped the table. "No. I guess we have politicians, just like you, and they do bad, like everywhere else. But, in your country – they don't teach you anything. It is all control of mind, right? It is all money – all your capitalism that runs everything. I have friend – he is British and he was in U.S. soon after September the 11. He told me that, after the attack, the government told the Americans that the best way to help their country was to shop - to spend money! It was not to learn, about the world, or Islam, or history, or maybe why people don't like you so much. It was to shop – is this right? He tell me there was saying everywhere – America, Open for Business. This crazy to me!"

I suddenly tired of defending my screwed up country. "Yeah – it's true. Look – let's not talk about this now, okay? This is a great night out – yeah?" At this I threw back the last shot of the third bottle and slammed the bottle back down into its bucket.

Bugra's face lost all traces of anger and his laugh lines wrinkled again. "Mohammed – you crazy! It is time we go – we will take you for hamburger, yes?"

We grabbed Dinar and headed out, back up Istiklal Caddesi and to the top of the hill, where the kebab/burger joints were still operating. Bugra bought ten burgers for the three of us – they were small ones a la White Castle – and we doused it in horseradish mustard and downed them with Turk Colas. Outside again, Bugra led us away from the main street, around Taksim square and onto another major road, this one with auto traffic and dotted with neon sign flashing awnings. We went into a place, paid a cover and then found ourselves at a disco, the dance floor empty but several people hanging at booths and tables. Bugra ordered more scotch and we were joined at our table by three girls almost immediately. Bugra entertained them while I stared at the beauty next to me, with huge blue eyes and full red lips.

"Ha – Mo – this Natasha."

I threw on a drunken debonair air and greeted her. "Natasha – you are the most beautiful girl I have ever seen," I said.

Bugra laughed so hard he had to slap the table three times just to stop. Composing himself, he said, "No English. But she no care – Natasha likes you."

"Oh really?" I smiled at her and she at me and I fell madly in lust with her.

"Yes – oh really. You can have her for 50 million."

"What?"

"She is a Natasha – they are all Natasha. They come from Russia for work, you know? 50 million lira and you are in."

The realization that I was at a whorehouse struck a chord with me that it was time to go – a line had been crossed. I stood up and walked out, weaving miraculously back in the direction of the hotel, through Taksim square. As I spied the Hotel Keban sign in the distance, the azan burst out from all around me, calling the faithful to the Fajr prayer. My inebriation and my religion thrown together for the first time, I could think of only one thing - getting plowed in a Muslim country is weird.

PICTURES:

The courtyard of the Kairouine Mosque in Fez, Morocco.

The prayer hall inside the Kairouine Mosque.

A *madressa* in Fez, Morocco.

Guide Abdullah and his son in an alley of the medina of Fez.

The Court of the Lions inside the Alhambra in Granada, Spain.

Turrets of the Alhambra looking over Granada below.

Inside of the dome of Aya Sofia in Istanbul, Turkey.

The minaret-studded skyline of Istanbul behind a lighthouse
in the Bosphorous Straits.

Rumi's tomb in Konya, Turkey.

Cha Cha and his baby girl.

Cha Cha's family's camp near the mosque in Margao, India.

Kids from Cha Cha's camp mugging for the camera.

The Petronas Twin Towers in Kuala Lumpur, Malaysia.

The KL Menara and Petronas Twin Towers, Kuala Lumpur.

My friend Noc from Koh Ngai in Thailand.

The beach on Koh Ngai, looking out at Koh Muk and Emerald Cave.

Chapter 10

A Love Supreme

Perhaps Islam's greatest crossover hit, the one part of the religion that has appealed more to modern Western consciousness than any other, is Sufism. Mysticism and song and dance are qualities that are much more appealing than long beards, hijabs, and stonings, and ever since the flower power 60s, Sufi poetry and music have been an increasing presence in Western bookshops and coffee houses. A common association is made between hippies and Sufis – in fact, I knew a few families growing up in San Francisco whose parents had made the successful transition between the two, oftentimes with a ten year yuppie phase sandwiched in between. But, in fact, the comparison is only skin deep – while hippies may have a certain mysticism/asceticism in common with Sufism, the basis of Sufi belief is not free love and weed but love of God and His Creation. There may be no better illustration of who Sufis are than the life of one of their greatest teachers, Maulana Jalaluddin Rumi.

Rumi was born on September 30, 1207 in the city of Balkh, in modern day Afghanistan. While he is now known popularly as Rumi, which means 'of Rome' in a nod to the Byzantine empire, many Afghans and Persians fondly refer to him as Balkhi, cementing their claim to him as their own. At the time he was born, the Persian empire was weakening in the face of growing peril from the east in the form of Ghengis Khan's Mongol hordes, and his father moved the family when he was five in a slow circuit westward, through Damascus and then into Anatolia, or Asia Minor, and into the Seljukid Kingdom, which held sway over much of modern day Turkey.

Rumi's father was an Islamic theologian, and he taught the Qu'ran and the Prophetic traditions at various learning centers as they moved through the Muslim world. In those days, a learned man schooled in Arabic could win work over a huge swath of land, from Africa to the Middle East and Asia. A man of good reputation, he was invited by the Seljuk King Alaeddin Kaykobad to come to their capital, in Konya, and teach, so the family finally settled down and Rumi grew up. After his father's death in 1231, Rumi took over his father's post as professor, spending fifteen years as a teacher and scholar. During this time he was introduced to the Sufi traditions by a former student of his father's, but his own transformation from religious scholar to Sufi master did not happen until October of 1244, when walking down the street in Konya he encountered a traveling stranger, a dervish, who posed a question to him.

The dervish was named Shamsuddin, which translates to 'Sun of Religion,' and legend holds that he had been wandering throughout the Islamic world, in search of anyone who could comprehend the beauty of God the way he could. His question raised a philosophical point – who was greater, the Prophet Muhammad or the Persian mystic Bayezid Bistami, who was a fashionable thinker of the time. The outrageousness of the question shocked Rumi, but as they began to debate Rumi became fascinated by the traveler and the two became inseparable.

In the Sufi tradition, there is a teacher/student relationship. The metaphysical and spiritual quest of student is attained through the guidance of a spiritual teacher, often known as a sheikh. The sheikh has achieved a level of knowledge (usually through years of intense meditation and study) that allows them to subsist almost solely on love of God, and the greater their love of God and knowledge of faith, the greater their following usually becomes. All the major branches of Sufis subscribe to one charismatic teacher as the originator of their order, just as Rumi is the orginal teacher of the Mevlevi Order of Sufis, who are also known as the whirling dervishes.

Shams inspired the passionate love of God in Rumi, a man already well versed in Islamic thought and practice. The two spent months together, barely leaving the room where they discussed religion and God and divine love, and it got to the point where the residents of Konya, outraged at the scandal of one of their pre-imminent teachers shirking his educational responsibilities to associate with a questionable foreigner, conspired to run Shams out of town. Perhaps sensing their jealousy, Shams split town as mysteriously as he had appeared, leaving Rumi heartbroken to have lost his companion in divine love.

But, inside him a transformation had begun. Rumi began to write incredible poetry, many of his lines comparing Shams to the Sun that had ignited within him love for God which burned fiercely. He began to listen to music and whirl around for hours, spinning himself into a state of ecstasy. What Shams had shown him was the pureness of Creation, and the way back to the pureness could only be through love, not intellect, as love was the most mysterious and powerful of humanity's tools. This pureness is an expression of Sufi philosophy – that we are born pure and made to worship God, Who had provided us with everything that we need on Earth so that we may glorify Him. Created in a divine state, we were sullied by life and experience, and the only way back to our divine state was through study and love. In his poetry, Rumi often compares people to vessels for divine love that just need time to mature and age until our love can be at its highest and most ripe.

The rest of his life Rumi spent writing poetry and dancing, extolling the virtues of both Shams, his igniting light, and God. The love poems that have made him popular in the West are, in fact, more about a platonic love for another man and complete love for God than about any earthly sensuality – they are Rumi's attempt to explain the love, the 'Divine Mystery', that to he himself is almost unexplainable. He tries, with poems such as:

> *Through Love all that is bitter will be sweet,*
> *Through Love all that is copper will be gold.*
> *Through Love all dregs will turn to purest wine*
> *Through Love all pain will turn to medicine.*
> *Through Love the dead will all become alive,*
> *Through Love the king does turn into a slave!*

Rumi's opus, the *Masnewi*, is in fact a long treatise on the complexity of love, told in verse and allegory. It is only by total embrace of love can the human being truly attain happiness, which is his natural state, Rumi argued. And his poetry, written in the beautiful Persian language, is perhaps the greatest expression of Love ever.

I learned all this by reading some books I had picked up in Istanbul, on yet another overnight bus, this one going from Istanbul to Konya. At midnight we crossed the Bosphorous Straits into Asia, by 3 AM we were into the flatlands of Anatolia (Asia Minor) and by 6 AM we rolled into the ancient capital of Konya, where a light snow was falling in the dawn light as we pulled into the *otogar*, or bus terminal. The Turkish bus system is fabulous, and can get you anywhere in the country for relatively cheap. The buses were modern, big and clean, and I had no fear as we plugged along in the snow on the Turkish highways, as I might have if in a similar situation in Pakistan.

Once in Konya, the local train took me into town. The streets were sparsely populated with early risers, scurrying hurriedly about through the cold. The few women I saw out and about wore hijabs, in marked contrast to their European-style Istanbul counterparts. I checked into a nice looking hotel on the main drag of town and crashed for a while, letting Turkish Pop MTV play in the background. I woke up around noon to the roar of a jet over the city – my water bottle shook as it thundered by.

Awake, I decided to satisfy Khizr's request and go see Rumi immediately. It was colder out at noon than before dawn – the snow that had started when I arrived was now falling faster, creating bigger drifts on the sidewalks. As I walked down the main street, called Mevlana Caddessi, I remembered what the old lady on the plane had told me – Konya was boring. I looked about and decided that, from what I could see, she was absolutely right. There were the typical Ottoman-style spiked minarets here and there, but on the whole the old buildings were drab. But, as I neared the end of the street, a great green dome rose up to the right, startling in its contrast with the surroundings. It was the Mevlana Museum – 20 million lira entrance fee and you're inside the courtyard, bordered by tombs, a mosque, and a *semahane* hall for dervish performances.

The green tiled dome was for Rumi's tomb. It was beautiful inside – full of Islamic calligraphy, glittering in gold and the customary geometric tile patterns. Lined along the insides of the walls were sarcophaguses, each covered with gold embroidered velvet. Some had a green or white turban perched on the end, and three feet high calligraphy ringed the walls. At the far end of the room the sarcophaguses were more closely bunched, leading up to the biggest one, which was set alone against the most brilliantly tiled and calligraphy section of the room. Rumi lay surrounded by beauty, just as he should.

The only other people in the place were pilgrims – mostly older people who were there with their adult children. They prayed to Rumi – spending several minutes facing him and quietly reciting Qu'ranic verses in Arabic. The look on their face was one of relief – they were emptying the burdens of their spirit to their greatest spiritual son, the one who had come closest to God. I was compelled to recite *Sura Fatihah* and wish for peace, so touching was the belief of the few pilgrims in the room.

I moved into a second room full of things from Rumi's time - manuscripts of the Masnewi, old dervish clothes, carved wood doors, and beautiful old carpets. I was struck at the decidedly non-touristy feel to the place – no English anywhere, from the attendants to the signs - it seemed geared more to pilgrims than to foreigners.

I lingered for only a short time before going back into the courtyard and into the semahane, which had mannequins dressed in the traditional white dress of the whirling dancers, posed in swirling position. Next I went into the bookstore, where I found an English translation of a work on Rumi's life by a Turkish professor at the University of Konya. I went across the street into a restaurant, tried to order (no English meant they brought me whatever they wanted, which was a delicious chicken kebab with bread and salad), and read more about the man I just met.

I spent the rest of the day wandering around the bleak town, from old building to old building, where I was the only tourist on an otherwise dull winter day. I saw the mosque dedicated to Rumi's muse, Shams, and the mostly empty market square, where a few vendors were trying to sell winter hats and gloves to no one in particular. No one spoke English, and the overall chill in the air made up for a very drab day.

Having seen enough, I retired back to the hotel, where afternoon was turning in to evening and there was a hustle and bustle in the lobby. Back in Istanbul Bugra had given me the cell number of one of Dinar's pals and I thought of calling him, but I didn't have the energy and decided to try and stick around the hotel area. I saw the concierge and approached.

"Um hello," I said, "you speak English?"

"Yes sir, of course sir. What you need?"

"I would like a good restaurant, to eat in later. Maybe around nine tonight?"

He proceeded to give me many options and then, after getting to know my current state of boredom, suggested I go to a *hammam*, or Turkish bath.

"Really, mister, you go to bath. It will be good for you – it is real Turkish tradition."

After a little hesitation I accepted, figuring that I had nothing better to do and Turkish TV sucked, and the concierge gave me directions to a bath a few streets from the hotel. I followed the directions and came to a small red door on the corner of two side streets. I walked in to a blast of hot air – it was at least 50 degrees hotter inside than out – and I had to defog my glasses before I could see the room. It was tiled, with lockers on one end and benches on the other. Several men in various states of undress were either lounging on the benches or chatting at the lockers. In the middle of the room was another door next to a small office, where two old men were pointing at my boots with disapproving looks.

I looked down and saw I had tracked some dirty snow into the clean room and quickly took off my boots. None of the men spoke English, but I was able to communicate my desire to go in and I was led to a locker. A man came out from the little office and pantomimed for me to undress to my underwear while letting me know it cost 20 million lira to go in. I complied and he then pointed to another door, outside which stood a large man wearing only swim trunks and holding a large bucket. He signaled me that it would be 30 million lira to get washed by the big man, and I began to panic real quick, realizing that I wasn't quite sure what I had just signed up for. I began to protest, but the man from the office waved me off to the point where I felt I was beginning to insult the whole place. I acquiesced, and was motioned to enter the next chamber.

The room was steamy, but through my blurred vision I could see two rooms, a smaller one with no door and lots of steam blowing out and a bigger one, ringed with troughs of water and taps. It was hot – much hotter than the outer room had been. A man was sitting in the smaller room with his young son – after a few moments he recognized that I had no idea what I was doing and led me to the bigger room. We went near one of the taps and he mimed for me to lie down on the hot tiles. I wasn't so sure – to lay so much of my skin on a surface where many men had sweated before didn't sound so great. But, he was insistent in his miming and I finally lay down on the warm tiles.

I must have been there for ten minutes. Men came and went, coming to the trough to get water and dumping it over their heads. As the sweat beads started to multiply on my back a man came up right next to me and dumped four bucketfuls over his sweaty body, creating a small river of dirty water and sweat that came right at me but then veered at the last second and went into a drain towards the middle of the room. I closed my eyes and counted, the heat becoming more and more intense and the sweat getting more and more extreme every minute.

My count reached 242 before the washing man lumbered up next to me. From my blurred position on the floor I could not see his face – it was obstructed by his huge belly. He held in his hand something that looked like a cross between a pad and a hand towel. As he wrapped it around his hand, he instructed me with hand signs to get up and sit on my butt, facing away from him.

He went to work on my back with a vengeance, scrubbing with vigor and purpose. Every few strokes he would put his full weight behind the blow and my spine would heave forward, threatening to break under the 200 plus pounds of his girth. I felt as though the skin on my back was being ripped to shreds under the brillo cloth's unyielding swipes – a few involuntary grunts came out of my mouth but fell on apparently deaf ears.

He moved to my arms and neck before going over to the trough and filling his bucket with water. After an unceremonious dump of the warm water over my head, he turned me over and went to work on my legs.

Lying on my back, I just closed my eyes and prayed that he doesn't touch my dick, as I was sure that brillo-ing that part of my body would be too much to take.

He stopped just short of my worst nightmare and moved on to my chest, at which point it felt like he was bent on removing half of the hairs on my body. I could see little hairs from all parts being washed away with each bucket dump, and the skin left behind felt raw. Although a shock to my system, I had to admit that it was the cleanest that I had been in a long time.

He then produced a bar of soap and lathered me up, head to toe but with a bypass over the crotch region. After washing away the soap, I was made to lie down on my stomach while the washing man went around back. He grabbed my legs and raised them into the air, driving my torso and face into the warm tiles while he jerked my legs this way and that for several moments. He then sat me up, put his foot in my back and pulled both my arms straight backwards. My chest felt like it was about to come apart, but this latest abuse lasted only a few seconds before he was roughly massaging my neck and shoulders with his huge hands. He finished the job with one more bucketful of water over my head.

I lay on the tile for another five minutes, soaking up the sauna-like heat before getting up and going back into the outer room. The man who I had paid brought me a glass of apple tea, and I sat in my wet underwear for a bit, sipping the tea and letting the willies that come from being manhandled in a Turkish bath melt away. In their place came an oddly calm sensation - my skin tingling from the beating it had just taken and my body feeling loose and limber and rejuvenated after days of travel grime. That night, I slept longer and harder than I had in months.

Chapter 11

Back to Basics

In my dream I am walking in a crazy valley – rocks on the valley floor jut out suddenly and are shaped into little teepee-like structures. They are lined up row after row, in what looks to me like a suburb on the moon. At the end of a row I turn, and sitting at a table, in the middle of the street, is Khizr. There is a chair in front of him and he motions me to take a seat.

"Hey Mo – so nice of you to make it. Please – have a seat." He looks different – his hair and beard are short and he is dressed in a beige tunic with brown trousers and a grey fez cocked on the left side of his head.

"What up G? Good to see you man." I say, offering my fist for a fist bump.

He daps me back and bids me to eat some dates and nuts that are spread out on the table. While he watches me I feel that he is tired, that his emerald green eyes are a bit dimmer than before.

"Things aren't going too well," he starts. "Things seem to be escalating. People want the truth less and less, you know? They're clamming up, retreating to their old assumptions because it's easier. It's easier for them to hate than to love."

I have been out of the news for a while but I sense that maybe the war has taken a turn for the worse. "Islam v. West, winner takes all, huh?" I say.

"Something like that I guess," says Khizr, his voice trailing off at the end. He sits in silence for a second, seems to take a gathering breath, and then says, "but, that is not the way this world needs to be – that is not what was intended. We just need to spread the knowledge, harness what means we have." He stops and picks up a date, turning it over every which way before taking a bite and looking deeply in to my eyes. "So, what do you think of the Mevlana?"

"He was the man," I say. "It's amazing how powerful his poems are, even after all this time."

"Hmm, hmm," Khizr ruminates. "Poetry is perhaps the greatest form of expression, really. I've really thought that for a long time now. It is language, which is our means of communication for thought, right? And it is art, which is our means of communication for feelings. I love Rumi – he was a great man. I unfortunately never met him – back then I was working the whole Crusades thing – but I do love one of his poems the best – for me, it sums it all up. It sums up the meaning of our existence."

"Which one?"

"It's about the beauty of the heart, which is our most important organ. It goes:

> *The beauty of the heart*
> *is the lasting beauty:*
> *its lips give to drink*
> *of the water of life.*
>
> *Truly it is the water,*
> *that which pours,*
> *and the one who drinks.*
>
> *All three become one when*
> *your talisman is shattered.*
>
> *That oneness you can't know*
> *by reasoning.*
>
> *Mathnawi II, 716-718*

To me, this is the essence of belief, and this is why I asked you to come here. People of faith have made pilgrimages since the beginning of time – I wanted you to make a pilgrimage here, to see the man who captured the essence of belief."

"What do you mean, G?" I ask.

"It's all in the poetry, man. Rumi's talking about heart – it's all in here," he points to his chest with both hands, "all in here. These people – these passionate religofreaks who say they Believe but then set about killing thousands of innocent people because of something their *mind* has justified for them to do – that's so f'd up, if you'll pardon the French. The problem is that if they just took that emotion - that belief that drives them to their justifications – took it and turned it into love, for them and everyone around them, then we would have none of this. Because if you believe, then you believe that The Man Upstairs created everything, right? And if He did, and you love Him, then you gotta love everything and everyone else too, because He made it, right?"

"I guess so."

"Damn straight. Ain't no need to second guess, my friend. We always try to make things harder than they really need to be."

"But," I venture, "you have to admit that the way the message was brought – I mean with the different Prophets over the centuries creating confusion and stuff – left a lot of room for factions. You know – there is a lot of friction between the various God fearing people."

Khizr screws his old face up before responding. "That's just politics, Mo – it has nothing to do with belief. Belief is beautiful, bro, but greed is ugly. And politics, more often than not, has to do with greed. You know where you are at right now, my friend Mo?"

I look around at the fairy-like stone castles along the street and shake my head. "Wherever it is, it is some crazy dream land."

"This ain't no dream land, buddy. It is one of the most beautiful places in the world – in the province of Cappadocia, Turkey. This place is called Goreme – it's not a three hour drive from Konya. Here, for centuries and centuries, East met West in the most fantastical place on the planet. This street was where the two sides met, in fact – right here in this little village. On the west side of the street were churches, to the east there were mosques. Everyone got along here for years – everyone was equal in their love for God, so they didn't sweat each other. And that's what we're missing these days – people have forgotten to love God, they only fear him. In fact, for some strange reason the fools who call themselves the most pious are praying the hardest for apocalypse right now – I mean, surely they don't think that the Big Man is gonna spring it on them when everyone expects it? He is the Ultimate Trickster, you know – slippery. He does things when you least expect it because He likes to remind you He's in control – He likes to try and keep you humble."

"So, the end of the world is not imminent?"

"Well, I didn't say that. I don't know really – only He does. But I've seen the way He works, and I don't think you've got anything to worry about – you'll be long gone before it comes. I'm the sorry sap who has to stay around until the End of Time, not you."

I sense the source of his weariness and press. "Man, that must be hard, huh? Being eternal and all, I mean. It must be hard to have relationships with people and stuff. Don't all humans need that kind of thing?"

"Yes – it is hard. We do need interaction with others of our kind. Lasting and meaningful interaction. But, I get it at a surface level with all living things around me, and at this point that's fine with me. I draw energy and life at all times from all of God's Creation, so love is always surrounding me. Because, we don't really need a lot to survive, really. Just some shelter, some food, water – that's it really. And Love, as the Mevlana would say. That is also why Ramadan is important for Muslims – it is why it has been prescribed. Men and women should reduce their lives to these basic elements once in a while – get rid of all the excess. It is purifying – grounding."

"My uncle says Ramadan is the most important thing God has asked us to do."

"Yes – your uncle would say that. It is pretty much true – I'll give him that. That's why I'd like you to go to see him. Your uncle, I mean, in Pakistan. Ramadan is starting in a few days, and I want you to spend it with your family there – get to know what it is like to participate in the fast inside a Muslim country. It is the holiest of our months. And enjoy your family – they are the most precious thing in the world, you know. They are your blood, and that is one of the greatest bonds of love known to man."

At that, Khizr leaves the table and slowly walks down the street, leaving me alone with my new task of going to Pakistan. As I watch him disappear from my sight, I can't help feeling a bit sorry for the burden that he has to bear.

Chapter 12

The Frontline

Khizr's directive was clear, and Konya was bleak, so I hightailed it back to Istanbul and caught a flight for Karachi the next morning. As I touched down at Jinnah International Airport in Karachi, I felt the same pang, dull and fearful, that I always feel when I think about Pakistan.

Since I was young, when the subject of ethnicity came up, I would struggle to make my fellow Californians understand. 'Pakistan – it's near the Himalayas' or 'Pakistan, which is pretty much the same as India' were the two answers that came to be most common until I turned twelve and decided to stop explaining. It was much easier to just say 'I'm Indian', because everyone understands curry, right?

But now, Pakistan is famous – or maybe infamous. It is the only Muslim country with nukes. It hates India, which also has nukes. It has mega-earthquakes. It has a dictator who backs the U.S., but on shaky ground, and with mullahs plotting his downfall at every turn. It is where the most Al Qaeda suspects have been captured and turned over to U.S. authorities, but also where Bin Laden himself may be hiding. It is with us, but could just as easily be against us, and it is the inherent contradictions within Pakistan that make it one of the most difficult places to understand in the world today.

This shift in profile for my home country had not changed my feelings for it – I had always known Pakistan's fickleness. I remember my father talking to his friends, all ex-pat Pakistanis living in the Bay Area and watching their country twist in the geopolitical wind from afar. I remember talks of wars with India, sham democracies, military coups, outside meddling, sectarian violence, feudal lords – all factors that they blamed for Pakistan's inability to live up to its potential.

Our family's most direct connection back was through three visits, the last of which happened when I was sixteen, in addition to weekly telephone calls to the grandparents. All of my parents' brothers and sisters had left the country and spread out over the globe, and I remember the obvious ache in my grandparents' collective voice when speaking with their children, especially as they began to get sick and pass away. Dadi-jaan, my father and YuMa's mother, was the only one left, holding on to the old values and traditions fiercely in her old age. Nobody in the family knew how old she was, and nobody cared – she was still as vibrant as anyone remembered.

I landed the day before Ramadan started, which was one of the busiest times of the year for YuMa at his clinic. During the month of Ramadan it is encouraged to feed the poor, and YuMa's clinic was preparing to offer dinner to anyone who wanted it, every night during the holy month. He had sent his driver to get me, and as we rolled through the city, its dusty highways and crammed tenements reminded me of how much I disliked this place – how boring and oppressive it had seemed to me. Pakistan is a dry country, an Islamic Republic – there are no nightclubs, no bars to speak of. For an American youth like me, it can be the most boring place on the planet. My last visit there had been for three months in the summer of 1991 to visit the grandparents, and I had spent that entire summer sweating in the heat and being bitter about leaving my punk band back home.

But, as we neared the old family house in Defence, an upscale Karachi residential area near the Arabian Sea coastline, my feelings changed to warm ones, to the greatest redeeming quality of Pakistan – family. I had not seen my grandmother in thirteen years, and a mix of guilt and happiness rose in me as I recognized Zamzama Street, the main thoroughfare near the house.

The house sat inside a compound of about twenty villas, and access could only be gained through a security checkpoint with armed guards, as some bigwig government minister had a home inside. AK-47s are commonplace in Pakistan, and as the policeman waved us in with the barrel of his gun pointing haphazardly at us, I was reminded of that. Once inside the compound we came up to our own gate, and the *chowkidar* (security guard) opened it after a couple of honks from the driver. He too had a weapon, a shotgun, slung over his shoulder, which he quickly put down after closing the gate so that he could take my bags upstairs. I noticed that there were more armed guards inside, looking like they were wearing police uniforms, and noted that the security posture around the house was much larger than I remembered.

The chowkidar grabbed my bags and I followed him inside, where I found Dadi-jaan in the T.V. room, having a cup of tea and watching Faulty Towers (she had lived in England as a young woman and had a huge library of British comedies on tape). She saw me, and her face lit up immediately.

"Salaam Alaikum. *Bhaita*, you are here!" As she struggled to get up I went to her.

"Walaikum Salaam Dadi-jaan – can I help you?"

She waved me away. "I may be old, Mohammed, but I can still get up and hug my grandson." She grabbed her cane, steadied herself, straightened up, and smoothed out her blue *shalwar kameez* before coming to me. She had been a beautiful woman when she was young, and even now, in her old age, she always presented herself well. Her hair, which she still applied henna to for a nice blackish red color, was parted neatly down the middle and pulled into a long braid going down her back, and she still wore diamond studs in her nose and ears.

She came over and hugged me, ordering Momin, the cook, to get me some tea and samosas before turning off the T.V. and peppering me with question after question on the status of my life. Her most immediate concern, as was always the case when we chatted on the phone, was my marital status. As she hinted around that there were plenty of nice girls in Karachi for me to meet, I playfully dodged her attack and started telling her about the Kairouine Mosque in Morocco. Halfway through my story, the azan called out from a nearby mosque and Dadi-jaan excused herself to pray. I decided to go upstairs to the guestroom to shower and change. Feeling as good as new, I decided to take a tour of the old place.

The house was built in 1988 – YuMa and my father had built it for Dada and Dadi-jaan to enjoy their retirement from the military, where Dada had been a General. It had two stories, with two bedrooms downstairs and four bedrooms upstairs, and a spiral marble staircase connecting the two. There were three different balconies on the top floor, all looking out to a small park that was directly in front of the house. Dadi-jaan's room was downstairs, with a door that led into a vegetable garden that, other than getting all her grandchildren married off to good Shias, was her main project. On the other side of Dadi-jaan's room was the dining room, which led to a sitting room and then to a library facing the front lawn.

Dada had always been a great lover of books, and as I entered the library I could see that YuMa had preserved and expanded Dada's passion – all the furniture had been taken out of the room except for a leather chair in the middle of the room, with a low table and reading light, and various books thrown about on the ground. The room was ringed by bookcases, all overflowing with books from around the world. I started to make my way around the room, first through the Urdu section, then what looked like Persian and Arabic, and then to English. There were books of all kinds, with a heavy bent towards history, politics, and religion, but with liberal sprinklings of fiction and poetry too.

I came upon a section that dealt with the Partition in 1947, when Pakistan and India were born amidst great bloodshed and controversy. I thumbed through it to refresh my memory. It was estimated that more than one million people had died during Partition, and millions more were moved from their ancestral homes to new and strange parts of the subcontinent. My family had been part of the mass migration – we had moved from near Delhi to Karachi in 1948 when my father was only two. I had never fully understood this watershed moment in my family's history, and as I brought down another book titled *Pakistan: A Modern History*, I heard a car horn honk outside and the front gate open, followed quickly by YuMa striding through the door.

"Salaam Alaikum nephew! Welcome home, young man. Welcome to Pakistan."

We embraced in a bear hug before YuMa ushered me into the dining room, went and greeted Dadi-jaan, and then bade Momin to bring out dinner. YuMa had aged, though not much since I had seen him in London a few years before. He had the fair coloring and high cheek bones of Dadi-jaan, and he was a mountain of a man – 6'2' and over 200 lbs. His beard had become whiter and bushier, and maybe his hair a little thinner, but his eyes still held a spark of youthful idealism, and as he looked at me I could feel his excitement.

"So," he said as plate after plate was brought out from the kitchen, "the great traveler is here. My nephew, the follower of Khizr. You don't know how much joy your trip has brought me – I am so blessed to see my favorite nephew undertake such a noble quest! Subhan'allah!"

"Yeah well – thank you. Just the right place at the right time, I guess."

"Yes, indeed. You know, when I was young I did a trip similar to yours. I bought a VW Beetle, straight from the factory, in 1967. I had just graduated medical school in London, and my friend and I, we went straight to the factory in Germany and bought one." YuMa stopped for a moment, poured himself a glass of water and helped himself to some salad.

"So, we got the car – brand new and the most beautiful thing my twenty-four year old eyes had ever seen. We drove from Germany to Pakistan in three weeks – ah, what a magical journey that was!" YuMa launched into the story, and we spent dinner recounting the exploits of YuMa's carefree youth, driving through the Middle East in a foreign time of relative safety.

The rest of the evening I re-hashed my travels for him and Dadi-jaan, with YuMa urging me to provide him with even the tiniest of details. Dadi-jaan then steered the conversation to family politics, and as we listened to her gripes YuMa shot me an undercover roll of the eyes while he put his arm around her.

As we said goodnight, YuMa came with me to my room.

"So listen," he said, "you and I have some things to discuss. All the emails in the world cannot replace face to face communication – while you are here, I want you to get to know this place. As an adult, Mohammed. September 11th should show you that you are not part of the West – they will never accept you." This was classic YuMa, shooting to the heart of the matter without hesitation.

"Well, I don't know about that, YuMa. That is my home." I said.

"It is the only home you know. There are others out there, and I hope you give this one a chance while you are here, okay? Now, Khizr sent you here to learn about Ramadan, right? Well – it begins tomorrow – we will eat at 5:30. Momin will wake you."

He winked at me and headed off to bed.

The next two weeks I spent adjusting to the life of the fast. Life changes in a Muslim country during Ramadan – hours are shortened, people take longer lunch breaks, and prayers are given more diligently. Most activities switch to nighttime, after people have broken their fast, and if you go to the main drag of any Muslim city at night during Ramadan you'll find a bustling night market, with people shopping for *Eid* clothes or presents (Eid is the day after the month of Ramadan ends and is a Muslim Christmas equivalent) or eating snacks and drinking tea.

In YuMa's house, life revolved around eating. YuMa, Dadi-jaan and I had breakfast before dawn (it turned out that Momin's wakeup call was not needed, as the numerous mosques within earshot of us would do the trick by turning up their loudspeakers and yelling to the masses in Urdu "Get up, Get up! Fasters rise and do your duty to God!"). Then, we would go back to sleep for an hour, with YuMa getting up around 7AM and going to work. Dadi-jaan and I would wake a bit later and spend our day chatting and watching T.V. I took a special interest in the library, and tried to ward off the hunger of the late afternoons by focusing on reading as many books about Partition as possible. During the fast, you are not allowed any food or drink from sunrise to sunset, and it seemed like the afternoon hours before sunset were the longest and hungriest I had ever known.

I also fell into the rhythm of offering my prayers five times a day; whenever possible offering them with YuMa when he was home, in a special prayer room he had set up next to his bedroom. It was a solitary room – small and sparse, with just a few prayer rugs and pillows lying about on the floor. As the month progressed, I looked forward to each prayer time, as offering them had a meditative effect on my mind and began to wound deep hostilities regarding the modern world and my place in it that I had not fully realized existed within me.

Ramadan is about self-discipline, and every morning and night, our discipline was rewarded with the finest of foods. Our breakfast meals were especially heavy – *parathas*, eggs, *keema*, *shami kebabs*. Momin would be up and eagerly awaiting each morning's requests. At night, after breaking the fast with the traditional dates, snacks, and juice, Momin would cook up a feast of Indo-Pak delicacies – *pulao* and *korma* and *nihari* and *haleem*. Dadi-jaan, who still kept every fast even at her advanced age, would always venture into the kitchen in the late afternoon to make sure Momin had something extra special on the stove for that night, so that her two generations of sons would be able to break the fast properly. She was especially happy at my willingness to participate in the ritual, and I learned more about the breadth and depth of the foods of the Subcontinent during Ramadan than I had during any previous point in my life.

It was easier to fast in this environment – in the house, no one had food or water during the day, and your schedule revolved around the fast. YuMa told me of how much harder it was to fast in the West, when all your co-workers are eating seemingly constantly around you. It made sense – I had never dreamed of doing it back at home. It seemed so drastic. But here it was normal, and after a few days I had seemed to come to a balance – a slight weakening of my physical health in exchange for a large measure of mental discipline. The daily breaking of the fast became a mini celebration of my nascent piousness, and keeping the fast helped me feel absolved of my sinful past.

There are strict rules for the Muslim fast. A faster is supposed to enter a state of physical and mental purity between dawn and dusk. They are not to eat, drink, or smoke. They are not to lie, cheat, or get angry. They are not to have sex, and are required even more than normal to complete the five daily prayers. Many people read the Qu'ran during Ramadan, and there are a few nights in the month when people stay up all night, reading the holy book and praying for their sins. It is a month for reflection – one is supposed to take stock of themselves and their relationship to God.

I had always wondered about the seeming conflict between the joy and partying at night and the harsh fasting of the day. One day after breaking the fast at *iftar*, Dadi-jaan and I talked about it.

"Dadi-jaan – I don't understand something," I began innocently enough after asking her to pass a *pakora*. "Ramadan is supposed to be about inward reflection, isn't it?"

"Why yes, bhaita, yes. It is a most holy month. It is when we become pure for God," she said.

"Yes, but it seems like things would be different. People seem more happy – more jovial. The bazaars are packed at night. It strikes me as oddly Muslim – finding joy in something that makes you suffer."

Dadi-jaan smiled and put her fork down. "What makes you think it is suffering, Mohammed?"

"Well, you can't eat or drink during the day. I mean – what if you lived in the desert and you desperately needed water? Isn't that the way the Prophet lived, in the Arabian desert? What if it was 110 degrees out? Wouldn't you call that suffering, being in the desert without water?"

Dadi-jaan furrowed her brow and thought for a second before responding. "In some ways – yes, I guess it is. But, it is only physical suffering, and it is always temporary. It is a small price to pay for the wonderful gift that it brings."

"What gift is that?" I asked.

"It gives us the gift of being closer to God. It is the only thing He really asks of us. It is the time when we can show Him that we know Him. I mean – do you love God?"

"Yes."

"So, wouldn't you be happy to do what He asked of you?"

I thought about my trip, the haphazardness of it. I was flying around the world at the drop of a hat, questing after knowledge I never knew I wanted. And I was happy – the happiest I had been in a long time, because I was doing something that I felt mattered. Because I was defining myself through my beliefs, which had long simmered in a stew of contradiction.

"Yes," I slowly responded. "Yes – it would make me happy."

"Well – Ramadan is the month in which He communicated the Qu'ran to our great Prophet Mohammed, through the Angel Gabriel. It is a holy month, and God has told us to purify in the month of Ramadan – to fast and abstain and become closer to Him, and it is with sheer joy that we do this small thing that He has asked."

"Well said Dadi-jaan. Now, excuse my interruption, but I must take Mo away." YuMa had entered while we talked and was standing in the archway, listening to our conversation. He came over and kissed Dadi-jaan gently on the cheek before looking at me with a twinkle in his eye. "I've taken off early from the clinic so that we may break the fast and then go for a stroll down by the beach. We haven't gotten any time together - what do you say Mo?'

"Sure – sounds good to me."

YuMa had some dates and samosas, and we then said our evening prayer together. Afterwards, we took a short ride in his jeep to the coast of the Arabian Sea, on the south side of Karachi. As we pulled up to a parking spot, he thanked me for coming.

"Mo – it is so great to see you here. I have always worried that you would never know your real home – your real country."

"Thanks for having me, YuMa. It's nice to know I have a home here to come to."

"Nonsense – this is where you are from. You don't have to thank me for your home. I have often wondered how long it would take before you came here Mohammed – you should get to know your homeland. It is a beautiful place, with wonderful people. People who look like you, you know?"

We got out of the car and started walking along the promenade above the beach. In the twilight, various food and toy vendors were setting up, getting ready for the crush of people who would come out and enjoy the warm evening after filling up their bellies.

"Someone like you could make a real difference here," Yuma continued. "I mean a real difference, not like back in America. You could see it – see the people's lives improve because of your work. That, I think, would be much harder to do in your America. Pakistan presents us with a huge opportunity to do good – Subhan'allah!"

"I don't know about that YuMa," I protested. "There are plenty of places in America where people can be helped. And besides – it seems like things are looking up here, right? I mean, President Musharraf seems to be getting this country going in the right direction, taking on the mullahs and all that."

YuMa's face darkened at the mention of Pakistan's leader. "He's running a sham democracy that everyone knows is a sham democracy.

He's just another general running the country – the fourth we've had in fifty-five years. I can't really see that Musharraf is doing anything that will make this country better in the long run."

"I don't get it YuMa," this was a subject that always puzzled me – the murkiness of Pakistani politics, "Why is it that this country can't elect responsible leaders? Every government produced from democracy in Pakistan seems to have been a total failure."

He drew a deep, contemplative breath before beginning. "Well, I wouldn't go so far as to say 'total' failure. Some good has come, but not much. It's complicated – hey look!" Yuma pointed out to a crowd gathering a short ways away. We went over and found a show going on – a beach entrepreneur had a cobra in one hand and a bag containing a mongoose in the other. For twenty rupees each, he assured the crowd, he would let two of nature's enemies fight to the death. YuMa smiled at me and plunked down the money, and we watched a grizzly fight ensure, with the cobra flaring up and striking at the mongoose a dozen times before finally getting mauled to death by the ferocious little animal.

"Wow," I said as we walked away. "I can't believe the mongoose survived all those bites."

"They de-venom the snakes – the fight was fixed. It is much easier to catch cobras than mongooses," YuMa laughed and slapped me on the back, the weight of his arm making me lurch forward a bit before catching myself. "But, back to our topic at hand - perhaps one way to understand Pakistani history is by comparing it to your new homeland. How much do you know about American history?"

"Um – I dunno. The basics I guess."

"So – when was the Declaration of Independence signed?"

"July 4th, 1776." I said.

"And when was the Constitution created?" asked YuMa.

"Um – I don't know. At the same time?"

"Actually, I believe it was in 1789 – a full twelve years after the Declaration. During that interlude, there were lots of questions. The ideology of American government was slowly formed and addressed by men of high education and character, men who had fought against the British. It was really amazing, if you think about it. The confluence of circumstances that brought so many talented and learned men – men like Ben Franklin and Thomas Jefferson – together for the purpose of making a country was incredible. And they knew they were making history – that whatever country they made would be an immediate power on earth, what with its already robust economy and seemingly unlimited natural resources. Their words and actions created a Constitution that was, and still is, the envy of the world."

As YuMa went on he assumed a more teacherly manner, speaking easily to inform but not preach.

"But even with this serendipity came problems – the issue of slaves being one. While the Declaration said that 'all men are created equal,' in reality it was that only all white men were equal. Did you know, in an effort to compromise between the landed slave-owners of the South and the wealthy elites of the North, the original Constitution allowed that slaves counted as three-fifths of a person? Women, of course, did not even count as citizens. Remember all this, Mohammed, in the context of today. It is important to note our place in the greater story of recorded history."

At this point YuMa's face became even more earnest – more serious. He bought a *keenoo* from a vendor and started peeling it, throwing the peels to the beach below as he proceeded.

"This contradiction – of declaring all men free but also declaring some men to be only three-fifths a man – was a seed that festered and grew until war was declared seventy years later. The American Civil War. But, after the North won, an amendment – I think it was the fourteenth – changed this question of who counted as a person and said that all men over the age of twenty-one could vote. Of course, this still excluded some Indians and all women, but those rules were eventually changed as well. That is one of the beauties of the American Constitution, its provisions for amendments. The framers of America realized that flexibility is essential if any government is to endure, so they built in a strong, institutionalized process for change. The amendment system has allowed the U.S. to grow and adapt to the ever changing face of their populace."

He offered me a slice of his fruit, and then pointed for us to follow a side street, leading away from the beach. We played a successful game of chicken to cross the main road, which was moving in a chaotic swirl of brightly colored buses, small Japanese and Korean cars, motorbikes, donkey carts and blasting horns, and only after both of us safely entered the little street did YuMa take up his train of thought.

"Come Mohammed – this way. So – anyway. Back to America. I have always admired the other beauty of America's birth - the separation of powers. The Constitution set up three distinct bodies of the federal government, each with important checks on the other. The most important checks were that on the President, so that he would not become a tyrant. The system was designed to be bigger than one man, and for a lot of reasons that is why it worked so well for so long. I'm speaking of the past, mind you – now the American governmental system is a shell of its former self. It's probably unrecognizable to the American forefathers. They didn't provision for things like the Pentagon or the CIA or the NSC – all those things came much later and drastically affected how things worked." YuMa stopped short and offered me his last piece of his fruit before asking, "I'm not boring you, am I?"

"Not at all." It was a pleasure to hear him speak – his knowledge was both empirical and theoretical, and few people I knew could match him. "Please continue."

Before he did we had to sidestep some beggars who had spied us as potential targets. YuMa gave them ten rupees each and said, "The poverty here is so heartbreaking, so needless. It pains me - fills me up with sorrow on a daily basis. You see, Mo, Pakistan didn't have to be like this."

He pulled me gently to the side as a car came racing by from behind, a young boy not older than fourteen behind the wheel had swerved to avoid a donkey and was going way too fast in his tiny Dihatsu.

"I told you the American story, as I see it, to contrast it with the story of Pakistan's nationhood," continued YuMa, undeterred by the reckless traffic around us. "America declared its independence from Britain on July 4th, 1776, right? Well, Pakistan declared its independence from Britain on August 14th, 1947. Both countries had bloody wars in the immediate aftermath of their self-stated independence, but then history diverged for the two fledgling democracies. The serendipity of the American revolution and the cacophony of Pakistan's birth." YuMa seemed to like this last line and chuckled a bit to himself before taking up his lecture again.

"Right from the beginning we were in trouble. While America already had territorial integrity and a vast ocean between it and its chief protagonist, England, our split with the British and with India left us with a most untenable position. There were two parts of Pakistan –West and East, which is now modern day Bangladesh. Between the two parts of the country lay India, Pakistan's natural enemy. Throw in the dispute over Kashmir, and you've got real problems. It was like putting the Soviet Union right between California and New York."

"I never thought of it like that." I said.

"It's history, nephew! Plain for all to see. We also did not have the kind of time that America did. After kicking the Brits out, America had time. For a period the states did whatever they wanted, and then the Constitution was written, and then there was thirty odd years of peace until the war of 1812 broke out. We, however, did not have that luxury – less than a year after our independence, we were given a war with India over Kashmir. Now – do you know how profoundly war can affect a society?"

I thought about the changes in America since 9/11. Polarization. Blind patriotism. Secrecy. Religious agendas. As I nodded, YuMa took us through another alley, which came out to a park. It was as impressive as it was misplaced in the barren landscape – a huge track surrounding landscaped green lawns, with big sitting areas and sculptures dotting the inner area. As we came closer, I saw people on the track, some running, some walking. We got to an entrance and YuMa paid the ten rupees each for us to go in. The exercising multitudes were a cavalcade of Pakistani characters – the young Westernized men and women, running in Nike sweats and listening to their iPods; the ponch-laden middle-aged guy sweating in his shalwar kameez; the *burka*-clad women in black speed-walking in pairs.

YuMa and I joined the rounds on the outside ring, walking briskly. Our conversation had been one sided, as they often were. But this time it felt different – he had urgency in his voice. Like he was making a pitch. It had been six years since we last saw each other, in San Francisco for my brother's wedding, but lots had happened in that time.

We lived in the New World, the Post Twin Towers world. Everything had changed, and we both knew it. My two worlds, which had always known a delicate dance of co-existence, had crashed into each other and exploded. YuMa's cause, which he had fought his whole life for, had just crystallized – this was the point of his life.

"Look at our leaders, too. The Father of America is?"

"George Washington."

"Yes – General George Washington. Who led the Continental Army and beat the British on the battlefield. Who was the first President, but was so gracious and such a patriot that he stepped down after two terms, citing nervousness about becoming too powerful. I mean – what a way to start out! You get this amazing Constitution, and then an amazing, unifying figure as leader for eight solid years! Now, who is the Father of Pakistan?"

"Mohammed Ali Jinnah."

"Yes – and he died less than a year after the country was born. His efforts were much different from Washington's – he had 'won' (if you could call the Partition a victory) on the political battlefield, not via arms. He had led the Muslim League, which was first a branch and then a rival of Ghandi's Indian National Congress, in its efforts to create a Muslim homeland on the Subcontinent. I mean – it was a very romantic idea. The Muslims of India, 200 million strong, had a very distinct history, a distinct culture from the Hindus and the rest. With the breakup of British India, Jinnah and his cohorts saw their chance to get the Muslims out of a minority and into a majority, so they pursued it."

YuMa sidestepped a lady in a black burka and glow-in-the-dark Nike running shoes struggling to keep up the pace and continued.

"And they won – Jinnah won independence for Pakistan. But at what cost? Pakistan was born amidst bloodshed and massive homelessness, huge populations of Muslims, Hindus, and Sikhs were forced to leave their ancestral lands and relocate. Our own family made the choice to migrate from Delhi in India to Karachi in Pakistan – have you ever thought about why? Can you imagine – Dada had a wife and a two-year-old child – me. But he decided to move, as did your other grandfather, your mom's dad. They decided to leave everything, their jobs and their lands, and make a dangerous journey to an uncertain land and an uncertain future. Why do you think they did that?"

"I don't know," I said.

"Because of the romance – the ideal of a Muslim homeland. Pakistan means 'Land of the Pure' – did you know that? Do you know his background, Jinnah's?"

"Wasn't he a lawyer?" I only remembered from a report I had done about him in high school.

"Yes – a lawyer. He was a British lawyer, actually, and completely Westernized. Jinnah was a Muslim and was the voice of the Muslims of India, but in practice his Islam was very different than that of the masses for which he spoke. He saw no incompatibility between his form of Islam and Western political thought. He saw, in democracy, the ancient Islamic practice of *ijma*, which means consensus of the community. He saw tolerance and progressiveness in *ijtihad*, which allowed for continuing evolution and interpretation of Islamic law. But, these were theoretical ideas – justifications. In practice, no institutions were built to map the tolerant Islamic practices to actual governmental functions. And Jinnah died so soon after independence that he had no time to go about drafting a constitution that could execute the promise of Pakistan as a tolerant Islamic state. His was a new proposal, revolutionary, if you will. While an Islamic democracy, in his theoretical world, was quite possible, the reality was that there was no organized way to incorporate his theories into practice."

"But weren't there other people," I asked, "other leaders around that could have continued his vision? I mean – if George Washington had died, there would have been plenty of other men ready to lead America."

"Yes – you are right. America's was an amazing revolution – very lucky to have so many great leaders. There was no such thing in Pakistan – Jinnah was the only one with the revolutionary thought, and after his death Pakistan descended into the partisan politics that it still suffers from. Punjabis, Bengalis, Sindhis, Muhajirs – all the groups of the country started to pull it apart, each vying for power and influence. After Jinnah's death what followed was calamity after calamity – the loss of Kashmir in 1948, the assassination of Jinnah's successor Liaquat Ali Khan in 1951, the adoption of a first Constitution in 1956 only to have it suspended under martial law in 1958. This was done by General Ayub Khan, who then introduced a new Constitution in 1962. Then another war with India in the Rann of Kutch in 1965, then another declaring of martial law in the 1969 coup by General Yahya Khan. The list goes on and on."

YuMa had started the track on a brisk pace but slowed a bit now. He had always seemed larger than life to me, both in mind and body, but I could see age beginning to creep in on him. His back was not as straight, and his beard had no black hairs left. He sidestepped to let a younger pair of joggers go by, looked at me and pointed to the next exit to signal we'd be done soon before continuing with his lecture.

"Compare this first twenty odd years of Pakistan's history with that of America's. America's first twenty years had zero wars, three legitimately elected executives - Washington, Adams, and Jefferson - and one Constitution. Pakistan had two wars, two different Constitutions, two different military coups, and an assassination in the same timeframe. Mohammed, I am not telling you this as an apologist – I am telling you the history. Recent history, mind you – this all happened to our country in my lifetime, and it only got worse from there."

We had made a complete circle around the park and came back out on the street, backtracking towards the beach and our car.

"In 1971 there was the inevitable civil war between the two Pakistans, and East Pakistan succeeded and became Bangladesh – a humiliating blow to our country. Then came another Constitution, this one in 1973 at the behest of Zulfikar Ali Bhutto, who tried to put civilian controls back on the military, land reforms against the elite, and nationalize several major industries. But, he was discredited and eventually hung in a coup by General Zia-ul-Haq in 1977, who remade the country with a Wahabbi/extremist bent."

There it was – that magic word again. Wahabbi. "Really," I said, "I didn't know Zia was a Wahabbi."

"Oh yes, of course. He was the one who gave Pakistan over to the Saudis, made us their puppet for the last twenty-five years. It was through him that the Saudis and Americans poured millions of dollars into the Afghan Mujahideen, to fight the Soviets, and it was through him that the Taliban came to pass. Thousands of Wahabbi schools were built for the poor, mostly in Baluchistan and the Frontier provinces, on his watch. When I was fighting, in the early 80s, it was all just starting. Now, hundreds of thousands of young boys have been brainwashed into believing in hatred and intolerance. And, this radicalization under Zia intensified with the fight against the Soviets, and then further with the uprising in 1990 in Kashmir. Every politician since has had to deal with this volatile force – with armed religious militants exerting their will on the country at their leisure. Throw in millions of Afghan refugees, sanctions from the rest of the world, tensions with India, and now, the so-called War on Terrorism, and you've got a recipe for a failed state."

We were coming closer to the beach and YuMa slowed his pace, trying to catch more of my eye as he talked. "Mohammed, I tell you all this because I love you. Even with this seemingly hopeless situation, I feel as though it is my duty to help – as though God himself has created such a situation so as to see how we, not only us Pakistanis but all the Muslims of the world, will react. And I will do what I can – I will help educate and grow the people of this country, to make them proud of their religion, to make them progressive."

We had come back to the promenade, which was more crowded than before. Kids were taking camel rides up and down the beach, and the toy stands were doing a brisk business, selling kites and tops and glow sticks. We made it through the crowd and got back to the car before YuMa continued.

"I want there to be a new generation of leaders of Pakistan, Mohammed my dear. A new generation who are educated as well as any in the West, but that have a sense of duty and pride in their culture and in their religion. All of our politicians have failed because they did not have this sense of duty – but we can plant seeds now. My quest is to prepare for an Islamic Renaissance, one that you or I might not see but that your children might, or your grandchildren. This is the front line, here, to fight the good fight. I know why it is that Allah sent you here. It is so that you can make a difference. It is so that you can be free – to know in your heart that you are finally doing something of true worth to the world."

I was silent, not knowing what to say or do. We got home, and YuMa laughed as he pulled us back into the compound and then into the house's carport.

"I know I come on strong - I learned that from your Dada. These are serious times – I'm delighted that you are not hiding from yourself, that you have come back to your Muslim roots. I have some things I think you may be interested in here, okay? Ways to spend your time wisely."

YuMa got out of the car and strode into the house, greeting the policemen sitting by the door before stooping through the entrance. I sat in the car for a second, thinking about YuMa's stance, not sure if I agreed with him that moving to Pakistan was the only way to help.

Chapter 13

Zindabad Pakistan

Ramadan continued to unfold, with each successive day of the thirty days seeing me become better and better at keeping the fast. It becomes your new routine – you still eat, but just not as much and at different times of the day. But, the times of day are prescribed (basically before dawn and after dusk), and like anything else, the body adapts, and even thrives, off the regularity of it. Granted – my month of fasting was easy, as I had no physical or mental labor to do whatsoever, but I must say that it wasn't as hard as I thought it would be.

I spent a lot of time with my grandmother, who would tell me stories of my dad as a kid or about the different places she'd been in her life. With my grandfather having been in the army, they had traveled all over the world, to Europe and Africa, and my grandmother had taken great joy in the trip I was on and in sharing her own travel stories with me.

But, always lurking beneath her stories, Dadi-jaan would slip in an occasional anecdote about one of the seemingly dozens of great couples she had hooked up, and after a week or so she began to put the full court press on me. An old lady with nothing but time on her hands, she had become consumed with my marriage, to the point where me showing up, single and so completely marketable, was almost an affront to her and her entire way of being. I would see her staring at me, from across the dinner table, the intensity of her look making her seem closer to seven feet tall than her actual five feet of shrunken height. Her bifocal glasses, which were coke-bottle thick due to her multiple cataracts and a bout with glaucoma, would make her eyes look like an owl's, and as she watched me pick through my *biryani*, I could see her sizing me and my girl preferences up.

Dadi-jaan started her attack pragmatically by first trying to put
a timeframe to my visit. She kept pestering me about the specifics
of my plans, about how I would decide my departure date and
when I would buy my ticket. I knew it was half for herself, but half
to see how many marriage appointments she could schedule. My
vagueness only lent to her sense of urgency, and soon she started
to tell me stories about the wonderful daughters or granddaughters
of her friends and acquaintances, all of who, she assured me, were
beautiful and Shia. Amazingly, she always had a picture ready of the
young woman in question, invariably a glamour shot with a fuzzy
white background and a preponderance of makeup dominating the
shot. Beauty was, indeed, in the eye of the beholder, as Dadi-jaan
subscribed to the classic *desi* 'the whiter the better' opinion, as every
girl was whiter than the tanned white girls back in Cali. Funny how
in the East the brown girls try to be white, while in the West the
white girls try to be brown.

Dadi-jaan's gambit to get me hitched had almost a sporting nature
to it - the art of matchmaking has a long and proud tradition in Pakistan,
and I remember when I was young and my grandfather, who had
brought Dadi-jaan and stayed with us for a year in California, also had
told me about the countless couples he had been personally responsible
for hooking up. Making an introduction that leads to marriage is worn
like a badge of honor to the matchmaker, and my grandfather went even
one step further, saying that you get special credit from God, *sawaab,*
anytime you make a match.

Matches are usually dreamed up based primarily on religion, with
a strong undercurrent of subculture. So, while it is preferable that
Punjabis marry Punjabis and Sindhis marry Sindhis, it is almost required
that Shia marry Shia and Sunni marry Sunni. Primary selling points
may include level of education, a good job, looks, a good family, or
citizenship in a Western country, with looks being especially important
for girls.

So, as Dadi-jaan began showing me candidates every so often until
it built to two or three pictures a day coming out from a seemingly
unlimited stash, I would laugh them away or quickly change the subject,
and usually she would let me get away with it. Every time she would

show me a new one she would watch me very closely, hoping for any sign of interest that she could pounce upon.

After a few days, she showed me a picture of a girl who was undeniably hot – with large, doe-shaped eyes, a pretty smile, and full lips. Her name was Yasmine, and Dadi-jaan immediately laid it on thick, telling me how this girl had been to school in Canada and was pretty much a Westerner, just like me. She also told me that our families went way back, and that Dada and Yasmine's grandfather had been in the Army together. After a few more minutes of getting worked over, I gave in, and told Dadi-jaan that she could arrange a meeting if she liked. I figured that it would be less pain for me to indulge her than to battle an old lady for the rest of Ramadan.

Dadi-jaan got on the horn immediately and was able to arrange a meeting for the following Friday. When YuMa found out, he thought it was hilarious.

"So, Nephew, seems as if your Dadi has it in for you, huh?" he teased one morning as we breakfasted together before dawn.

"I guess so. She's got me going to see some girl this week. On Friday, I guess."

"Well son – don't despair. She's been working on me for over fifty years, and she still hasn't won. But you are different – she seems to be bending the rules for you."

"What rules?" I asked.

"Usually, these summit meetings are not done during Ramadan. But, she has successfully sold the urgency of this meeting to her counterpart on the girl's side, Jafari Aunty. She is Yasmine's grandmother – a wonderful family."

I wasn't sure if he was joining in the pitch. "You too, huh YuMa?"

He laughed my accusation off. "Mohammed – I am the last person to speak on the benefits of marriage, and I know you know that, so I know you are probably not taking this too seriously."

"Yup."

"But, Dadi-jaan spoke to me, said she wanted me to come along. These things are always about the family, you know, and she wants a good showing on the part of the Khans. Your father called as well, from America, and your parents are both excited by this prospect."

"Man. I didn't know this was taking on such global implications."

"Look at it as an opportunity – an opportunity to see the age old mating rituals of the Subcontinent. And, you will get to meet Jafari Sahib – Yasmine's grandfather. He is a guiding light in this world – an old soul. I often go on my own to see him, just to sit and chat with him, and listen to his wisdom. You know, as a young man he was published for legal and philosophical books, both in English and in Urdu."

"Cool," I said. "And I'm glad you're going, so that you can help me. I want to be as nice and non-committal as possible. There is no chance of success, so I want to make sure we follow protocol, you know? I don't want to be responsible for bad feelings between our families."

YuMa patted my back sympathetically. "Don't you worry, nephew. You are not the first boy to go to a girl's house with this attitude in mind – just be yourself and everything will be fine."

Friday night came around and we broke our fast after the dusk prayer. I ate the chicken korma carefully, trying not to spill any of the broth on my new white shirt. Dadi-jaan had brought a barber over during the day to tidy up my hair, and the day before we had gone to do some shopping at a Western-style mall called Park Towers, so that I would look my best for my 'date.' I happily indulged my grandmother in her preparations, as it was plain to see the joy she was getting from them.

We finished up and got in the car. Dadi-jaan gave her instructions to her driver, Shahid, and we rolled down Zamzama Street. After about a mile, we came to a large roundabout that separated YuMa's neighborhood from the affluent sea-side neighborhood next door – Clifton. In the middle of the roundabout were three huge stone swords, each about thirty feet high and with Pakistan's national motto inscribed on each – Faith, Unity, and Discipline. We circled around the swords, avoiding a donkey cart that was clogging the flow of traffic, and proceeded in to Clifton, taking a couple of more turns and winding up in front of a large, fenced in lot. Shahid parked the car and YuMa, Dadi-jaan and I got out and rang a doorbell in the iron gate.

A man in a traditional shalwar kameez and long, henna-dyed beard opened the door and asked us our business, a sawed off shotgun standing to his side. YuMa told him who we were, and we were escorted onto the grounds. We followed a pathway that cut between a carport on the left and a large, well-manicured lawn stretched to the right before getting to the front door of the house proper. Dadi-jaan gave me a last look over before the door opened up and we were greeted by a good looking, middle aged woman.

"Aunty," she said to Dadi-jaan, "Salaam Alaikum. So wonderful to see you."

"Walaikum Salaam," said Dadi-jaan.

"Please come in," said the lady. "Hello Yousuf," she said to YuMa, "you are looking well. And, you - you must be Mohammed, right? From California? I am an old friend of your dad's – my name is Zoha."

"Salaam Alaikum, Aunty Zoha." I said.

We came into the foyer, which was decorated with a framed page of the Quran in ornate calligraphy. We walked in to a spacious living room, where an old couple sat, waiting to receive us. I didn't see the girl anywhere.

We exchanged greetings with the elders and sat down. I was seated next to the grandfather, who was introduced to me as Jafari Sahib. After some initial chitchat, regarding my travels and plans, the two grandmothers and Aunty Zoha started their own discussion while Jafari Sahib, YuMa, and I were left to our own devices.

The old man looked fairly weak – he had struggled to get up when greeting us, precariously trying to balance on a cane and shake our hands at the same time. He was completely bald, and wore large tinted glasses that dominated his face. He was dressed in a white shalwar kameez, with a khaki vest and matching socks on his feet.

"So, young man" he began, in thickly, Indian-accented English, "you are from America, yes?"

"Yes uncle, I am. From California."

"Regarding the USA," he started right in, "I hate what happened on September 11th. I have profound regard and respect for the USA because of the advancement they have made to the human knowledge and to the scientific progress and to the human effort to advance what you call democracy throughout the world."

The way he spoke was hilarious to me – he shook his head side to side and sounded like a caricature of the classic Indian accent that my brothers and I had mocked since we were young. But, his vocabulary seemed advanced, and from the book next to him (a rather large treatise in English on South Africa during apartheid) and what YuMa had told me I was already beginning to feel in awe of him.

"USA is very, very good," he continued. "When you read lives of such men as Abraham Lincoln and Thomas Edison and such, you find that these people are the real human mind, that these people are real human beings. They were in a foreign land, but they put two and two together and they have reached the pinnacle of progress - material and scientific progress. The effort they have made - in their laws, their trade, their methods of governance – these efforts are all so good for all humans, everywhere we will benefit from the USA's studies. And, well," he paused for a second, changing which legs were crossed before continuing, "at least they were not sadists, they were not overly cruel, right? The ideals they have, I mean. It was something you can understand, though they did deal with the local inhabitants - the Red Indians - very badly. Those poor people deserve sympathy because they were people of the Earth - you should have charity and sympathy with them instead of allowing them to remain in the state they are in. But, overall, I like the USA – I wish my country could have been more like them."

His unsolicited opinion of my country was interesting, so I pressed him a bit. "And what about America, post September 11th?" I asked.

"Later on they have committed aggression in the world, in the name of fighting terrorism. But, they themselves have proven to be the worst criminals on Earth - what are they crying about? They did the same thing to the Japanese! Hiroshima and Nagasaki - by throwing a couple of bombs, they destroyed hundreds of thousands of people, and some people were sick for fifty, sixty years afterwards. You know, some people think that September 11th was organized by the Japanese? Because, I don't think that Osama Bin Laden and a few others - sitting in Tora Bora thousands of miles away, with their one yard beards - could have managed to arrange a simultaneous assault with five or six planes on the World Trade Center. Simultaneous! It must have been arranged by either the Israelis or the Japanese, who are equally scientifically mature. It is not Osama. Perhaps it will take him a half century more to achieve that level of smartness and efficiency."

"So why do you think America blamed him?" interjected YuMa, seemingly enjoying the chance to probe Jafari Sahib on the subject.

"There must be other reasons, which you will come to know after twenty years. Nowadays, the politics are one of fear - everything is covert. The media, the newspapers - they create such a smoky screen that it is impossible to find out what is the truth. I do not know about Iraq, but I do know about Afghanistan. I have been to Afghanistan, I know Afghans, I know their history - and these are poor people. Other people - Pakistanis and Arabs, all with long beards and similar ideas - they are the ones who came and threw a few bombs in that country. The Afghans had nothing to do with it – they are not to blame for Osama. They hate him. So - why bomb them? War should be equal. You cannot put Hercules on one side and a man from Liliput on the other side - it is not justice. An elephant stepping on a lizard – is this a fair fight? America is the greatest power - it is the only one who can dictate. It is a superpower, no doubt about it. And no one, not even China and Russia combined, can challenge it. But they should be careful, because it is the law of nature that their time will come."

"So," I ventured, "are you are saying that there is a natural law of retribution, and one way or another something will happen to America to even things out?"

"Yes, they cannot get away from it. Because, you see - I have been reading history. Throughout time - where there is land once upon a time there was water, where there is a volcano once upon a time there were clouds. Stars change, rivers change, climates change, empires change, Earth changes - everything under the sun changes except for one thing - and that is human nature. Human nature doesn't change, but everything else does. And it is in our nature to die. My father, my grandfather - thousands of people, they are all gone. Nothing of them is here - they are in the graveyard. If I was to take you to see them you would say 'Where are they?' Right? Because you would not see them – they are dead! And, whatever little bit there is now, it will also be gone. This Earth does not belong to anyone - this is like a traveler's inn, like a hotel. We are only checking in for a few days. Everything will be taken away. Death has another key to the safe where you lock up your money. It comes and takes everything away from everyone."

His talk of death was not morbid – he spoke like a man facing it soon and completely at peace with this undeniable truth of life. "And this will happen to America?" I asked.

"This happens to all over," said Jafari Sahib. "You see lots of civilizations that have been destroyed - people in Mesopotamia, people in Moenjadaro, you know, places where now there are ancient mounds and ruins. Cities have been destroyed, and this is not just for sport. There is something behind it. Human beings have a short life, and so do societies. The murder that America engages in is as senseless as a common street murder. I don't understand why Mr. A kills Mr. B - he is going to die anyway! Humans are destined to die - both of them! Why expedite it? Nobody has lived more than 150 years. People die."

YuMa couldn't resist stoking the philosophical fire. "But isn't that the ultimate expression of power - for one man to kill another? Mr. A cuts short Mr. B's life to show his power over him. America kills people to show its power, and to force its stance on the rest of the world."

Jafari Sahib chuckled. "But Mr. A will die himself, so this is foolish. Even a mosquito bite can kill the strongest man. You don't need a tank or a bomber - people die anyway. The question of murder is - what does it bring for the murderer? If you pull a mango plant out of the Earth, what good does it do anyone? People rotting in jails, people hanging - I don't understand this. A father should punish his son so that he won't steal again - if he kills him, then what point does it make? Nobody is learning anything. The human being is a very poor creature - he has a time limit. The point is that certain things are useless - America is a giant, Afghanistan is a baby, and Iraq is a child - for America to go and kill them and call them terrorists is useless. Who the hell are you? You are the father and mother of terror."

He said this last statement with a smile – it was not combative towards me at all. You could tell he was speaking from a detached, academic viewpoint, and each time he said anything vaguely offensive about America he would pat my right knee and look at me, to make sure I wasn't getting upset. I decided to ask him a question that had always bothered me. "So, Jafari Sahib, you say America is the father of terror. How do you define terrorism?"

"Terrorists create a certain atmosphere so that other people, normal people, are unable to breathe for fear. Because in fear your senses are worthless - you are stupefied. I have seen this - you know in this country, men who are sentenced to hanging can appeal, but if the appeal is denied they will be hung the next day usually. One man was denied his appeal, and overnight his hair turned grey. I worked as a lawyer – I saw it! This is fear. You know that Christ, when he was being led to the cross, due to fear, blood started oozing from his skin pores. With fear, you cannot work, you cannot walk. I know about fear. Once, a long time ago when I was a young man, my house was on the banks of the river Indus. I went to walk to the bathroom - they used to say my house kissed the Indus, and I used to say as long as they don't embrace I'm all right." He and YuMa both laughed at this one, and when I realized what he implied by 'embrace' I joined in before he continued. "So, one day when I entered the bathroom there was a black cobra sitting there looking at me. The bathroom was small, and I was already inside - I think he came in from a pipe that went into the river. He was about seven to eight feet - a very dangerous snake. And he started hissing and flared out like cobras do. And I was forced - when I go to the bathroom, I must be on the verge or I cannot go - and when I saw him everything came out in my pants." We laughed again and the ladies on the other side of the room began to look over with wondering glances. "But, I was so scared it didn't matter. I grabbed a hold of a bar on the ceiling and raised my bare feet up off the ground and was worried - what do I do? Well, I decided to jump on his head - if I missed I was dead, but what else could I do? So, when I saw my opportunity, I jumped on its head with one foot, and with the other heel I started to hit it. It wrapped it's whole body around my leg and started to squeeze - to this day this leg (pointing to the left one) is weaker than the other. But, I was able to kill it - I think it was due to that extra energy a person gets in such situations."

"You mean adrenaline?" I offered.

"Yes yes. I have felt this a few times - when I was in the Royal Indian Navy and my life was at stake a few times, I felt it then too."

"And this to you is terror?"

"Yes - after I killed it I had a terrible fever for six or seven days. I had killed it, but I was still so scared that my body shut down. Terrorism does this - it affects every part of a person's being. Those who threaten terror are like those who take the knife and say 'Believe me or I will kill you.' I don't believe them because they are wrong. Certain people take the knife and say 'Believe as I believe' - how can I? It is mathematically impossible, because each creation is unique. We humans are not mass produced by machines - every human being is a world in itself. It has likes, it has dislikes, it has beliefs - everyone is different and nobody knows what is going on in someone else's top story," he pointed to his own bald head for emphasis. "You have to accept this. Before you discuss human beings, you must accept the uniqueness of our creation. If all women look alike - then why do you fall in love with one particular woman? She has the same two eyes, the same two ears, same mouth. Why do certain people say if they don't marry her they will kill themselves? Why?"

At this he smiled slyly, looking at me from the corner of his eye. "This is why you are here, no? Surely you do not think that all humans look alike, or you would not have come here to meet my granddaughter."

I had been so interested in his ramblings that I had almost forgotten my reason for being there. Of course, Dadi-jaan had not, and I immediately became aware of her looking at me, from across the room. She seemed to be straining to hear our conversation, and I smiled at her to let her know everything was okay. Jafari Sahib continued to eyeball me, and I felt he was waiting for a response.

"Well, Jafari Sahib, it is a pleasure to meet you. And if your granddaughter can speak with a fraction of the eloquence you have just displayed, I will count my trip well worth it."

This pacified him, and he turned to YuMa to chat about common friends from the past. As they talked I began to wonder when this meeting might actually occur. Yasmine was nowhere to be seen, and while the prospect of marriage seemed the furthest thing from my mind, the prospect of being introduced to a pretty girl was always a good thing.

After about a half hour more, she finally made an appearance. She came in carrying a tray of tea and cookies, walking slowly and elegantly through a swinging door to the side of the room. She was dressed in a pretty, western-influenced shalwar kameez, full of bright blue and orange colors and tight on the hips. She wore a modest amount of gold jewelry, on her ankles and wrists, and her hair was blow-dried straight. She served tea to Jafari Sahib first, then Dadi-jaan, and then YuMa before finally coming over to me. I tried to make eye contact with her as she asked me how much sugar I took, but our whole tea interaction was done with her eyes lowered, on the ground in front of her.

When she was done serving everyone, Yasmine took a seat next to her mother. Dadi-jaan tried to engage her, but she answered with very short, yes or no answers. I couldn't tell if she was pissed off or just shy, but I didn't have a lot of time to figure it out. Within a few minutes Dadi-jaan rose, cleared her throat, and said it was time for us to leave, as it was getting late and everyone needed to get up early to prepare for tomorrow's fast. Jafari Sahib protested.

"Please, before you go, I must give this boy something. He has been so nice to speak with an old man like me, and I want him to have something of mine."

Jafari Sahib struggled to his feet and shuffled over to a large bookcase on the back wall of the room. He selected a worn out hardback, and brought it back over to me.

"This book, it is my favorite of all time, except for the Qu'ran, of course, which is the most complete and beautiful book ever written, because it was written by God. But, this book, I think, may be the best book ever written by man. It is the story of life and death, and of man's relationship with these two certainties of his existence."

He handed me the book, and I could just make out the faded title on the cover to say *The Story of San Michelle*. I tried to refuse his generosity, but he insisted, saying that it was pointless for old men to keep books away from the young minds that needed them. I thanked him, and he gave me a hug before we started to the door.

Yasmine had taken cover behind her mother, and as we left she mumbled a goodbye to the three of us, all the while refusing to look in my direction. We left, went through the gate and back to our waiting car, and I had not once spoken to the girl I had come to meet.

As we drove off, Dadi-jaan grabbed my hand and looked at me, her eyes beaming. "So, bhaita, what do you think? She is stunning, isn't she? And so polite! She has fair skin, just like your mother. She is very beautiful, don't you think?"

"Yes, Dadi-jaan, she is."

"So, what do you think? Do you have some interest? We could go back and call your parents, and if they agree, send the proposal this evening."

YuMa coughed a laugh up in the front seat, and I could see I had to tread carefully with my old grandmother here. She was pumped up – the thrill of the bridal hunt had her forgetting that I was not from the old world, but from the cynical new one.

"Dadi-jaan - I didn't even talk to her."

She cut me off before I could go any further. "Hogwash! What is there to talk about? Your families like each other, you are both Shia, and you think she is pretty. This is all that matters – talk will only confuse things."

I tried to contain a laugh but could not hold it, which only made matters worse. Dadi-jaan seemed to immediately realize that I had never seriously considered this route to matrimony, and she launched into a diatribe against the corrupt society I had been raised in. I had heard it before, and tried to console her and calm her down. YuMa finally stepped in on my behalf, re-directing her anger at my father for moving to America in the first place. When we got home she immediately called my dad, her son, and let him have it, and then proceeded to stay up for half the night, worrying about what she would tell the Jafari family about the Khan family's interest in their daughter. I'm not sure what she ended up telling them, but in the end, I'm not sure if humoring her in her quest to marry me off had been such a smart thing.

The days seemed to drag longer and longer. The month was almost up and I had lost ten pounds from my already trimmed down travel weight. My mind was dulled – I gave up more and more reading and writing and watched more and more weird Pakistani TV and old British comedies. I stayed mostly at the house, and slowly started becoming bored out of my mind.

The most action I saw would be on occasional walks I would take around the neighborhood. Much to Dadi-jaan's chagrin, I would take off unprotected and walk to the beach, going along side streets and sometimes getting lost on the way. Dadi-jaan worried about the violence that always seemed to bubble below the surface in Karachi, but I got clearance from YuMa, as long as I stayed in certain areas.

On one trip I got completely turned around and found myself a bit lost. Some exchanges in broken Urdu with food vendors (the main items were hot peanuts and corn on the cob) led me back down a main drag, away from the sea. The street was lined with trees in the middle and huge mansions on either side. Each mansion had a group of guards outside, all armed with rifles or Kalashnikovs, and they all surveyed me suspiciously as I walked past until I would ring out a "Salaam Alaikum (peace be upon you)" and their demeanor would change instantly. It was kind of a fun game – to watch the guards' angry scowl and then have it change almost immediately after being greeted.

Even though most of the Muslims in the world don't speak it fluently, the influence of Arabic in Islamic culture is undeniable. It is the language in which the Qu'ran was sent down. It is God's language, the language of prayer. And even though the explosion of the Islamic world encompassed many different lands with long standing languages, Arabic still found its way into a position of importance. Persian and Hindi, for example, eventually had successors, Farsi and Urdu, which drew heavily from Arabic vocabulary and were written in modified Arabic script, significant changes from what they had been before the advent of Islam. And, it was always the goal of the pious Muslim, no matter what culture he or she came from, to learn Arabic and read the Qu'ran in its true natural state. And, more practically, it had given Muslims a few universal terms, like a greeting, to bind them together. Saying "Salaam Alaikum" to a Muslim is almost like a secret handshake – it signifies to them that you are in their club and are okay to pass.

So, I walked on down the road, laying Salaam Alaikums on all the heavily armed men along the way and feeling like I pretty well fit in. About a half mile down I came upon a huge wall – it was sectioning off a compound about half a block long, with barbed wire fence ringing the top and Pakistan Rangers (the equivalent to the US National Guard) and Karachi Policemen posted every 200 feet or so around the perimeter. At the front of the compound was a truck, fitted with armor plating and a machine gun, standing next to a checkpoint. Inside the checkpoint were half a dozen or so Rangers, wearing both fatigues and menacing stares. I decided to say nothing and keep going – and as my step quickened I looked up and saw what the hubbub was all about. It was the American consulate, a.k.a. the biggest target in Karachi.

I walked on until I made it back to the *"Theen Talwar"* of Faith, Unity, and Discpline. I knew the way from here, and was back at home in less than fifteen minutes. Once inside, the aircon hit me and I collapsed onto the sofa in the TV room. This mild exercise, which paled in comparison to my daily schedule back home, took almost everything out of me, and I realized that Ramadan had taken its toll on my body. I turned on the T.V. and mindlessly watched a Pakistan cricket match, thinking vaguely that there would be no more walking for me while Ramadan was still on.

I fell asleep and was woken by YuMa, who said it was time to break the fast. While we ate our dates and samosas, we chitchatted about his work and some of the political news stories of the day, and I could feel him wanting to ask about my plans. I avoided the subject because I knew the answer would disappoint him, and when we both turned in early, I think he already knew the answer. My heart was not yet into diving into the mess of my homeland, as I needed to figure out my own mess before doing anything else.

Chapter 14

Zero Sum Game

That night he comes back. He is wearing his standard green robe, but this time he has come to my bedroom at YuMa's house.

"Howdy Mo!" he says brightly, as he walks in and takes a seat on the edge of the bed.

"Yo, wazzup G?"

"Not much, my friend, not much. Just been jetting around, taking care of business, you know? Business like yours. So – how's Ramadan going?"

I think a bit before responding. My life has slowed down. It has become more elemental, revolving around meal times and conserving energy. It has become more spiritual, and the intent of the fast is never far from your thoughts during the day.

"I've found it pretty easy, actually. There is a minimalism to it that I like, you know? The meals are set, and you just kind of revolve around that. Every morning you eat at home, and every night you eat at home. And, it instills discipline, when you give up something because of your belief. I like it."

Khizr smiles. "Yes – I like the way you see it, Mo. That is my view too. It is unnatural, I must say, to have the amount of choices for eating that Western humans do today. Fruits and vegetables were meant to be eaten in season, straight from the vines and trees where they grow. And meat and poultry were to be eaten with the greatest respect, for their spirits and for God who provided them. Nowadays, a burger from the BK Lounge might have six different friggin cows packed together in it, you know? And a hot dog - who knows how many!"

"Yeah but, whaddya gonna do? That's mass production, that's what happens when we have billions of people on the planet."

"Yeah, maybe you're right." Khizr gets up and lies down on the floor, kicking his sandals off and cracking his ankles. I protest and try to give him the bed I am in, but he waves me off and closes his eyes, apparently enjoying the hard floor.

"I long ago gave up soft beds, my young friend. A weak spine is a weak mind!"

We fall silent for a while as he keeps his eyes closed and starts to breathe deeply. When he speaks again, his eyes are still closed.

"Mo, I have often marveled at the way human history has unfolded. How, again and again, humans keep re-inventing how they organize themselves. You talking about billions of people reminds me of that, of how all these billions of people have organized themselves in different ways. Imagine that – we have had organized civilizations for thousands of years on this planet, and we still haven't figured out the best system!"

He has dropped the vernacular and levity from his tone and opened his eyes.

"You will never have one political system for all peoples, you know that? It is impossible. Humans are free wills – it is impossible for two men to see the same thing the same way. It is impossible – they may agree on ninety nine point nine nine plus percent, but there will still be a fraction that is different. It is the uniqueness of man's creation – it is what we are, by definition." His green eyes are firing bright as he drives home this point.

"Yes – I had a conversation with a wise old man here about this as well." I think I see where he is going and venture further. "But - don't you think that democracy is the right way then? That way, every unique one of us gets a vote."

Khizr raises his head from the ground to look up at me on the bed. "Democracy is the closest we have come, because it embraces the free will of humans. A human can understand he has his vote, and no one can take from him, and that the vote is his expression of his free will towards society, because he decides where it goes. But, democracies are not immune to corruption; just as all other systems of government are not immune. And democracies only work if formed internally, over a long period of time, when there are social institutions present in the society that ensure justice and fairness as cornerstones of the country. After all, American democracy is a lot different than Pakistani democracy, right? In Pakistan, the vote only counts if the Army approves it."

"Why, G? Why is it that the Muslim countries can't get it together?"

"I think politically the Islamic world has never been more disunited than it is now. All of the structures that express political will are decrepit. Politically, it is divided into a large number of states that are manipulated individually, and individually they all seem to see their survival as based on relationships with non-Muslim countries. The amount of inter-Islamic cooperation is really limited. So, from the point of view of divisiveness, from the point of view of dislocation, from the point of view of powerlessness, I think we are at or near the worst level we have had in the Islamic world's history. And, there is no sign on the horizon that tells me we are likely to improve the situation. The tragedy of the Muslim world is that its political language is one of unity - it is the language of the *Ummah*, which is the community of all Muslims worldwide. But, its reality is extremely fragmented, extremely disparate. I don't see anything on the horizon that may act as a catalyst to bring the Ummah together, or that will allow the Islamic identity to take hold over the other forms of identity given to peoples by states or governments."

"What was it like?" I ask. "You were around then, right? In the Islamic heyday?"

"Yes, yes I was. It was good, Mohammed – as fair a time as any other the world has seen. Cities like Damascus and Baghdad – these were the London and Paris of their time. They were very cultured, and rich. Someone like Osama would have been a nutcase – outlawed and probably killed by the rulers of the day. That is the Muslim problem of today – there are no rulers out there strong enough to stand up to Osama and the West, and to implement proper Islamic justice, which is neither what the Americans nor what Osama wants. There are other options to what is being presented today, my friend."

"But, don't you think that Osama's goal is to unite the Ummah?" I ask.

"Well, I don't really know the man, so I can't say what his goals are. But, I have tracked his past, and it is interesting to note that before his days as an international terrorist, in the mid to late 80s he was a very important element in the Afghan war. If you rummage through articles and newspapers you'll find his name mentioned quite a bit."

"You mean for building roads and hospitals, in partnership with America?" I have always loved referencing America's former support for the likes of Saddam and bin Laden in political arguments back home, as it is the ultimate truth for those who claim America is perfect, and without fault in foreign policy.

"Not just for that," Khizr continues, "he actually participated in combat - organizing fighting units and such. Bin Laden, I think, does see the potential of uniting the Ummah, is disgusted by the reality of Western rule, and wants to help the Muslim countries. If he has a program, then this must be it - to catalyze the Muslims and make them realize their potential. The program would probably destroy him in the end, because he can never speak for a united Ummah. He is too radical, what with his Wahabbi rules and such. Osama probably is not in this for personal power, as he knows that is not realistic. I think he is happy to instigate, if for nothing else to shake up the status quo."

"So you think Osama has seen the low point of Islam and views war as the only way out?" I ask. "But for what? To break America's unchecked power? Surely, he will not be able to bring down the U.S. – it is an impossible task. This has always bothered me about the war – why fight a war that has no clear end goal? Osama and his ilk ask for things like the removal of Israel as their demands for peace – things that will never happen."

Khizr closes his eyes, and after a few seconds starts doing leg lifts. Slowly, he raises his three thousand year old legs an inch above the ground, and then slowly he brings them back down. He does a set of twelve, and as he exhales on his last one opens his eyes and smiles at me. "Strength, my boy, it comes from the gut. A man's gut is the window to his discipline – if he has one, then he's got none." Khizr patted his own belly and chuckled before swinging around his legs and sitting up Indian-style, all in one motion.

"I think," he begins slowly, "that nothing lasts. If you are a person who is a Muslim, then you believe in the Quran. In this great book, there are lots of instances where God tells you to look at examples in the past to see that nothing survives - that great nations crash, and that great powers crash. There are no indications or signs right now that this sort of American hegemony is about to crumble, but it's almost a given that it will happen. Fifteen years from now, probably not, but a hundred years from now it is very likely. And, generally these powers crumble internally. I mean - look at the exhaustion of the British as a result of carrying a financial and political burden which was far greater than their abilities. Look at Rome - it was divided because the state itself was unable to muster the energy to defend its countries. America itself is changing - I mean, the browning of America itself is a clear long term trend."

"The browning – what do you mean the browning?"

"Yes - the increasing Hispanic or non-white European influence in America will in time create a new type of America. In time it will create tensions and resistance to certain parts of the Anglo-Saxon white European power structure that defines American culture right now. All imperial forces carry with them signs of decay – we have already seen a breakdown in true democracy in America, where money and religion have come to play big parts in every election these days."

"Sounds like you're not a big fan of the U.S., huh G?"

"Not at all, Mo, not at all. I think America has done some great things, especially in the fields of science and technology. America is the greatest experiment civilization has ever undertaken on this planet, a place where peoples from all over the world come to live as one. I have always loved that aspect of it. I mean, the reconstruction of Europe after World War II – the Marshall Plan and all that - was really altruistic, and it was smart. That element in American policy, that moral element, seems to have disappeared now, and has been replaced with a sort of hard-nosed realism which doesn't sit well with the rest of the world. So, it isn't whether I am or am not a fan, because I don't matter. It is a question of humanity living together in peace, and I think America's actions today are hurting that. I think the Muslims also have a lot of work to do, and before long the Chinese and the Indians will have their fair share in the say too."

"Do you believe that Islam and the West can co-exist?" I venture. "Or put another way, are we in a zero-sum game between the two, where one must win and the other must lose?" And there it is, the magic question of my life since 2001.

"Well, again the answer would be both yes and no, depending on what you mean. There is no doubt that so-called Western thought - that is the various issues related to democracy, human rights, civil rights, women's issues and so on - are defined in the Western terms because it is the West that has all the power. That is not to say these values are not good – they all are, and are to be aspired to by everyone. But, right now we are being told that the West has the answer in their specific form of democracy, and I think Islamic thought doesn't necessarily buy this line of reasoning from the West. They may buy the values or principles - for example, the underlying principle of democracy is popular participation, and Islam agrees with that, but the forms in which these principles are expressed might not necessarily be acceptable for all cultures. So defining rights in Western terms puts a Western spin on it. It doesn't mean that these rights don't exist in Islam - they are just expressed in different ways. What people should look for are the underlying principles behind these rights and express them in ways that are culturally specific and acceptable. There will be tension in applying Western concerns and current issues - and their resolutions - to other places. I mean, things like women voting are important, but they are less important than rights such as access to clean water, or education or health, which are the fundamental problems facing most Muslim countries, ones that they must solve while the West demands that they become 'free' overnight. True freedom takes time to develop, and it must develop naturally, based on the values of the people. Just as it did in the West."

"G, you are not answering the question. Is this going to be World War III or not?"

"No – this is something bigger, I think. Islam is probably the only existing civilization that has an entire political and moral alternative to the West. Well, at least other civilizations don't claim such a thing yet – both the Chinese and the Indians have ridden American capitalism on their rise to global prominence. So, Islam is in essence fighting a rearguard action toward these underlying problems that arise as a result of wholesale acceptance of Western-paradigm values, as it were.

Because, these Western values are temporary, in a sense that they are capable of changing. Fifty years ago in the U.S. racism was a part of government, and fifty years from now there may be a school of thought in the West that calls for the governance of women - I don't know. I mean, these things are not permanent, but they are made to appear so in the West. People in America think things will always be like today, but Western history shows that nothing ever lasts. American power is severely flawed, and Islam is the first of perhaps multiple different paradigms that could challenge the West for supremacy."

"So, is there no one right answer, politically or spiritually, for man?"

"Well, there is One Truth and many truths." Khizr looks sideways at me and lets out a mischievous laugh. "That is the Sufi in me talking. What I mean to say is, Islam tells you that there is One Truth that is expressed in many ways, and that the manifestation of these many truths also points back to the One Truth. It is not an either/or situation - it can't be. Truth with a capital T is one, but truth with a small t is many, and there are many paths to Truth. So, from my perspective the question is not formulated correctly. It is not an either/or situation - whether Islam or America has the truth and nobody else does. There is an expression of the Truth that Islam feels is complete, but there are other expressions that may be equally valid if they are used to confirm the existence of the One, the control of the One, and the dominance of the One. So, there is no single right way - there is a single right way only if it leads to the divine objective."

"Meaning the belief in one God?"

"Yes - meaning the source of power, the source of all being is the One True God. Now, Muslims believe that the Truth is manifested in a certain way, and for us to understand this power we have to constrain our lives in certain ways. If you don't allow constraints or certain forces of guidance in our daily lives, then what we have is the belief in the West that everything is possible and there are no constraints. This is the West's greatest fallacy – the elephant in the room that the West has missed. The West believes change to be good, and is always striving for it. But, in fact, it is the opposite of what the human soul craves. The soul craves truth and knowledge, and wants to know that once it has the Truth, it can never change. This is why the fasting of Ramadan is so important – it is a demonstration of your acknowledgement of the Truth of the message which the Prophet Mohammed brought, and what Jesus and Moses and Abraham before him brought. It is the Truth of the One God."

As I ponder this, Khizr gets to his feet and fumbles in the folds of his cloak before bringing out a picture. It shows a small hunchbacked man, sitting on a beach with a drum in his hand. He has a dark brown complexion, and a thick moustache to match his dark, shaggy black hair.

"Eid is approaching," Khizr says, "and I want you to spend it with some of the less fortunate. This is Mustafa. He sells drums in Goa. I want you to go meet him – I want you to spend your Eid with him and his family."

"Goa, that's India, right?"

"Yes – he lives on Palolem beach. I want you to go there tomorrow, okay? Spend your Eid with him – see what his life is like."

"Okay – I can do that. But, you know G, this whole thing is pretty crazy – my family won't like me leaving here before Eid."

"Your YuMa understands – trust me. He is a good man. Your Dadi-jaan will be upset, but don't worry. She's a tough old lady – come back on your own time when your trip is done and she'll be fine."

He laughs at this and leaves the room without another word.

Chapter 15

Hindustan's Forgotten

The slang term desi refers to a person from the Indian Subcontinent. In its current political manifestation, this includes people primarily from India, Pakistan, and Bangladesh, with Sri Lanka, Nepal, Maldives, Bhutan, and Burma being on the outer fringes of *desiness,* depending on who you talk to.

There are now satellite desi communities almost everywhere in the world - from Auckland and Amsterdam to Singapore and San Francisco and everywhere in between you can find the South Asian diaspora thriving. In some places they have taken over whole neighborhoods, like in Jackson Heights in New York City or South Hall in London, and in other places they have established themselves as the convenience store clerks or doctors and are now woven into the fabric everyday life, getting their own T.V. personas like Apu 'Thank you, come again' Nahasapeemapetilon or CNN's Dr. Sanjay Gupta.

Desis have gone everywhere, leaving the subcontinent largely to look for better economic opportunity. What binds the desis together is a mostly common food, language, and pop culture, with Bollywood movies symbolizing the cultural currency that flows throughout the desi world. The desis' bond is comparable to the Germans and the Austrians, or maybe Aussie to Kiwi - outsiders view them as pretty much the same because, when viewed from a distance, their commonalities seem stronger than the ethnic, religious, and political differences that separate them back home. The desis are no different – in America, Pakistanis and Indians are the best of friends, but back on the Subcontinent, their national and religious differences are quite often

insurmountable, and the wounds from centuries of upheaval still have
plenty of hurt and blame to go around.

In particular, the 20th century was not kind to the area. The Partition
of 1947- where in one last grand act of imperial hubris the British carved
up great sections of land to parcel out based on religion- is the cataclysm
that shapes South Asia as we know it today. My grandfather, who
fought in wars on behalf of both Pakistan and India during his forty year
military career, once told me that it had all been a big mistake, and that
Pakistan, India, and Bangladesh should have all stayed together. This,
coming from a man who had lived and fought his whole life on the soil
in question, had always left an impression on me, as he was a great man,
and the sadness I heard in his voice had somehow translated for me into
the sadness of a billion people who may have known a better life today.

This is what I thought I knew of India before I went there. I knew
we desis were the same – but that we were different. Like Tupac and
Biggie or the Hatfields and McCoys. I knew that political and religious
differences had split the land half a century ago. And I had been to
Pakistan a few times as a kid, which I had always assumed was the same
as India, just with more mosques. Khizr's next mission for me filled me
with excitement, as I had always been curious to see what Mother India
really looked like.

YuMa took my leaving in stride, and Dadi-jaan was upset, just
as Khizr had predicted. She was upset on two fronts; first that I was
leaving Pakistan without a bride, and second that I was going to her
birthplace, to India, and that she would not be going too. She kept telling
me how much a shame it was that she couldn't go with me – if only I'd
wait a couple of months she said she would hook us up with long lost
relatives. She had not been since leaving in 1947, and my sudden travel
plans there awoke within her a desire to go back to where she grew up
in the Uttar Pradesh province. It broke my heart to do it, but I had to go
it alone, so I promised I would return soon and accompany her back to
her ancestral village, at her leisure. This seemed to pacify her, and I was
able to get out of Karachi without too much grief.

They both gave me last minute advice – YuMa telling me to tell
the Indians my heritage was from India, not Pakistan, and Dadi-jaan
telling me to take a bite out of onion in each city I visited, to steel my

stomach against bacteria. This, she assured me, is what the Imam Ali did whenever he traveled. YuMa drove me himself to the airport, where we finally had a chance to clear the air a bit before I left.

"YuMa," I said after we had made small talk for a bit, "I'm sorry I'm not staying for longer – I know that is what you wanted."

"Nephew, you are on a grand adventure, and you should be apologizing for nothing."

"No, I want to," I insisted. "The life you live is extraordinary – I respect you more than almost anyone else I know. You have always lived according to your principles, which are clearly defined for you. I wish things were clearer for me, but they are not. YuMa – you are a son of Pakistan – you have seen it from its birth. Your whole life has been tied to this land. I feel that tie too, but my relationship with this country is different. I have America in me too, and that side of me is strong. And that side is also worried – that America might do something terribly foolish. America is a great country, but it is only as great as its citizens. I may be able to help Pakistan more by being in America, you know? I'm really not sure."

We came to a traffic light and beggars flooded around the car. A little girl of about eight came up to my window and started tapping on the car with a hideously deformed hand – she had two fingers and two stumps where the rest of her fingers should be. She was filthy, and as I looked at her I wondered if what I was telling my uncle, and myself, was crap.

"Really, YuMa, I'm not sure of anything anymore. I'm not sure what I believe..."

YuMa let out a howl of a laugh and then honked the beggars off the car before taking off through the intersection. "If those begging kids have you confused, then you shouldn't be here at all! They are professionals – did you see the belly on the one on my side, complete with double chin? They do not need our help at all!" He honked again at a slow moving bus and passed on its left as the airport tower appeared in the distance. "Nephew – all I request is one thing."

He swung us around another truck and onto an exit lane before continuing.

"You must believe in something. Anything really, but be a Believer, with a capital B. Hinduism, Christianity, Judaism, Islam – anything, but just believe. It is most important that you believe in something – that is the only way that a human can get through this life in the right way, with regard for the greater good. Those who sit on the sidelines, the agnostics, I feel pity for them. How can you not make up your mind about the most important thing, the question of why we exist? Mohammed – do your travels, follow your saint, find out what you believe in. And then, and only then, will you be ready to come and help as I want you to, here, in America, or anywhere else."

We arrived at the terminal and YuMa and I embraced before parting, he back to his philanthropy and me back to the unknown. My time with him during Ramadan had been special, and as I navigated the bureaucratic mess of leaving on an international flight from Pakistan, I silently thanked Khizr for sending me to Pakistan after so long an absence.

There were no direct flights from Pakistan to India – the neighboring countries had severed air links after a particularly ghastly terrorist attack on the Indian capital a few months before, so I had to transition through Dubai. As I boarded my flight from Dubai to Mumbai, I felt like I had already arrived in India - from the curry smells wafting out of the airplane's galley to the incessant jostling and howling of seemingly every passenger on board. If the English are the masters of politeness - with a 'sorry' or 'excuse me' always at hand for the most trivial of matters – desis are the opposite. They will cut in line or honk the horn and not think twice. I have always attributed this to the fact that there is overpopulation on the subcontinent, but maybe I am an apologist.

I fought my way through the throng of passengers trying to fit their gigantic carry-ons into the overmatched overhead bins and finally found my seat, only to find an elderly lady already sitting in it, dressed in a pink sari and holding a newborn baby high against her shoulder. Over the bawling infant, I tried to inform the lady that she was in my seat, but she said she didn't speak English. I switched to broken Hindi, but when she saw that I spoke her language she just shrugged her shoulders and stared at the back of the seat in front of her, ignoring me completely. I pushed my way back to the hostess and asked for help, and after ten minutes of standing in the way, I was ushered into a new seat – a much better one that was on the aisle and next to a grown-up.

I settled in and started taking the 'all desis are similar to each other' train of thought again. I started to think about how little I really knew about India – about how everything I knew was through the filters of my parents and grandparents – people who had fled that country and whose own feelings were still raw and unformed, fifty odd years later. I started to think about the Muslims of India – still 140 million strong (the world's largest minority group). I began to wonder about the man Khizr had sent me to meet, Mustafa, and what he might teach me.

I landed in Mumbai at midnight, my haphazard itinerary calling for me to catch a train to Goa at 3:30AM from a station on the outskirts of the city. After being quickly introduced to the legendary Indian bureaucracy (I was made to show my visa to no less than four people in an almost deserted airport), I hopped a cab and took it straight to the train station, named Lokmanya Tilak. My cab slithered through the thick exhaust-filled night, having to swerve between piles of trash fires and roaming herds of cows before making its way through worsening shanty town after shanty town and finally to the station.

The cabby dropped me off about a hundred yards from the entrance, and after negotiating a ten deep line of taxis, rickshaws, and motorbikes I made it inside. It looked like some kind of post-war refugee scene – hundreds of people were strewn about the floor, their meager belongings arranged into makeshift pillows and mats. There were flies everywhere, and the floors were covered in a thick cake of dust. There were no guards or terminal workers anywhere – it took me ten minutes to find an information guy, who pointed out track three and the Shatabdi Express, my train to Goa.

As I left the big city I wished I had diverted some time to checking it out – I had always heard that Mumbai was like the NYC of South Asia - the media mecca of a one billion person democracy. But soon we cleared the metropolis' reach, and as dawn broke we were chugging through farmland, every so often passing small villages just starting to stir. Down the aisles of my packed second class carriage came vendors with breakfast on wheels, advertising eggs or biryani or *chai* like hot dogs and beers at a ballgame. I hadn't eaten an onion yet, so in honor of Dadi-jaan I declined the food and eventually slept.

The train arrived, six hours later, in Goa. After negotiating the long and hot bus and taxi legs of the journey, I was dropped at Palolem beach. The immediate approach to the beach was lined with tourist-type shops – clothing stores and souvenir stands, catered almost strictly to Western backpacker clientele. Before I even got off the bus there were three guys on me, offering the best accommodations at the lowest prices.

"Hello brother – coco hut? You want coco hut?" All three men were giving me this sales pitch in unison. The biggest of the three started to box out the smaller guys and put his hand on my backpack before I gave him a stern 'No, thank you' and walked on to the beach.

It was scorching hot, and the three men followed me for a minute or two before giving up and going back to the entrance. There were people strewn about everywhere on the dirty blonde beach – mostly white tourists, playing volleyball or soccer or sunbathing on brightly colored sarongs. A cow ambled by, decorated in bells and ribbon.

A young boy approached and gave me his coco hut pitch. He seemed harmless enough, so I followed him about fifteen minutes down the beach to the huts he was pitching. The beach was lined with bars, bungalows and huts, all shabby-chic and pulsing out techno-ambient music at low volume. The boy introduced me to his father, who owned a place named 'Village CocoHuts,' where I rented a hut for 200 rupees (about five dollars) a night.

It was hot, and for some idiotic reason I had been wearing jeans and a full sleeved shirt for my entire journey, so my first order of business was to get into trunks and jump into the Indian Ocean. After accomplishing this, I lay down on my towel and closed my eyes, letting the cramped compartment travel of the last seventeen hours slowly wash away with the gentle lapping of the tide. Planes, trains, and Indian taxi rides can really wear on the traveler's soul, and I felt happy to just lie on the beach and stare up at the burning blue sky.

In the evening I ate dinner alone on the beach. Village CocoHut's restaurant was seven or eight tables placed in front of the entrance to the bungalows and facing the beach, with a small but tasty selection of desi food – all your standard curries and *chaat* fare. The waiters found my Hindi hilarious and kept me company through most of my meal, telling me stories about drunk Westerners making fools of themselves at the various nightspots on the beach. They were also self-proclaimed experts on assessing the looseness of the foreign girls who came and went from their tables in varying states of beach undress, with their rating system being largely weighted towards nationality. Their top slut awards, they happily informed me, went to the British women.

I enjoyed their banter, but even more enjoyed their protection from the ravenous dogs roaming the beach. In India, nothing comes easy – even a picturesque chicken kebab at a nice beach resort can become uncomfortable, at the drop of a hat. The stray mutts on the beach rarely tasted meat, so when they smelled the *tandoor* it drove them mad. They inched closer and closer to my table, growling at me, until one of the waiters would shoo them away for a few seconds. But they would come almost immediately back, eyes still fully on their prize, so I ate on the edge of my seat – ready to pop away from the table should one of the beasts get by my waiters and make it to my feet.

As I dined dusk turned to night. The complexion of Palolem changed with the time of day – the music was now turned up, and all sorts of lights had been strung up at all the different party shacks lining the beach. I finished my meal and started walking, passing one bar after another along the beachfront, but it was early and not many people were out. As I spotted a few men sitting around a campfire not too far off in the distance, the entire beach went black in an apparent power outage, and with the overcast night providing no light I was surrounded in pitch black. I went straight to the light of the fire, unable to help sneaking up on the men out of the darkness.

"Um, Hello," I said, as the men drew silent after seeing me pull up.

"Hello," said the man tending the fire.

"My name is Mo, Mohammed, there are no lights on the beach, do you mind if I sit?" I said this in Hindi, and the man broke into a smile.

"Of course, sit down. Please – your name is Mohammed, you are Muslim?"

"Yes."

"Salaam Alaikum," he said immediately.

"Wailakum Salaam," I returned, "What is your name?"

"Mustafa," he said.

My heart jumped. In the flicker of the firelight I could only see his face, and I had not recognized it from the picture Khizr had shown – all I had remembered of it was the hump on Mustafa's back. But, it was him – as he turned to get another log I detected the shadow on his back before he turned back, putting a log on the fire and waving me over to a seat.

"Where are you from, brother Mohammed? How is it that you know Hindi?"

I remembered YuMa's advice and said, "My family is from the UP, but I was born in America. But, my parents still speak Hindi at home and I picked it up from them, although not very well..."

He laughed and shook his head, "No – it is good. You can speak good. Me – English not good. We can speak Hindi?"

"Sure," I replied.

"I am also from the UP – where was your family from?" Mustafa, obviously delighted to have stumbled upon a geographical oddity such as myself, grinned with delight through his question. The other two at the fire were young boys, and they listened on with interest.

"My father was from Lucknow."

"Oh - that is also where we are from! Oh, Glory be to God – you are our brother! You must stay and sit with us. My friends are coming – my cousin is coming right now, he would like to meet you."

Before I could answer the power came back to the beach. A light atop the beach shack we were sitting in front of came on, illuminating Mustafa, the two boys, and rows of musical instruments lining the shacks shelves. There were mostly drums of all different sizes, *tablas* and *dhols* and bongos.

"Wow! You have so many tablas." I said.

Mustafa beamed with pride. He was a small man – about 5'6", but standing tall for every one of his inches, despite his deformity.

"Yes. I make them. It is our family business. My father, and his father before – we have made tablas for many years. But they made their's back home – now there are no jobs there. We moved here, to sell tablas to tourists, my Cha Cha and my brother and my cousin. You like tablas?"

"Well, I play drums at home in America. I love music," I said.

"Oh great! When everyone gets here, we will sing some *qawaalis*, okay? My cousin is a great *qawaali* singer. Please, sit down. You would like some chai?"

As Mustafa got up to serve me, another man emerged out of the shadows, coming in the direction from the road behind the beach. Mustafa did not see him before he said, "Oi! What's going on here? Who is this?" His tone was joking as he came up next to me.

"Cha Cha, Salaam Alaikum! Look at who I have met – I want you to meet him too!" Mustafa excitedly introduced me, and Cha Cha bade me sit down on a log next to the shop. When he heard of my UP heritage, he broke into a big grin and gave me a hug. He was short and had a smooth shaven, handsome face and a dark complexion. When Mustafa had called him Cha Cha I had thought he would be an older man, as Cha Cha traditionally means your father's brother on the Subcontinent, but this Cha Cha didn't look more than thirty-five.

"Hazrat Mohammad – Salaam Alaikum. You are like brother. What we have is yours. What brings you here?" Cha Cha spoke in slow, labored English, like each word took a half second too long to form in his brain before being sent out through his mouth.

"I am a traveler," I said, more easily able to explain my adventure now that I had been on the road for a while, "I am traveling all over the world, meeting Muslims. I have been to Morocco, and Turkey, and Pakistan. And now I am here."

Cha Cha listened attentively, nodding and making approving murmurs.

"And why have you done this, Hazrat Mohammed? It sounds costly?"

"Well – I, it is because I want to learn. I am looking to understand Islam." As I spoke I looked around their beach shack shop and saw that the men lived in it - there was cookware tucked in the corner and rolls of bedding under the workbench. Both the mens' and the boys' clothes were tattered – full of holes and stains, and they gave off a vibe of deference so often seen in poor people when in the presence of a perceived higher class. "And I am very lucky that I was born in America," I added, "it allows me to have earned enough money to travel in this way. I am very lucky."

"Yes – it is true. It is good for you – a good thing you do." Cha Cha spoke with such a directness that you could not doubt his genuineness – he seemed really happy for me. "We here in India – we have very strong Islam. I am glad you have come here – you can see our Islam."

That's exactly what I'm supposed to do, I thought.

Cha Cha started giving orders to the two boys, sending one running down the beach and the second to set up a pair of tablas and a harmonium. He and Mustafa excused themselves to say their Isha prayers, and asked me to join, which I did. One of the major differences between the Shia and Sunni prayer is the way you hold your hands – Sunnis hold them clasped in front, while Shias hold them straight down at your sides. I noticed that Cha Cha and Mustafa prayed in the Sunni manner, and I did the same, heeding YuMa's advice to play a 'when in Rome' type of strategy.

Everyone came back from their errand with more people – Cha Cha, Mustafa, and I picked up two other men dressed in shalwar kameez and beards from the small mosque around the corner that we prayed at, and the first boy came with two more men dressed in shalwar kameez and beards. The party started to take on a much more Muslim look.

"Hazrat Mohammed," said Cha Cha, switching to Hindi and taking the hand of one of the new comers. "This is my cousin Abdullah. He is also from the UP. And these boys here are my nephews – that is Tariq, and that is Hamzan, and over there is Mustafa, who you met before. And this here, he is our neighbor – this is Shanti. We are all from UP except Shanti – he is from Bombay." I gave my salaams to all the men and sat down next to Abdullah.

"Brother Mohammed," continued Cha Cha, "My cousin Abdullah is a fine *qawaal* – I have asked him to come here to meet you and sing for you tonight. Do you like qawaali music?"

"Yes, of course. My father loves it – Nusrat Fateh Ali Khan and the Sabri Brothers are his favorites." Qawaali music had been the one thing I had always loved from my culture. The power of the music was obvious, even if you couldn't understand the words that drove the passion – I had turned a number of my college friends on to Nusrat, and they still listened to him years later.

Abdullah nodded at me. "These men are good. They sing well. And what song is your favorite?"

"How about Allah Hoo?" It was the only one I really knew, as my dad had translated it for me when I was young.

Abdullah immediately launched into it, his eyes closing as he squeezed the first slow, dramatic notes out of his harmonium. Cha Cha waited a few measures until joining in with some tabla accompaniment, providing the raw rhythmic undertone that gives qawwali music such a tribal quality. A few more measures and the introduction was over – Abdullah launching into the first couplet of the song with fiery resonance, Cha Cha answering him, couplet for couplet:

> tere hi naam se har ibteda hai
> tere hi naam tak har inteha hai
> teri hamd-o-sanaa alhumdulillah
> ke tu mere Muhammad ka Khuda hai

> *(all beginnings begin with your name*
> *all ends end with your name*
> *your praise is praiseworthy*
> *because you are the God of my Muhammad)*

> Allah hoo Allah hoo
> Allah hoo Allah hoo

> *(Sufi mystic chants)*

As the song gathered strength, the others around the campfire started joining in the refrains being sung back to Abdullah. He slowly built the tempo and volume until it reached a fevered pitch, getting so swept up in the song that he didn't notice knocking over his chai with his outstretched left leg. He was gone – in another world as he sang in this one.

The love of poetry on the Indian Subcontinent is undeniable – for centuries it has been a pursuit enjoyed by all races and classes. Many of the leading intellectuals of the 19th and 20th centuries were poets, and men like Mohammed Iqbal and Faiz Ahmed Faiz were the ideological fathers of the two nation theory that seeded the split up of India and Pakistan.

Qawaali music is a special form of musical poetry. It is Muslim devotional music, putting the words of the religious poets of the Farsi and Urdu language traditions to driving beats and powerful voices. Qawaalis usually have large bands – they will have a harmonium (kind of like an accordion on its side), a tabla, various percussion instruments, and a host of backup singers. Usually, the head qawaal will sing a line and the backup singers will repeat it back to him, and they will build in volume until a chorus is sung, which usually ratchets the already up-tempo proceedings up to a higher level and can induce Sufis and other such mystics into states of God-loving ecstasy, their eyes rolling back into their heads as they convulse in harmony with divinity. The musical form is a powerful one on many levels – reaching people in tactile and spiritual ways at once.

Abdullah and Cha Cha were doing a good two-man interpretation of the music, kind of like an acoustic version of an epic rock band. The men sitting around us shook their head in appreciation, seemingly both for the poetry as well as the delivery. A couple of them played the part of backup to Abdullah's lead, and in the parts I recognized I joined in and sang along (much to the glee of Cha Cha and Abdullah). My Urdu being mediocre, I could only join once in a while, and was only singing the song from phonetic memory. Urdu is a multilayered language, and there is a big leap from my conversational knowledge of the language to the beauty of its poetic expression.

The song ended and Abdullah started right into another, warming up right into the medley. I knew this one (I was fairly certain it was a Sabri Brothers tune), but I didn't know the words at all and sat silently, watching and nodding my head in enjoyment. As the backup singers began again, everyone looked at me somewhat expectantly and seemed disheartened when I didn't join in.

Their concern with me was only momentary, as they were soon swept up in the passion of their song and bellowed it to the Indian Ocean behind us, attracting a few curious partygoers as their volume rose. After the third song, an even bigger crowd had gathered, enough so that it made Abdullah wave his hand and immediately halt the concert. The Westerners drifted over to the bar down the beach immediately, and Abdullah stared after them with disdain.

"Those unbelievers," he said slowly, "they don't deserve to listen to this song. This song is about the Prophet Mohammed, Peace Be Upon Him. It is about his perfection – he was the greatest human who ever lived. They do not deserve to hear about him, so I will not play for them."

The others nodded their approval, but seemed more afraid of Abdullah than mad at the Westerners.

"Well, you are a wonderful qawaal – congratulations," I ventured, "But, Mr. Abdullah, so what if they hear you? Maybe it will change them – maybe you can teach them about Islam?"

Cha Cha stirred at this.

"No. They are drunk. They do not care about the reason for the song – the power behind the song. They only like it because it sounds good to their heathen ears, like some big dance party for them. It must be hard for you, Brother Mohammed, to live amongst those people. They have so many wicked ways. Brother Mohammed, do you drink?"

All eyes were on me, and I figured this was not the time to make some philosophical everyone-in-the-West-does-it argument.

"No, I do not. But, it doesn't make them bad people. It's just what they do – I bet many of them are Christians who believe in God just like we do."

"It doesn't matter," said Abdullah, bringing the hammer down quickly. "There is only one God, and Mohammed is His Prophet. If you do not believe this, then you are an unbeliever." As Abdullah spoke he got up from behind the harmonium and walked into the shack, ending the discussion.

"Abdullah is right, of course," said Cha Cha, "but enough of that. Brother Mohammed, we are to return to our little village in two days, to see our families. We are hoping that will be Eid."

"Yes, I was going to ask you." I said. "When is Eid?"

"It should be in two days, but it depends on when we see the new moon. We go by what the Saudis say – when they see the new moon in Mecca, then Ramadan will be over and we can celebrate. And we would consider it an honor to have you come with us on Eid, to say our prayers together."

I accepted, and sat with the men for a while longer. They asked me about America, but it was only about the Islam in America that they cared. Was it true that Muslims were being shot (no)? Was it true that Islam was its fastest growing religion (yes)? Were there any mosques (yes)? After a while I began to tire, feeling the wear of my day's long journey, and I took leave of them with a promise to return the next day and check in.

As I lay in my hut I thought of the interaction with Abdullah. It donned on me that alcohol was one huge difference I hadn't counted on between India and Pakistan. Pakistan, being an Islamic Republic, is a dry country (at least officially). Once, when we visited when I was in high school, it was New Year's Eve and I remember my older cousin had gotten a bottle of something he said was Russian vodka. I took a swig and felt as though my throat was covered in gasoline (it might as well have been moonshine from Uncle Jessie's still), but this was the exception to the rule. Almost all activities enjoyed by the Pakistani public at large have no alcohol present.

In Islam it is a sin to drink, and I believe it is not a trivial difference between Islam and the West. Western culture, it can be argued, lives to drink. Weddings, funerals, parties, happy hour, a good day, a bad day – it doesn't matter, because booze always makes it better. Even in religious ceremonies, alcohol can play a major role in Western life. It is how Westerners let off steam – how Westerners bond with their peers. What could be more social than getting a beer with someone?

But in Islam, the only outlet is God - He is all you need. I suppose drinking is banned because it only blunts that devotion – it only inhibits your ability to remember the real order of things. The Muslims have a more institutionalized system for letting off steam – they pray five times a day, and instead of getting a beer with a buddy you are supposed to go pray with him. The design within the Islamic system is to keep your eye on the prize the whole time – the prize of heaven – and to shun all things that divert you even a little bit from that one true goal of this life. In Western eyes this way of life is viewed as suffocating – through the Islamic lens, it can be seen as liberating, as it makes it easy for humans to find peace while living out a life in which we are guaranteed to die.

Chapter 16

Death & Taxes

I spent the last two days of Ramadan on the beach in Goa, alternately swimming and reading and generally being happy to have some time to myself. The discipline of the fast had stayed with me, and I rose before dawn both days, said prayers, and ate the morning meal with Cha Cha and the boys from the music shack. After dusk, I tried a couple of the restaurants sprawled along the beach and found some excellent local fare - the food of Goa was nice and spicy, with seafood, curry, and rice being staples in most meals.

Palolem beach, more than anything, was a backpacker haven. Situated at the southern part of a stretch of beaches made famous by free-flowing drugs and all-night raves, Palolem had no high-rise hotels and only a few sturdy buildings. Lining the half-mile stretch of beach were dozens of stilted, coconut wood and palm constructed shacks that passed for lodgings, while distributed haphazardly among them were little bungalow store fronts selling cheap clothes, trinkets, food, booze, travel arrangements, massages, internet access, and anything else that the typical twenty-two year old Westerner might have need for when on a travel budget of $15 a day.

Before leaving Pakistan I had emailed some friends to apprise them of my next stop, and in Palolem, I checked my email and received word that an old high school friend of mine, Lauren, would be rolling through in three days time. I immediately emailed Lauren and told her where I was staying - I was excited to see a familiar face from home and even more excited to see her, as she was beautiful and always traveled in packs with other hot women.

On my third night in Goa I again sat with Cha Cha, Abdullah, and their crew and sang qawwali songs. About midway through the concert word came that the new moon had been seen in Arabia and that the month of Ramadan was over, signifying that tomorrow was *Eid ul-Fitr*, or the Celebration of the Breaking of the Fast. We all rejoiced and continued to sing while Cha Cha busily started making plans for the next day. We were all to show up by 7 AM, showered and in our Eid clothes (the cleanest and nicest you have), to take a bus to Margao, the capital of southern Goa, where I was told there was a small but thriving Muslim community. Cha Cha was to hand over his shop to Shanti, their one Hindu friend, who would take care of his shop with the agreement that during the Hindu festival of *Diwali* Cha Cha would do the same for him.

The next day I showed up on time and there were about twelve young men, all in their best shalwar kameez and sequined vests, milling about in a buoyant mood. Cha Cha strode out from inside his shop and after giving some last minute direction to Shanti, came and embraced me.

"*Eid Mubarak*, Hazrat Mohammed!"

"*Eid Mubarak*, Cha Cha," I said.

"We are so glad you are coming with us – God Bless you and your family." Cha Cha was in bright spirits and put an arm around me while we walked up the beach.

"My family lives in Margao," Cha Cha continued in Urdu, which is all they spoke with me at this point. "My wife and three children. It is too expensive to live here in Palolem – this is for the tourists. They came with us from UP and live with my wife's brother in Margao."

"How often do you get to see your family?" I asked.

"Oh, about once a month. It is hard, but this is what I have to do to make money. All the tourists are here, and we must sell our drums to them," he said.

"Do you sell a lot of drums?"

"Maybe five or six big ones in one month. The big ones are 250 rupees each. And then we sell some little ones, maybe ten or so. They are around 100 rupees each. So, although it is not much, this is what our families live on. My family, Mustafa's family, and many other cousins who live with us in Margao."

I did a quick calculation and estimated their annual income generously at $720 for a family that sounded like it was well in the teens in numbers.

As the extent of their poverty hit me, we made a right turn from the beach onto the main street, where halfway up a bus was parked. Abdullah was waiting for us there, along with three other men, and both groups exchanged greetings before boarding the bus. Cha Cha secured a seat near the front and we sat down – I in the window and he in the aisle. I quickly saw how lucky I was to get my seat - within two stops the bus was overflowing with Indians, all pressed together in a menagerie of body parts that looked like a clown car from the inside.

As the old bus lurched forward under its ungodly weight, Cha Cha had a far off look in his eye.

"It is a wonderful day – praise God!" he said, while looking dreamily past me and out the window at the coconut trees passing by outside.

His happiness was contagious, and we started trading stories about our childhoods, his in a small village in India and mine in a big city in America. Though my Urdu was limited, we really bonded on the hour-long trip – his stories about growing up as a poor kid were tinged with love and humility. He did not complain or whine once about the poverty he was born into, and he always attributed all his good things (wife, children, parents) to God. He was as pure in his belief as anyone I had ever met.

We descended out of the hills and into the city. Indian traffic anarchy reigned, and the bus skillfully nosed its way through two traffic circles crowded with hundreds of vehicles before coming to rest at a depot. We all got off, and Cha Cha led the small group through the busy intersection and down a side street. We passed some hotels and restaurants and, after about a half mile, came to some railroad tracks. We crossed and went up an embankment, and when we came down the other side the poverty level had noticeably risen. The colonial mansions and high-rise hotels of the city center had given way to a shanty town where everything, from the people to the roads to the flimsy shacks stretching out around us, seemed to have a pale brown hue to it.

Cha Cha smiled at me. "Here, Hazrat Mohammed, is the Muslim part of town. Please – follow me. We are almost there, and just in time! The prayers will start soon!"

We trudged on through the ghetto, and I started to think about how different this was from Eids past. Eid is like Christmas for the Muslim world – it is accompanied by gift giving, feasts, and general merriment. The prayer in the morning is akin to Midnight Mass, and it is traditional to offer it at the mosque, together. Growing up in San Francisco, the only time my parents had ever taken me to the mosque was for Eid prayer, at a mosque in Mill Valley. Some years we didn't go if my father couldn't get work off, but our family would still celebrate when he got home – it was like a badge of honor for us, to not celebrate Christmas but to celebrate a lunar holiday that fell at random times throughout the year.

I thought about that beautiful mosque in that beautiful part of the world as I walked down the street with these strangers, and thanked God that my father had moved to America. Most of the believers were poor, like these men, and I was fortunate to be experiencing their world for only a day and not a lifetime. I wasn't sure of what the proper course of action was, as this was the first time I had been confronted with my relative modern affluence and the humility I felt thrust upon me.

We progressed through the shanty town and into some fields. Down a country lane we came to a clearing and a small house. Outside the house, men were gathered in groups, sitting on straw mats. Little boys were running around, pretending to shoot one another with sticks for guns. There were no women anywhere.

"This is our mosque – it is not much, but it is all we have," said Cha Cha humbly. "You, Hazrat Mohammed, you are like my brother. You have come from so far, praise God, and you have honored me by coming to give prayers at our little mosque."

He had tears in his eyes and gave me a hug. An amazing feeling swamped me – a feeling of togetherness and belonging I had rarely felt before. I was in my homeland, being embraced by a total stranger because of our common beliefs. I did feel like his brother as we hugged, and I thanked him for his words.

As we entered the grounds I was swarmed (I am not more than six feet tall, but in this place I was a giant – more than a few inches taller than the next man there) - all the kids gathered around me and asked questions at once while Cha Cha swatted them away and brought me to the mosque's entrance. I was introduced to an older man, named Khalid, who was dressed in traditional clothes but whose close-cropped beard and designer eyeglasses made him standout amongst the congregants.

"Salaam Alaikum, brother. Eid Mubarak brother," Khalid said to me. "You will have to excuse the children, they do not see foreigners every day." His English was flawless and spoken in a British accent.

"Oh no, that's okay. Makes me feel like someone important, I guess," I said.

"And are you someone important?" Khalid asked, his eyebrow raising just a bit.

"No, I don't think so. I'm just a traveler, lucky enough to have met Cha Cha and Abdullah in Palolem and get invited to Eid prayer here."

"And tell me," continued Khalid, "why is it that a Muslim brother like you went to Palolem? Don't you know that that is where those heathens go to drink alcohol and fornicate?" The severity of his tone startled me. While Cha Cha's cousin Abdullah had said some strange things to me, I had not thought them to have much malice – they were generally nice and simple people, telling you their beliefs in a straightforward and honest way. Khalid, however, had a probing intelligence in his eyes and a knowing smirk on his face.

"I did not know that," I said in a quick-thinking defense. "I only went there because I had heard it was beautiful, and I wanted to see a beautiful part of India. And, by God's grace, I met Cha Cha and Abdullah and have found my way here."

Khalid's face broke into a smile and he seemed to relent. "Yes, yes – lucky for us to have a stranger from America here on our most festive day. A Muslim brother, no less. It is truly a blessing. Come – please come sit with us before the prayers. They will begin shortly."

Khalid took my arm and led me into a circle of men sitting cross-legged at the entrance to the mosque. Most had long beards, but their dress was noticeably nicer than that of Cha Cha and Abdullah, who had followed us but sat behind me and out of the circle. Khalid introduced me and we all exchanged Eid greetings. There was a man at the head of the circle, crouched over a shoebox full of money and scribbling on a piece of paper.

"This is Abdul Latif," said Khalid. "He will take your *Zakat*."

"Salaam Alaikum. How much money did you make last year?" asked Abdul Latif. As he asked he looked up and I caught the face of this religious accountant – he had a glass eye and seven tobacco stained teeth.

"Um, excuse me?"

"This is for the alms, your zakat," said Khalid. "It is what a believer returns out of his or her wealth to the neediest of Muslims. It is for the sake of the Almighty Allah. It is called zakat because it comes from *Zakaa*, which means to increase, purify, and bless. This is how you bless your money – by giving to the needy. You are to give 2.5% of your earnings to the mosque, for distribution amongst the needy."

I knew what Zakat was before Khalid lectured me – when I had started earning my mom had encouraged me to put a little aside every year and to give it to her so she could send it to poor family members in Pakistan. I was not, however, too excited about being made to forcibly give up my charity by these men.

"How much did you make last year?" insisted the gap-toothed assessor.

"Um, I'm not sure. I am traveling right now, as well, and I do not have money on me."

This caused a murmur among the men watching the transaction, and it seemed as though I had committed an unpardonable faux pas. I saw one man point to my nice Puma shoes and another point to the camera slung around my shoulder, as the group began muttering that I was wealthy and not doing my duty.

I fumbled for my wallet and saw I had 2,000 rupees. I took it out and gave it to the assessor, who grabbed it and wrote me a receipt for my alms amongst apparent approval by everyone watching. Another man started in with his calculations as Khalid took my elbow and escorted me into the little building where the prayers were to be given.

"2,000 rupees is a very generous offer, Brother Mohammed, to our little mosque here. We thank you for it," he said.

I sensed some sarcasm in his tone. "Well, Khalid, I usually give all my zakat to my family, you see, and I plan to do so again when I get home."

"Yes – that is good. I am sure you will. But, just remember, that all the Muslims are your family, and if you give the zakat today, on Eid, it is said to be worth 70 times the amount in the eyes of God."

I looked around for Cha Cha to save me from this sales pitch, but he had drifted over to a corner in the back of the room. Khalid had brought me to the middle, where we sat in a line and waited for the mullah to begin the sermon. The room had become crowded, with men of all ages and young boys filling in to evenly spaced lines stretching from the front to the back of the room.

"Where do the sisters pray?" I asked Khalid.

"We are a humble community – we do not have enough space for them. They pray at home."

The mullah got up and cleared his throat, and the mosque fell quiet. He was big – bigger than most of the men there. His belly was wide, and he wore long flowing robes and a turban, all in black. His appearance was menacing – he looked the part of the zealot. But, when he opened his mouth he spoke in soft tones and smiled repeatedly through his opening sermon. It was short and quick – he thanked God for Ramadan, which had physically and spiritually cleaned the congregation, and he made sure to remind everyone that it was now their duty to pay zakat – that no matter how much or how little a man made, he should always give of himself to those less fortunate. Looking around at the poor people in the room, I couldn't imagine them parting ways with their meager sums of money, and I began to feel a little guilty that I didn't have more to give on me.

The sermon over, we gave our prayers behind the mullah's leadership – two rakats of thanks and blessing. Eid prayers are some of the most sacred in Islam, and as we gave them I felt a bit more at ease, forgetting the strangeness of the situation and enjoying the familiarity of praying in a group. At home, after Eid prayers my brothers and Dad would pray together in the morning before my Mom served a huge breakfast feast. Afterwards, we would get money from our Dad and then go to the mall and spend it as frivolously as possible.

176

The prayers ended and we all did the traditional post-Eid prayer hug and three-cheek kiss greeting. Cha Cha re-appeared at my elbow, hugging me and then requesting that I accompany him back to their family home for Eid breakfast. I happily agreed, but before we could leave Khalid made his way back to me.

"Brother Mohammed," Khalid said, "I was just speaking with the mullah – he would like to meet you. It is not often that he has an American in his mosque."

"Well, that is very nice of him, but I have just accepted an invitation for breakfast at this brother's house," I said pointing to Cha Cha, who had automatically moved two steps away to a respectful distance at the sight of Khalid.

"Well, that is fine. I did not mean now. Why don't you go with them and then return after breakfast? The mullah has business to attend to right now anyway. I insist on it."

I said okay without much more of a fight and walked away with Cha Cha, who had now been joined by Abdullah and a couple of other boys from the beach. As we turned up the dirt road Cha Cha excitedly spoke up.

"Hazrat Mohammed – what is it that Brother Khalid spoke to you about?"

"Oh – he asked me to come back after breakfast to speak with the mullah."

"Oh, that is very excellent. God be praised! He is a very smart man, and you should speak with him. He is a great man." Cha Cha spoke with reverence about the mullah, and he was obviously pleased that the stray he had brought home from the beach was gaining such an important audience. "Now," he continued, "we will go celebrate. Brother Mohammed – our home is humble, but we welcome you to it."

"Not at all – it is my pleasure."

We walked on for a short while before coming upon a river. There were logs set across it as a makeshift bridge, and on the far bank there were forty or so people. We crossed the logs and I was mobbed by twelve or more kids, all barefoot and jumping up and down and giving me Eid greetings. Cha Cha laughed.

"They have never met a foreigner before," he said while scooping one of the little girls up into his arms. "This is Zohra my daughter."

I brought out my digital camera and the kids went even crazier, dancing and mugging and pleading with me to take even more pictures. Cha Cha gently dispersed the kids and led me further along the riverbank to the main area.

The encampment was not even a shanty town – there was not one solid structure on the river bank. There were about six different areas where a sheet had been propped up with heavy sticks, and under the sheet straw mats, blankets, clothes, cookware, and toys were strewn about in a haphazard sprawl. There was no sign of a refrigeration device, and no signs of any kind of bathroom at all. The scene was somehow worse than the homeless cities that pop up in empty lots and park spaces in San Francisco, but not altogether incomparable. The main difference was the amount of kids here – more than half the people looked to be under the age of twelve.

Cha Cha introduced me to his wife, a pretty woman sitting cross-legged on a straw mat and holding an infant in her arms. She was tending to a small pot, cooking over an open fire.

"Brother Mohammed – this is my wife, Syeda."

"Salaam Alaikum," I said. "Eid Mubarak."

She giggled and returned my greeting. The baby in her arms looked sick – it had a yellowish tinge to it and seemed very thin.

Cha Cha cleared a space for me on the mat and bade me sit down. "We do not have much, but we are honored that you are here. All these people here – we are family, from the UP. That is my brother's camp there, and over there is my wife's brother's family, and right next to us is Abdullah's family."

"It is nice that you all get to live together," I offered, trying to be positive.

"Yes – that is nice. Would you like some chai?"

"Yes, thank you."

I watched as Cha Cha produced some cups from under a blanket and dipped them into a pot sitting on some rocks. He gave me the cup and I looked in – there were tiny bugs flitting across the top film of chai, and I could feel the fear of dysentery rising up in my loins. But, with Cha Cha and Syeda eyeing me anxiously, I knew that to refuse would be to dishonor these poor people, so I sipped some and made a show of enjoying it immensely.

Syeda then produced a wooden plate and served up some *keer* (rice pudding traditionally served on Eid), which I dutifully put down over the grudging protests of my stomach and brain. As I ate Cha Cha proudly introduced me to all his relatives – most of the men worked as drum sellers at the coastal resorts. Their happiness to be home was evident – nearly all the men had kids draped all over them, and a cricket game amongst the men and kids was being organized in a small clearing next to the camp.

I was invited to play and did my best, trying to convert my ball and bat skills from years of beer league softball to rural cricket conditions. The ball is harder than a baseball, and no gloves are used. The field we were on was swamp-like, with sticks and rocks and trash at every turn. But the jokes were flowing and the family was into it – the wives were cheering from the sidelines while even the smallest of toddlers was allowed to take a bat. I was touched that Cha Cha's family had invited me to take part of their family fun, and as the game ended I thanked him for his warmth and generosity.

"It is you, Brother Mohammed, who should be thanked. You have come from far away to share this time with us, to give your Eid prayers with us. May Allah bless you and your family, always."

"Thank you Cha Cha, but I think I should get going. I am to meet the mullah back at the mosque."

"Yes, of course. I will walk you there."

I said my goodbyes and, after snapping a few more photos, went back over the river with Cha Cha. He walked me to the dirt road that led to the mosque, but then stopped.

"I will leave you here – I must go back. We are going to catch the bus from the depot – there is one at 5PM, and one at 7PM. Which one would you prefer?" he asked.

"I will prefer the 7PM one, I think – there is no need to rush. Please, spend time with your family and enjoy yourself. Are you sure – you can't come with me?" I felt as though he had my back, somewhat, and I would have liked him there with me as I met the mullah.

"No – I mustn't go in there. You will talk with the important people – it is no place for a man like me. I am only a poor, simple man." He said this humbly and without apology – like it was his lot in life and he accepted it. I thanked him again for his hospitality and he turned to head back.

I went down the dirt road and came upon the mosque's outer area. There was no one around, and when I poked my head into the mosque there was only an old man, sitting in apparent prayer. I looked around the back of the mosque and saw Khalid sitting on a tree stump. When he saw me he motioned me to take off my shoes and come to the back.

He was talking to two other men, whom he introduced as Hakim and Lefak. Both men greeted me in perfect English after their salaams. Both were in their late twenties, with long beards and black turbans that made them look like Talibans. But their demeanor was respectful, and their English made them seem highly educated. After a few minutes of chitchat the door to a small shack behind us opened and the mullah invited us in.

Inside, the room was sparsely furnished. A cot was nestled along one side of the small room, and books crowded in along the walls and floor. Seated next to the mullah on the ground were two men, both with the long-beard-black-turban look that was the apparent fashion in these parts. We all sat down and the men started talking about finances, estimating how much money the mosque took in today. I was largely ignored, until after fifteen minutes or so Khalid turned to me.

"Mullah Usman, this is Brother Mohammed. He has come from America to spend Eid with us."

"God be praised and God bless you Brother Mohammed," said Mullah Usman, in Urdu and smiling widely. "Eid Mubarak."

"Eid Mubarak. It is nice to meet you," I said.

"So, Khalid says you are from America?"

"Yes – I am."

"And you are Muslim?"

"Yes."

"What kind of Muslim? Which school do you follow?"

YuMa had warned me of theological questions like this – you never know who you are talking to.

"My family is Sufi."

"And which school do you follow?"

I hesitated, forgetting all I had once learned about the five schools of Islamic thought. As I fumbled for an answer I could hear Khalid say sneeringly in Urdu that, "he is only a born Muslim" to Mullah Usman.

"I am sorry – I forget which school we follow, as I am not so strict a Muslim."

"We here, we are Hanbali. We follow his school of thought, as we feel it is the best one. But, what is this, you are not a strict Muslim? There is only one kind, Brother Mohammed. You either are or you aren't."

The other men grunted in agreement while I began to panic a bit. Was I safe here, being grilled by men in long beards miles from anyone who might help me?

"Of course, I am a Muslim. But, it is different in America – we don't have so much time to devote. We are living in another culture."

"Yes, a culture which is evil and decrepit," said Khalid, jumping at the chance to dog America. "I feel bad for you, Brother, that you must live there amongst the infidels."

"No, Khalid, do not say this," said Mullah Usman, "everywhere is God's house, even America. It is good that our Brother lives there. He can help more than we can. Tell me, Brother Mohammed, do you know many Muslims there?"

"Well," I began, thinking of my motley S.F. crew, "not really. There are not many where I live, but more in places like New York and Houston. I live in San Francisco, on the western side of the country."

"You know I have heard that more people in America are becoming Muslim than anywhere else in the world right now?" said Hakim, breaking into the conversation. "I heard that even after Somalia, the American soldiers who came back from that mission all converted to Islam."

"Well, I'm not sure about that, but I do hear it is the fastest growing religion in the States," I offered. "But, that's because there are so many people – 280 million, I think. Of all those people, only 6 million or so are Muslim, and that's not very much."

"Yes – and there are more Jews than Muslims. That is our problem," said Khalid, looking straight at me as he said it. "The Jews have control over America, and they are making it difficult on the Muslims everywhere."

The gathering all agreed to this assertion, the mere mentioning of Jews causing looks of disgust on their faces.

"But," I ventured, "what is wrong with Jews? They are People of the Book, right? Didn't God give them a book, the Torah? Aren't we told to respect the People of the Book?"

"Yes, they did get a book," answered Mullah Usman, "but they forgot it, they strayed. That is why God sent the Bible, but then the Christians strayed too. Then He sent the Qu'ran, and that was the most perfect of all religions. All the rules are spelled out, for all to see. But, even we have strayed, and that is why we are in the state we are in. We have not been real Muslims for a long time. Tell me, Brother Mohammed, why have you come to India?"

"I am traveling the world, going to Muslim countries and learning about the people. I have been to Morocco, Turkey, and Pakistan. And now I am here."

"This is very good. It is very good for a young man to see so much. And tell me – what have you learned?" asked the mullah.

"Well, it is hard to say. What I can say is that most people are nice – most people have taken me in wherever I have been and showed me warmth and compassion."

"Yes – this is the true nature of man – this is how God made us. But, it is unfortunate when we cannot be happy like this – it is unfortunate that many people in the world today, including most of our Muslim brothers, are suffering. This is what we are faced with, the test that God has put down before the Muslims. Tell me, brother, what do you think about Osama bin Laden?"

The men leaned forward expectantly, and I had the distinct feeling that I was among some of his staunchest supporters.

"Well," I began diplomatically, "I'm not sure. If he was behind the attacks of September 11th in New York, then I think he is a bad man, because many people, including Muslims, died that day. But, if he did not do it, then I think that maybe he is not so bad, because he is standing up for his people against a powerful enemy, and he deserves respect for that."

My answer seemed to mollify them, and Mullah Usman was quick to assure me. "Of course, whoever was behind 9/11 was a bad person. You cannot justify killing so many innocent people. But, Osama has said he did not do it, and no one has shown any proof."

"Yes – it is true," chimed in Lefak, "when the Americans asked the Taliban for Osama, they said that they will give him up – they just wanted to see the proof. But, America did not have any, so they just dropped the bombs anyway."

"Well, I guess you're right," I said, not wanting to get too confrontational. "We don't really know who did it. But in America, he is guilty."

"But, this is wrong," said the mullah, "don't you see? Your country, which talks so much about freedom and democracy and human rights, has already made a man guilty of a terrible crime without ever proving it! This is what is wrong with America – you say one thing and do another."

"Well, I agree with you. America has a double standard, and it is unfortunate."

"That is why it is important for you to understand this. It is up to you, the Muslims of America, to make them understand this. Personally, I believe in Osama – he is a great man. Who follows Hanbali thought, just like we do. He is the one trying to get us back to the true Islam, the one of the Qu'ran. He cares about the poor people – he always speaks the truth. He is the only one who has stood up for the Muslims, while all the governments have only been puppets of Western power. He has brought us pride and courage – he has given us strength and wisdom." Mullah Usman's voice was starting to sound more sermon-like, and I quickly realized that if these guys and Osama were the same kind of Muslims, then these guys were Wahabbis.

"Wait," I said. "I thought that Osama was a Wahabbi?"

The men grumbled at my question and Khalid jumped on it. "The word Wahabbi," he said in English, "is a made up term. It means nothing. Osama follows the Hanbali school of Islamic jurisprudence, which is the only true school and the one we follow as well. Wahabbi is not a word we take very kindly to around here – it is a label given to us by others that we reject."

My mind started racing and I started to feel the fear creeping into my gut. Had I lost all sense to be sitting here in rural India with a bunch of Wahabbi nuts, debating Osama's virtuousness and my salary?

"Osama is one with us – he is our leader," continued the mullah. "He has proclaimed a jihad only because it is necessary – because the infidels have plundered our homes and our oil fields. We would happily co-exist with the infidels – let them have their heathen ways and let us have God. But, they would not leave us alone, and decade after decade they have come to our lands and spilled the blood of our brothers. So, we now strike back – we would never strike the first blow. Osama is only responding to their aggression."

"But surely, Mullah Usman, killing innocent women and men in suicide bombs is wrong, isn't it?" I said, trying to seem interested but racing to find an acceptable excuse for an exit.

"If you are poor and that is all you have, then how can it be wrong? God says that it is your duty to spread your religion and defend it against attack. This is the only way for us to defend ourselves. Brother Mohammed," he continued, "one of the most important things Osama has done is show us that we must organize for what is true and right. We are followers of the *Tabliqi masjid* here – it is an organization throughout all of India that helps Muslims – we feed and clothe Muslims from all over the country, and we teach them the true ways of Hanbali thought. It is only through organization that we can do this – we have donors from all over the world who give to our office in New Delhi, and then that money gets spread throughout the rest of the country. And then we feed poor people, like the people you have seen here today."

I felt like this was an extended sales pitch and the punch line was about to become apparent.

"And, when we meet a man like you," said Mullah Usman, "we like to talk to him, to try to get him involved. There is so much you can do to help."

"Well, I'm not sure," I said, trying to not sound too disgusted about the prospect of joining Osama bin Laden's cause. "I'm not very important – I'm just a traveler."

"Yes, but with an American passport, right?"

"Yes, right."

"So, you can come and go freely – this is something we cannot do. And you speak perfect American English – this is something we don't do. You can do much for us – I want you to do me one favor. Will you be going to New Delhi?"

"I'm not sure."

"Well, you must. You must go there and meet our leadership at the Tabliqi Masjid – you must go and meet with my friends there."

"Well, I'm not sure..."

"It is okay – I understand. But you must ask yourself – why have you come this far? What is it that you are seeking? I am here to provide you with answers, but only if you want them. Here is my card – please take it with you to New Delhi and show them at the Tabliqi Masjid – they will give you a free place to stay and free food. Now, we must busy ourselves with cooking food for our congregation – we are providing food for all the families tonight as part of our Eid celebration. It was very nice to meet you, Brother Mohammed. May God bless you and keep you and your family safe and happy."

I thanked him for his time and got up to walk out. Khalid and Latif followed me out.

"I will go with you to New Delhi," said Latif. "I have been putting off a trip there for a long time. We will go to the Tabliqi Masjid together, okay?"

I did not want to make any twenty-plus hour travel plans with some Wahabbi nut. "I'm sorry – I am not sure what my plans currently are, so I do not know when I might be going North." I started walking to the road while Khalid and Latif tried to convince me to go to Delhi immediately. I was able to beat back their advances and walk back up the road alone, through the ghetto and into town.

My anger began to rise as I walked and realized Cha Cha and his family were all Wahabbis. I had spent the day celebrating with the very people who I blamed for most of the war today, the same people who had been responsible for most terror acts of the 21st century. The word Wahabbi was, in my mind, as racially charged as Nazi or Nigger, they were the ones who had killed and oppressed the things that I knew and loved. I had even given them money – a thought that was so outrageous to me that, as I boarded the early bus back for Palolem alone, I began to curse Khizr for sending me to celebrate with the enemy.

Chapter 17

Purification

Back at Palolem that night, I resolved to drown my inner angst. Lauren had arrived and left word that she and her traveling buddies were staying up the beach from my spot. I gladly headed over to her spot, which was far away from Cha Cha's shop and the source of my confused anger.

In typical fashion, Lauren had found the hippest place on the beach to stay. I found her and her two friends Zadie and Emily (whom I had met at a Halloween party in Isla Vista years back) lounging on beach chairs in front of a low lying beach bar, where a DJ spun down tempo grooves on one side and a bartender slung *feni* drinks on the other.

Goa is an anomaly in the Indian union of states – it was ruled by the Portuguese well after Indian independence from the British, for over 400 years (it only became part of modern India in 1961, after being forcibly retaken from Portugal). The Catholic Church has a strong hold on the majority of the population, and western dress is the norm over the saris and shalwar kameez seen throughout the rest of India. Along with a distinct culture and religion, the Goans have their own alcohol, called feni. The two types of feni come from either coconut trees or cashew apples, and are distilled to be thirty to thirty-five percent alcohol before being served to unsuspecting tourists on the beach.

Lauren screamed when she saw me and jumped into my arms. She looked as good as ever – her tan, lean, surfer-girl body barely clothed with a bikini and sarong wrapped loosely around her waist.

"Yo, Mo! Wassup dude? It's been ages, hasn't it?"

"Hey Lauren – good to see you're still living large." I turned and saluted her friends. "Ladies, a pleasure to see you both."

I settled in with them and we started trading travel stories over cashew feni drinks. The feni was served neat and, because both the aroma and aftertaste were so strong, we were drinking Kingfishers as chasers. The girls had been on a month-long expedition, through Nepal, Myanmar, and India, and I was happy to let their chatter sweep me away from my own world, which felt only serious and heavy at the moment.

As the girls made friends with a group of good-looking Aussie guys sitting next to us, I began to zone out, pounding feni and Kingfishers absentmindedly while thinking about why Khizr could have possibly asked me to come here, to this place, to find out about Islam. This beach was full of partying Westerners and poor Wahabbis, it seemed – what was I to learn here? And what good was any of it anyway, what with fronts open in the clash of cultures seemingly all over the world?

My thoughts were interrupted when the power went out on the beach, and the party around us went quiet without the help of the DJ's speakers. Lauren called for a skinny dip, and a major part of the bar whooped in agreement and took off for the water. I stayed behind, and while sitting in the darkness felt a presence next to me.

"Hello?" I asked.

Nothing came back. The sky was completely clear, with a full ceiling of stars stretching out to infinity above me, but with no moon and no power the beach was completely black.

"Is someone there?"

I thought I heard a slow, guttural moan, but it was too faint to confirm. In my feni haze I had a bright idea and whipped out the monitor on my digital camera, to use as a flashlight. The camera showed me two pairs of eyes about ten feet from my chair, and the light made the growl louder and more menacing. Realizing I had been joined by one of the scavenging dogs of the beach was enough to sober me up fast, and I slowly slid out of my chair and walked away, figuring that there must be some food in the bar area the dog had scoped out. I seemed to be right, as the eyes did not follow me and I heard some rustling around in the zone I had just left.

I turned and ran, the idea of a pack of dogs milling about spurring me on to get out of there fast. I must have run down half the beach, in the pitch black, all the while with a building panic propelling me through the darkness. The last thing I remember before tripping and spilling forward was the fear of the dogs giving way to an acute fear of the future, which seemed to have gripped my belly the minute I heard about the World Trade Center and hadn't let go since.

I hazily recall a wet moment, with urgent voices shouting around me. The next clear moment I remember was the morning, waking up in Cha Cha's shop with Mustafa looking worriedly at me.

"Cha Cha!" he yelled when he saw my open eyes. "Hazrat Mohammad is awake!"

Cha Cha came rushing from outside and came to me with a bottle of water, insisting that I drink some.

"How are you feeling, Brother?" he asked kindly.

My head ached and when I touched it I felt a large bandage had been wrapped around it.

"What happened to me?"

"We found you, on the beach last night. I had become worried – you were not at the bus stop, in Margao, but when we returned to Palolem I went to your cocohut, and the owner said that he had seen you come back that day but had not seen you in the night. Mustafa and I – we were worried and went looking on the beach for you, and found you being taken out to tide. There was a big cut on the side of your head. Did someone attack you?"

"Uh – no, I don't think so. I think I tripped and fell, when there was no power."

"Oh, praise God we found you, Hazrat Mohammad. If we had not, you would be out to sea right now. The tide is strong at night, and when we found you, you were completely out – we could not wake you at all. You had already been dragged – your face was covered with sand."

The tenderness in his voice betrayed the real affection he had for me, and as I looked at this small, poor man who had just saved my life, it was hard to equate him with the Wahabbi menace I had spoken about to Toby and so many others back on my soap box in San Francisco.

"Thank you, Cha Cha. Thank you so much." I rose but became woozy and sat back down. Both Mustafa and Cha Cha jumped and caught my arms to steady me back down.

"You need rest," said Cha Cha. "Please, stay here and rest."

I looked around at Cha Cha's inventory of instruments and realized he could not be doing any business while I lay sprawled in his tiny shop. I insisted that I go back to my hut, and Cha Cha finally backed down, ordering Mustafa to assist me back. He got me back, with a few breaks to rest, to my shack, and I fumbled through my gear, found my Advil, popped two, and collapsed on to my bunk.

Chapter 18

Fear and Arithmetic

I am back in Margao, sitting on the floor of the mosque where I gave my Eid prayers the day before. Khizr is standing in front of me, with a chalkboard propped up on an easel and the number 2,000 written on it.

"Hey Mo – nice battle wound."

"Thanks man," I say sheepishly. "Pretty stupid, huh?"

"More like predictable. Fear is always around the corner, my friend. It is an emotion programmed into the genetic makeup of every living thing on this planet. You ran out of fear of the mongrel – down a pitch-black beach and headlong into God knows what. You put yourself more at risk because you were irrational, because of your fear."

"It's irrational to be afraid of being torn to pieces?"

"It's irrational to forget that there are many others close by, and to think that running in the dark is ever good. But, that is beside the point. I am glad you are okay, and that you have made such good friends here as to have them concerned for your well being."

"Well," I say, beginning to recollect my state of mind, "it is understandable, don't you think? That I was in an agitated state of mind? I mean, what's the deal with sending me here, G? Eid prayers with Wahabbis? Did you want me to get recruited?"

"Now how is that even possible, to join something that you have professed to hate so many times?" Khizr asks.

I am quiet as he plops down next to me in the prayer line.

"Mo – I wanted you to come here to understand something of the darker side of humans. And of yourself, in particular. I want you to know – there are things that we all have inside us that must be kept in check, and fear is one of them. The hatred you have for Wahabbis is really fear – you have always feared your own Muslimness, ever since you were a little kid. 9/11 just amplified that fear. Your whole deal with Wahabbis is just an apology, concocted by your fear of being ostracized from the community in which you live."

I know he is right instinctively. I have always had an insatiable appetite to be considered 'cool' by all the friends in my life, to be the one who always has something going on. But still, something doesn't sit right.

"But, what are you saying? That the Wahabbis aren't the problem?"

"Abso-freakin-lutely not. They are a huge part of the problem – they are an anti-modernization movement, and those are always a tough nut to crack. But the same rule applies to them that applies to almost every organization man has ever known – the 80-20 rule. 80 percent of folks are good – they want a clean living, food on the table and respect from their neighbors. Even with the Wahabbis, although somewhat skewed, this is true. 20 percent of people everywhere are bad, and will succumb to fear or hubris or greed - usually at the expense of everyone else. For the Wahabbis, this 20 percent is particularly harmful, because they see just about everyone as their enemy, and have become more and more aggressive over the last few decades."

"80-20 rule, huh? You'd think God would try and give us better odds than that, like 95-5, if He loved us so much."

"Ha! I don't know about that – this is my own thesis. 3,000 years of life make me an expert of human nature. How do you think I got you to run last night, huh? Controlling that which another fears is the ultimate weapon, whether used for combat or for sport." He winks at me and pops up onto his feet, before making like he is going to dog pile on top of me, his quick movements like those of a floor gymnast. He stops at the last second, tussles my hair and laughs.

"The 80-20 rule is a positive way to look at things, I think. It means that humans are, at their core, good. We want to do good, in general. It's just unfortunate that the ones who lust for power and who usually have the biggest impact on history are disproportionably from the 20 percent. It is one of the great ironies of our race, really – that the ones with the ambition to lead are usually the ones least fit to act for the common interest."

"So, Osama and other Wahabbi leaders are bad, but the common folk are good?"

"Mo – it isn't about bad or good. No one person is bad or good – this is what I am trying to tell you. Every person has a battle going on within, where they must choose every day what is right and what is wrong for them. Once someone is in the 80 percent, they still may fall into the 20 percent, if they lose their way. And the flip side is true too – people can reform and be made to see the error of their ways. It is the joy of our creation – we are fluid spiritual objects, if you will. Each one of us unique and constantly in flux."

I think about Cha Cha, and how he has seemed like an older brother to me since we first met. He saved me, and did so only because he had genuine concern for my well being. I begin to realize that I have been employing a double standard, putting things in stark black and whites when talking politics and war when, in reality, these were the very categorizations that I was trying to speak against. Blaming Wahabbis for everything suddenly feels like certain Americans blaming all Muslims for everything, and that does not sit well with my liberal sensibilities.

"Well," I say, "I see your point. Maybe I have stereotyped some. But, Cha Cha seems like an anomaly amongst his people – all the other guys at his mosque seemed pretty aggressive."

"The men of the mosque are what is wrong with Wahabbism today. They have tried to intellectualize regressive behavior – things like oppression of women and technology. They do this in a misguided attempt to appease God, and this is a serious problem for today's world. Believe me – many people are working on this right now. Holding off the fundamentalists is one of our top priorities. But – Cha Cha is representative of many – he has chosen this path because it is one of the only ones open to him. There are no other mosques here, and there are no other people willing to assist his family with food and clothes."

Khizr waves off my next question before I can say anything. He points to the 2,000 up on the chalkboard.

"Now," he continues, "this is another one of man's inner demons that must be held in check at all times. Greed. This is why God has proclaimed that you must give charity – to purify yourself from caring too much about money."

He draws a line under the 2,000 and puts 50 underneath, and then next to the fraction an equals sign and a 40.

"Yesterday, when asked for zakat, you gave 2,000 rupees, which is roughly equivalent to 40 dollars. Now, by my calculations, taking into account your severance package and stock sales, in the last year you made 94,000 dollars." He puts this figure on the board and starts calculating. "Multiplying by .025, or 2.5 percent, we get 2,350, minus the 40 you already gave, which comes out to a grand total of 2,310 dollars that you still owe."

"Wow," I say, "does it really have to be taken so literally?"

"No," Khizr says with a smile. "Over the years, there have been many ways to calculate one's zakat. You must first be able to provide a basic living for you and your dependents, before you are required to pay – you obviously meet this requirement. Then, you must give some fixed amount, yearly, to the poor. The amount should be a percentage of earnings, as that is the only way to make it proportional. The 2.5 percent has been a standard measure – if a man makes 1,000, he gives 25, if he makes 1,000,000, he gives 25,000. He should not be so greedy, or it will consume him and all those around him."

"So, zakat is a purity tax, huh?"

"In some ways, you can say this. But, you can give it to anyone, and it is loosely defined on purpose. It is the spirit behind it that is important – a true believer should always be inclined towards charity. Charity is the most direct way to show you have conquered greed, which is one of the sins that God looks upon least favorably. Most people in the 20 percent, the ones that screw stuff up the most, they are motivated by greed."

As I think of all my possessions and money, I begin to understand him. "So, I owe more, but I can give it to anyone who needs it, right?"

"Well, yes. If you do not have poor people you know, you can give it to a charitable organization – you can give it anywhere where it is put to use for your fellow man."

"Cool," I say, while resolving to pay a big chunk of my zakat to the man who saved me on the beach.

Khizr seems satisfied and begins to erase the board. "And now, young friend, we are on the last leg of your journey. You have come far and I am proud of you – now comes the fun part. I want you to go to Koh Ngai – it is an island in the Gulf of Thailand. There, I want you to wait for me – we will have our last meeting there, and you will have completed your mission with us."

He draws a quick map and points out the tiny island.

"There is no rush this time – take your time, and I'll catch you later."

The dream is over, and I bolt upright in bed. I have a feeling that Khizr is in the room, but I look around and I am alone.

Chapter 19

The Asian Tiger

The next day I researched Koh Ngai online. It seemed about equidistant from Bangkok and Kuala Lumpur (KL), so I chose to make my way to Bombay and then take a flight through KL, as I had heard many great things about the city from YuMa. He had been involved in raising funding from Malaysia for various hospital projects in Pakistan for years, and had on many occasions told me that Malaysia was perhaps the world's best example of a modern Muslim country run well. I fired YuMa an email, inquiring about any contacts he may have for me there, and set about the long journey.

Before leaving, I went into town and cashed all one thousand dollars of my travelers checks. Resolved to make good on the lesson of charity that Khizr had given me, I put the money in an envelope and dropped it by Cha Cha's shop on the way out. He did not look inside the envelope and refused to take it until I insisted. I had decided, Wahabbis be damned, to make him a recipient of the rest of my zakat that year, so that he could maybe provide a better life for his family. Before I left, I made him promise not to give any to the mosque or to anyone else, and to keep it for his family only.

After forty hours of trains, buses, and planes, I landed in the ultra-modern Kuala Lumpur International Airport and took a twenty-five minute train ride through to the city proper. The scenery was tropical – lush palm trees and dense jungle lined the train tracks the entire way. It was night – around 9 PM local time as I spotted a Starbucks in the bus terminal and ordered an iced latte. The barista spoke flawless English, and when he found out I was new in town he suggested a travel agency on the second level for some information – his friends ran it, and he knew they were still there.

The travel agency turned out to be a godsend – within an hour of arriving in Malaysia I had arranged all my travel plans to Koh Ngai, which would take me on buses, trains, and boats up the Malay Peninsula. The trip didn't start for a few days, and they even reserved a bed for me at their friend's hostel – the Attapsana Hotel, in the Golden Triangle district of KL.

I thanked them and they me, as I'm sure my business was a welcome surprise to them that late in the evening. A cab whipped me through the hot, humid night, down a main boulevard lined with gigantic modern shopping malls and restaurants decked out in neon lights. I was shocked at how bright and new it all was – it looked as nice as any shopping district in America or Europe. In contrast to the frenetic and jarring Indian Subcontinent, Malaysia appeared to be a downright dream, with everything looking clean and orderly and all the cars staying between the lines.

It was Saturday night, and scores of people were out and about, carrying shopping bags and drinking at outdoor bars and generally having a blast. The diversity of the crowd was striking – there was white and yellow and every shade of brown, mixed together in total harmony. Almost everyone wore Western clothes, but I saw some hijabs sprinkled in - a daintier, more fashionable version to ones I had seen in other parts of the Muslim world. The headscarves here were smaller and of different colors, matched to the outfit the girl was wearing. The Muslim girls in KL seemed to have successfully accessorized it.

At one intersection I saw two teenage girls, maybe fifteen years old, holding hands and giggling. One looked Malay, brown and with a slight slant to the eye, while the other looked Chinese. The Malay girl wore a light pink hijab that matched a loose pink tunic and jeans, while the Chinese girl had on a mini skirt and halter top. Their outfits diametrically opposed, they walked down the street, giggling and chatting and looking for all the world to be the best of friends.

After getting lost in some back streets behind the malls, the cabbie finally found the Attapsana Hotel. The front of the hotel was small and sandwiched between a restaurant front and a bar, where live jazz music was being blown and a nicely dressed crowd seemed to be gathering. I rang a doorbell, was buzzed in, and ascended a long staircase before emerging into an air-conditioned room. A couple of long-haired European-types were watching T.V. on a sofa, and behind them was an open door to a room, where I could see two girls doing their makeup and wearing shiny, tight clubbing clothes. The hostel was small and intimate – the people who ran it had obviously converted it from a residence. The room I had entered must have been the living room, which now housed the front desk, T.V. room, and a bathroom. Stretching down a hall were what appeared to be the bedrooms, and then at the end of it, another bathroom. The whole place was wall to wall dark wood, which made it feel smaller than it actually was.

I stood there, being ignored by the guys watching T.V. and the girls getting ready. After a few minutes, a young Malaysian man came out and assigned me a bed. He was dressed all in black, with black Dickies pants, a black T shirt, and piercings throughout his nose and ears. He didn't have a lot of time for me – I was shown the bunk and he was gone. I could hear him in the next room, where he walked in and asked the ladies if they were ready, at which they yelped and I could hear the shuffle of multiple pairs of feet up and out the front door. I settled back on my bunk and started writing, determining to log as much of what I had been learning as possible on this great gift of a journey.

The next morning I awoke to a crash – someone in my dormitory had tripped and fallen on a bag. He cursed in another language and got up before going to the bathroom and puking. His dry heaving shot through the paper thin walls like an air horn, and I got out of bed, dressed, and went outside to explore KL by day.

I checked email and YuMa had given me the name of a good friend of his who lived in KL – a lawyer whom he called 'a gentleman and a Muslim.' I called and his wife, Hannaziera, answered the phone. He was away on business, she said, but she would be happy to show me around tomorrow, and I agreed.

Even though it was 86 degrees and humid, I decided to walk. I set out towards the Petronas twin towers, which dominated the skyline of the city and at one time were the world's tallest buildings. The walk took me through the Golden Triangle district, which was a shopping area mixed with large apartment buildings and Chinese residences, through some large office buildings, and into Kuala Lumpur City Center (KLCC). Built at the same time as the towers, the entire KLCC is brand new – a whole modern neighborhood, built in the last ten years in the middle of the city. Many of the buildings in KLCC share the stainless steel and tinted glass look of the towers, which serve as the centerpiece of the area.

The towers are huge, with a walkway joining them about halfway up and a large mall at their base called Suria KLCC. I went inside and got some coffee and took refuge in the A/C of the mall. Although the shop names were foreign, everything else inside made me feel as though I were in downtown San Francisco or New York – it was classy and modern, cutting edge all the way. I started wandering a bit and happened upon a bookstore called 'The Specialist Bookshop,' filled with Qu'rans and other Islamic texts on sleek new black shelves. It was the first reminder that I was still in the Muslim world, and was more akin to a Christian Science Reading Room than anything else.

I continued wandering and found myself at the back of the mall, which opened onto a landscaped descending terrace and then onto a large green park. I walked out onto the terrace and turned back around, realizing I had found the perfect vantage point for the towers. From that spot they rose straight to the heavens, two shining pillars of steel standing defiantly in the lush tropical forest around it. I snapped a few pictures and then went back to find the ticket counter – I wanted to go up.

Much to my chagrin, I learned that visitors are not allowed to the top of the Petronas towers, eighty-eight floors above the street. They are only allowed up to the 'Skybridge' walkway that joins the two towers at the 44th floor, so I got a ticket and stood in line for the elevators. There were placards in the waiting lounge that gave the story of the place.

The area known today as the chic Kuala Lumpur City Center (KLCC) was once a horseracing track, begun in 1896 by the British colonial governor Sir Frank Swettenham. The track maintained popularity for almost a century until the 1980s, when the government decided it should be moved to ease the stifling traffic jams that had begun to paralyze the city on race days. With the track gone, a huge piece of prime downtown real estate had opened up, and talks were begun on how to develop the land. After initially viewing it as a large park, it was decided that a mixed use commercial development would be best, and rights were given to Malaysia's national oil company, Petronas, to develop it.

The country was at that time booming – Prime Minister Dr. Mohatir Mohammed, who was at the beginning of his twenty-two year rule, had instituted economic reforms in the early 80s that had transformed Malaysia into one of the richest countries in the region. The country had always been rich in natural resources – besides having vast oil and gas reserves, Malaysia had been one of the world's largest providers of rubber and tin throughout the 20th century. But Dr. Mohatir had brought industry to Malaysia, and it now had thriving electronics, chemicals, and technology sectors. Together with Petronas, he urged the building of a world-class landmark that would announce Malaysia's arrival in the industrial world.

A by-invitation design competition was held and American Cesar Pelli, former dean of Yale's architecture school, won in 1991. His design embraced Malaysia's Islamic roots, with two slim twin towers rising up in decreasing circumference, seemingly stretching towards the heavens. The floor patterns were based on an eight-pointed star, a recurring motif in Islamic architecture which symbolizes the growth and spread of Islam. It was also designed to be functional, serving as headquarters to the nation's largest company as well as many other multinationals. As part of the development project, which had 7,000 people working on the site at its height, there were the two 1,493 feet towers, both taller than any other building in the world, the shopping mall, a world class symphony hall, a science and technology museum, and the surrounding landscaped gardens and park.

The twin towers opened in 1998 and reigned as the two tallest buildings in the world until 2003, when Taipei 101 came in at a whopping 1,667 feet. As I shuffled forward through the line with a huge throng of Chinese tourists I couldn't help think of the twin towers back home. Crazed Muslims had brought those down as a sign of anger – anger that the West had ruined their lives. But out here, on the eastern edge of the Islamic world, a Muslim country was showing a different path to the one championed by Osama – defiantly beating the West at their own game. These twin towers were just as much of an architectural and construction achievement as anything else in the world, and it had been done by the skill and ingenuity of Malaysia – why couldn't more Muslims channel their energy in such constructive ways?

The view from the Skybridge was nice, but not spectacular, and it was hard not to want to go to the top. But KL looked beautiful, with lush, equatorial greenery poking out everywhere and the KL Menara balancing the skyline across the way. While staring at the Menara I decided to go there and see if I couldn't get a better look at the city, my appetite for views now wet.

I took a short cab ride there and bought a ticket for the observation deck at the top. It was packed with tourists, but after a short wait I got an elevator and found myself on a 360 degree viewing platform. Immediately in front of me were the twin towers, which looked even more awesome from that height and distance. I toured the deck, checking out the views and reading the placards again. I found out that 'Menara' meant 'tower', and that Dr. Mohatir had been a driving force behind its completion as well. It served as the primary communications hub for Kuala Lumpur, and was also one of its top tourist attractions.

Sufficiently happy with my aerial views of KL, I spent the afternoon wandering around town, strolling through different neighborhoods and parks. Everywhere were reminders of the cultural diversity of the place – a British colonial building next to an old mosque or an ornate Hindu temple next to the gigantic Chinatown. Street vendors sold Indian, Malaysian, or Chinese food, and outlandishly exotic fruit was being hocked on almost every corner. The place was a true Asian metropolis for the 21st century – bold and bright, new and old, vibrant and on the rise. The more I saw, the more I liked.

The next day I was to meet YuMa's friend's wife, Hannaziera, at her office.

I hailed a cab and gave the guy the address, which turned out to be an office tower directly across from the twin towers. But, standing on the other side of the street, I got a completely different vibe from the one I had the day before – gone was the relaxed, landmark/museum feeling of wandering around the tourists parts of KLCC, and in its place was the go-go-go of a busy capitalist economy. Men and women in suits hurried by, briefcase in one hand and a cell phone stuck to the other. A Malay man in a suit was hording a bunch of English investors into the building, and as I waited for them to go in I heard gasps of awe – 'such a modern place!' or 'I don't think we have anythin' like this in London now, do we Jon.' I followed them in and found my way to the 10th floor, where Hannaziera's law practice was.

She was a successful lawyer – a partner in a corporate law practice dealing mostly with intellectual property rights. She was a mother of five, with kids ranging from two to fifteen. She was also a philosopher – staunchly feminist and even more so Islamic. She had achieved all this by the age of thirty-five, but when I came into her office I thought she looked more like a teenager, very slight and small and dressed in light blue, all the way from her hijab to her shoes.

She welcomed me in and told me to wait – she would be ready to go in a few minutes. She hurried out and then came back, handing me a water bottle while slipping on a phone headset over the hijab. She seemed to have an argument in Malay over the phone, and she rolled her eyes at me before finally hanging up.

"These stupid people – they can't get anything right!" she laughed.

"I hope it isn't important? Please don't feel as though you have to entertain me. I'll understand if you are busy."

"Don't be silly – we love your Uncle Yousuf, and he has emailed us about you. I have been waiting to meet you ever since my husband spoke of your arrival. He is sorry he couldn't be here, but he has business in Singapore. But, I have some things to do in the city today – you know, out and about. I thought it might be fun for you to come along – I can show you KL."

"That sounds great. Shall we go now?"

"Yes – but can you help me? I need to take these gift baskets downstairs to the car. It is Chinese New Year tomorrow and I have to deliver these gifts to our Chinese clients – it is tradition."

She piled three of the baskets into my hands – they were filled with fruit, candy, and fireworks, all wrapped in colored transparent paper. I struggled to balance the baskets while walking back to the elevators, Hannaziera giggling once when I almost lost control. But, I made it down to the curb, where an SUV pulled up and popped open it's back.

"This is us – put the things in the back and let's go," she said. She had the aura of someone who gives orders regularly – she said everything with a mix of confidence and respect.

I did as I was told and we were soon away, Hannaziera and I sitting in the back seat and the driver, Tariq, in the front. She informed me that he was her family's driver, and that without him her life would be intolerable.

"I mean, can you imagine, Mohammed? Can you imagine having five kids? Each one of them always needs something, and we are constantly running around town for them, dropping one of here and picking another one up over there. Without Tariq we would be ruined – right Tariq?"

Tariq just looked in his rearview mirror and smiled as his mistress quickly turned subjects.

"So, our first stop is at a real estate agency about thirty-five minutes from the city center – they are good clients of ours, and I want to keep them happy."

"Do you always hand deliver gift baskets for Chinese New Year?" I asked.

"Only to our Chinese clients. On Diwali I give sweets to all our Hindu clients, and on Eid we send cards and gifts to all our Malay clients."

"Wow – that must be hard to keep track of – so many holidays for so many different people."

"No – not really. That is our way here in Malaysia – we are a diverse land. But, not diverse in an American sense, where you have people from everywhere thrown together in a mishmash of humanity, but a more regulated diversity – a more state-controlled diversity."

"What do you mean?"

"Well, here we have three separate and distinct races – Malay, Chinese, and Indian. Each race has their own language and religion, but they are all Malaysians. Each race lives in certain areas, but they are all Malaysian. So, we have defined our diversity – we know what we are. In America, you have no idea who you are – you are changing constantly."

"Yeah – that's true. But I'm not sure it's such a bad thing. And besides, how can a state control diversity?"

"Easy – here in Malaysia, we are taught to respect all three of our cultures. Have you heard about the Open Houses?"

"No."

"The state encourages all three faiths here, the Chinese Buddhists and the Indian Hindus and the Malay Muslims, to celebrate any and all of their holidays and events. People are requested to open their homes on such days, and receive visitors to wish them well and celebrate with them. So, what you have is on Hindu holidays, the Muslims and Buddhists coming over to celebrate in Hindu homes, and on Muslim holidays, the Hindus and Buddhists go to Muslim homes, and so on. Even the Prime Minister – since he is a Muslim, he opens his house up during Eid, and complete strangers are invited in to have some food."

"Wow – that's pretty cool."

"Yes – and it makes us aware. When I have an Open House, I always make sure that there are enough vegetarian dishes, because I know the Hindus coming will not eat meat. And, when others invite us, they always make sure there is *halal* meat for us to eat – we are sensitive to each other's diets too."

"I like the concept," I said. "I wish we had this in America."

At the mention of my country she broke into a sneer.

"So it sounds like you are not too big a fan of the U.S.?" I said.

"Well, I think their nature is self-righteous. They are about preservation of their own culture and expansion of their own political hegemony. They are not about sharing, which is what our concept is about. Don't misunderstand me, Mohammed – we are not perfect here. We have had many problems with race in the past. But, our heart is good – the heart of our country is pure. It is not so with America, I think."

"You do not think America is good? How can you say that? Look at World War II. Look at Afghanistan. These places are better off because Americans came and spilled their blood there." I surprised myself with my defense of America, but being on the road had made me sensitive to America hating.

"We do not think that the wars America fights are about anything but money or Israel," she said defiantly. "Any good that may come is not the point of the war– it is a byproduct. We see their collaboration with Israel, and their shared imperial values with Israel. We see from the Palestinian issue that there is a link between the non-resolution of that situation and the alliance between the U.S. and Israel. The U.S. has the capability to make a stronger stand than the one they make now, and the fact that they refuse to do that shows they have some shared agenda with Israel. And apart from preservation of their political hegemony, they also want to enrich themselves by plundering wealth from other countries. I think that a lot of Malaysians feel that the war against Iraq is little more than a war to liberate oil and make Israel feel good about themselves. Remember – in the first Gulf War Saddam threw missiles at Israel, and they have always wanted him out since then. So here, we see these things, and it makes the war have very little credibility."

She suddenly stopped her tirade and yelled to the front seat. "Tariq – this is our exit!"

We were speeding down on a freeway and the driver had to cross two lanes quickly to get to the exit. Safely into suburban KL, we went down a street lined with cafes and shops. It looked like we were in an affluent part of town. After a few more miles down the road we stopped, and Hannaziera had me carry two baskets inside with her.

The real estate office was big, but most of the desks and chairs behind the reception desk were empty. Hannaziera motioned me to put the baskets down on a table near the door before engaging the receptionists in conversation. While they talked, I studied a model that was sitting on another table near the entrance – it was of a massive development project, filled with homes and condos and commercial space. The model had been done in great detail – little couples were walking their tiny dogs hand in hand and they had even drawn some artwork on the sides of the proposed mosque to show how it might eventually look. The scale of the project seemed huge and ambitious, and as I looked at it I became even more impressed with this small nation.

"This is their main project – it will take them one year to build it," said Hannaziera, who had come up behind me.

"It is very impressive – where will it be?"

"Right there – look," she said, pointing across the street to fields and jungle outcroppings. "This firm has built some of the best neighborhoods in all of KL – this one will be nice too. Come on – let's go get some lunch."

We headed out and Tariq took us back to the main drag, dropping us off in front of a restaurant that Hannaziera remembered to be good. We got a table outside on the patio and ordered before getting back to the heavy discussion.

"So," I started, wanting to understand this dynamic woman a little more. "You have told me what you think of the U.S. But what about the Islamic world? Surely you can't believe that it is better than America?"

"Well," she began, "the Ummah is in chaos, especially in the Arab world. We see them trying to preserve their status quo - they are afraid to let go of their wealth, and that is why they are not making a stronger stand on the Palestinian issue. They wish to preserve their status as rulers in their prospective countries. They've gotten used to wealth, and I don't think they want to compromise it. The Palestinians are Arabs - they are closer to the Arabs than anyone else in the world. But the reason their brothers have failed to come to their aid is because of wealth - they don't want to lose it. They don't know how to live without it."

"You are talking about the ruling Arab governments, right?"

"The lower Arab classes have probably been dissatisfied with their governments for a long time. There have been uprisings in the past, though scarce. I think Osama bin Laden, if he does exist, the first thing he should do, because he is a Saudi citizen, is not to bomb the twin towers but to topple the Saudi government, because that is the root of all evil in that region."

"So, you are not sure if Osama bin Laden exists? This is not the general viewpoint - in fact, most people believe he exists and that he was responsible for the attacks of September 11th," I said.

"Of course, the events have allowed the media to manipulate images as much as they want. As far as the West is concerned, it has really given Islam a bad name. The media has shown it as a terrorist act, and they have linked terrorism to Islam. But here in Malaysia, we also like to look at the causes that lead to such things."

Our food came, and Hannaziera took a break to take a few bites before continuing.

"A few weeks before 9/11, we were watching T.V. and saw pleas by Palestinian leaders for international help to aid them in the aggressions being committed against them by Israel. But of course not much was being done. I remember one Palestinian minister, while they were showing the bombings, said 'If this is not war then I do not know what is.' So you can really feel the genuine distress being felt by the Palestinians. While you watched that, you had a general feeling that something needed to be done. For a lot of us, we see 9/11 as that desperate act – done only because people have been suffering for much too long. If it was committed by Muslims, then it was probably a desperate act to bring attention to the Palestinian issue. However, it could be other things. It could also be a plot by the West - I don't discount that. It justifies the actions they have taken thus far, and it allows them to insert troops into whatever country they want. Because, before 9/11 it was hard to justify direct U.S. intervention into Muslim countries, but now it is much easier to gain European support for such interventions. America has certainly benefited from the attacks – don't you think? Well, at least the military has – can you imagine how much money they have made in the last few years?"

"I must say, Ms. Hannaziera, you do not seem very optimistic. Do you believe that Islam and the West can coexist in a peaceful world? Are we in a zero sum game between the two?"

She munched some rice and thought over the question a bit before responding. "I think that humans are, by nature, very adaptable. They can adapt to their environment. I have not traveled to the West much, but I don't see that much animosity towards Muslims in Europe. I think that Muslims have a higher burden, to show to other non-Muslims what is the proper way to live, according to Islamic tenets. Because, after all, we are the chosen people on this Earth."

"I thought that was what the Jews called themselves."

"Of course - I don't deny that. During Prophet Moses' time, they were the chosen people because they were monotheistic. Islam exists in many facets according to time. During Prophet Moses' time, they were Muslims because they believed in one God. We believe in the earlier prophets - in fact, it is mandatory for us to believe in them. So, basically, everyone who believes in one God is a Muslim."

"You are talking about the concept of the People of the Book?"

"Yes, but some of the books were distorted because of politics. Religion at that time gave dominance over other people. The Jews, for example, were able to gain dominance over the other populations by virtue of being People of the Book - they were literate and had more knowledge. Religion gave them a tool to dominate over others. Islam, however, is the perfect religion, and it is our duty to show others the right path."

I pressed her. "Islam is the perfect religion because, in the timeline of the prophets God sent to Earth, it was last, most complete, and its book was not tampered with, right?"

"Of course. And we have to persevere if the non-Muslims need more time to understand. We have to be patient."

"So your answer to my original question would be that Islam and the West can coexist because humans are adaptable, but since Islam is the most complete message it will eventually take over?"

"It is possible. But, eventually, the best one will win - Islam."

"So, you believe there is only one right answer for mankind?"

"Well, as a Muslim I must say Islam. The way that Islam should be portrayed is - we must highlight the universal values, meaning that anything that is good is Islamic. We cannot be so quick to brand things as Islamic and un-Islamic. For example, in Malaysia, the Chinese immigrants in the 19th century came here as miners and traders - they were mostly working in the tin mines. Malaysia was rich in tin, and the British were colonizing us and reaping the wealth from the tin mines. They brought many Chinese and Indians to work the mines, but mostly Chinese. Most of the Chinese who came were from the poorest provinces of China, and there used to be many social problems. Many of the Chinese were part of organized crime, and crime, abduction, extortion, and gambling were rampant. And, there were frequent gang fights between the rival Chinese gangs. They brought so many problems here, but over the years, because of their interactions with the Malays, they have acquired some of the Malay values - like tolerance, like patience, like the lackadaisical attitude," she laughed before continuing. "Which is good to a certain extent. So now, the Chinese here get along very well with each other and everyone else in Malaysia, although they may still have differences with mainland Chinese or Hong Kong Chinese. And Malay values, of course, are very influenced by Islam, because most Malay are Muslims. So you see - they are a more softer version of the Chinese. They still retain their culture, but they have become more tolerant, because they have taken our Islamic values."

"So, is the one right answer the Malay way?"

"No no - I don't believe that. What I am saying is that we should highlight the universal values which don't contravene *Sharia* (Islamic law) and are accepted by everyone as good. Basically, anything that is good and benefits society, no matter what society it comes from. Anything that is good and doesn't contradict Sharia is Islamic."

I found this woman fascinating. She was articulate and resolute in her beliefs, a tiny lady in a hijab speaking forcefully about politics and religion to a stranger over lunch at a sidewalk restaurant.

"You obviously believe very deeply in Islam. What would you say to those who would claim that Islam is oppressive to woman?" I asked.

"Well, in most Islamic countries it is not religion that prevails. So you see, the treatment of women is really a manifestation of thousands of years of culture. In the Arab world, women have always been second-class citizens – long before the arrival of Islam, women had no rights in their barbarian culture. But here in Malaysia, women play a vital role in the family - we are very much respected. We even have a few states where women are very much leaders of the whole group. For example, in the state of Negeri Sembilan, there is a culture where women are leaders of the tribe. When you marry into their culture, all the land goes to the woman - the man gets none. And in Kelantan, traditionally women are the ones who always bring in the money."

"And what do the men do?"

Hannaziera let out a big laugh before answering. "They sit in the coffee shop and talk politics. So, we have certain states where such cultures are prevalent, where women are very strong and in some cases in control. So, we benefit from our culture - the men are used to seeing women like this. We are completely liberated as women. But, our religion makes us feel comfortable with our role as women. We are feminists in one sense, in that we need to have our independence, but we are not feminists in the Western sense because we know our limitations, and we are comfortable with them."

I had never heard a feminist viewpoint like this and decided to ask more. "What are your limitations, as a woman?"

"Limitations in terms of roles, of responsibilities. I mean, we take the responsibility of bringing income to the family, but we relish our role as mothers. If there is an emergency, family always comes first. We don't view this as a sacrifice. It is very important to be comfortable being a woman - comfortable with who you are. Because, in the West there is the possibility that if a woman puts her family first she may think that she is making a big sacrifice. But when you have Islam as your guide, then you are comfortable with your limitations - which role should take priority. We have no questions on that."

We both fell silent for a bit, reflecting on our conversation while finishing off the last of our meal. Hannaziera signaled for the check, and when it came she would not hear of me paying anything.

After hooking back up with the car and Tariq, we delivered two more Chinese New Year gift baskets for Hannaziera's law firm – one to an accountant's office and one to a software firm. Afterwards, she took me to see a few of KL's most famous sites. Independence Square in the center of town, where she told me of Malaysia's independence from the British in the 1950s (they were one of the only colonies that gained freedom completely through negotiation, without violence). Little India, where rows and rows of tailors stood side by side with tourist shops and mosques. Hannaziera insisted on buying me a traditional Malay outfit at one of the shops – a pale blue wedding suit that I would never wear but accepted at her insistence. After taking me through Chinatown and back to the Golden Triangle, we stopped for coffee at a small place not far from my hotel and chatted for a little while longer.

"So tell me, Mohammed – what is it that made you travel so far and see so much?"

"I just wanted to meet my fellow Muslims, and to understand the Ummah better."

She sipped her coffee and gave me a knowing nod. "I think, if you don't mind me saying, that this trip was your destiny."

"How do you mean?"

"Well – I believe that God has given us all a path – a destiny that we must follow. It is not set in stone – we can of course do whatever we want because we have free will. But, if we are up to the challenge, then it is our mission to fulfill our God-given destiny."

"So what is your destiny?" I asked.

"Mine? Well, mine is to be the strongest mother I can be – to be a shining example to my children as to what you can accomplish in this world if you really try. I am a mother of five, I am a lawyer, I am teaching myself Arabic, I help other women to get into universities and to get good jobs. This is my destiny – it is not sexy, not exciting. But it is real, and I believe it is important. But you – you have been given an amazing chance. You can learn, and then you must teach – you must teach them the truth about Islam and the right path. Only you can do it – you are from there, and you speak their language. And they need it so bad – they are in desperate need of Islam."

"Well – I don't know about that. They seem to be pretty happy with what they have now."

"Hogwash! What they have now is capitalism, which pollutes their souls and destroys their hearts. And then they have what they call Christianity, which is nothing but a farce and a lie." She said this with a grin, knowing that I would press her further.

"What do you mean?"

"I mean just what I said. The Christians have been living a lie since the day their religion was born. Their legends and stories are the result of politics – they do not know what God truly intended for them. They lost their message before it even got started. Have you ever wondered about their concept of 'the original sin'?"

"Not really."

"Well – it is what their whole faith is based on, and it is quite ridiculous, if you think about it. The Christians believe that God came down in the form of Jesus Christ, and that he was killed for all of humanity's sins. So, all you need to do is swear allegiance to Jesus as God and then all will be forgiven. I mean, a man could murder and pillage – he could rape and he could plunder, and then on his death bed swear his belief in Jesus and be magically absolved. What kind of religion is that? How could a religion give someone such an escape clause? The whole point of religion is to bring you closer to your Creator, to strive every day to become a better person, in anticipation of your Judgment once the end comes. But these Christians – their doctrine is so twisted. Man is born bad? I cannot believe that. I do not believe in original sin."

"But doesn't Islam say that they are God's people?"

"Yes, because Jesus truly was a prophet. We believe in him – we believe he was one of God's greatest prophets. But, he was killed by his own people – the Romans killed him, and then when they realized that they had killed such a great man, they invented this whole thing about original sin, to justify their own actions. Within a hundred years of his death the whole Roman Empire was converted to Catholicism – they could not have done that if they had had no reason for killing him in the first place. So, they concocted this story so that they would be off the hook for killing their own prophet – and to make it even better, they made Jesus into God. The concept of the trinity goes against the fundamental belief of monotheism – that there is only one God. They did this all because of politics – they would not have survived unless they could justify their actions."

"But, Islam was born amidst politics as well, wasn't it?"

"Of course – any great religion is born with politics, because the truth of the prophet has such power that it mobilizes huge masses and makes it impossible for the current rulers to rule without acknowledging the religion. But, our religion was the last – we had the last prophet, and God tried to circumvent the problem of politics by giving us the Qu'ran, straight from His own mouth. Our holy book was recorded almost immediately after Prophet Mohammed's death, and so it survived the politics that invariably arose as Islam began to conquer the world. Of course, the politics caused all sorts of other problems – Sunnis, Shias, wars, *fitnas* – all of this affected our religion, but we have always had the truth of God's words in the Qu'ran, and no one can ever take that away from us."

Hannaziera glanced at her watch and abruptly stood up.

"It's time for me to go – I have to get home to my children. I lead them in Qu'ranic studies in the late afternoon."

"Oh, okay. Thank you so much for spending time with me."

"No – thank you, Mohammed. You will be in my prayers – I hope you fulfill your destiny. We are all counting on you and your brothers in the West."

With that, she signaled to Tariq and he pulled up, whisking her away into the KL evening and leaving me to finish my coffee and ponder my introduction to the liberated Muslim women of Malaysia.

Chapter 20

Freebird

I spent another couple of days in KL, writing and walking around and generally enjoying myself. The equatorial weather and the beauty of the city were intoxicating, and KL quickly shot near the top of my favorite cities in the world list. It was exotic and accessible, modern and traditional all at once, and I could see why YuMa loved it so.

As I considered why Malaysia could do this and why places like Pakistan could not, I came up with a theory – with two large minorities in the Hindu and Chinese, it was almost as if Malaysia was the only Muslim country in the modern world that was forced to address religious differences in a practical manner. The minorities within the country kept the Muslim majority honest, and as a result the focus of the government fell more to economic and civic advancements and less to enforcement of religion.

This was, and is, the source of successful democracy, in my opinion. You must have large segments of society who have large differences – this widens the pool of ideas and allows for greater study of the problems facing the society. In the Islamic world, most of the countries have a shallow pool to draw from, as there is little or no internal opposition to the various monarchies, dictatorships, and sham democracies that line its modern map. The free exchange of information between disparate groups of people is what creates a genuine consensus for the common good.

I left KL and over the next twenty-four hours traveled up the Malay Peninsula, on buses and trains, slowly making my way to Koh Ngai. Along the way I was becoming more and more excited – through the night, I rode a jungle train through Malaysia's National Forest and couldn't sleep, thinking only that the trip was almost over and wondering what I may do next. How do you follow up a trip like this with anything that isn't a letdown? The images of the cities and people I had experienced raced through my head, making me dizzy, and my wanderlust growled at the notion of going back to San Francisco, and back to my old life, within the next few weeks.

The train ended at the Thai border, which I walked across, cleared customs, and then caught another train, this time to the city of Trang on the Southwestern coast of Thailand. A bus and a boat got me to Koh Lanta in the mid-afternoon, the biggest island near Koh Ngai and the launching point for all boats going there. As I progressed further into the islands, the islander vibe started taking over, and things took on a slower pace. I recognized it from time I had spent in Hawaii – no matter where you are in the world, islanders always have the same chill, one-with-their-surroundings way about them. They move on island time, and I was quick and happy to adapt back to it.

The docks at Ban Saladdin, the small fishing village that served as Koh Lanta's main port, were packed with touts, trying to get you to their resort and promising the best and cheapest accommodations. Most of them seemed desperate, but one guy stood apart, with wild dreads standing straight up circa early Marley. He was dressed like a Lower East Side hipster in faded jeans, reflective police shades, and a Rolling Stones tour shirt straight from the 70s. I went over to him and he showed me a book with pictures of his resort – the Lanta Marine Village. The place looked nice, and he promised that there was a boat going to Koh Ngai from his resort in the morning that I could take for the bargain basement price of 200 bhat, or about five dollars.

I said yes and introduced myself to my new host. His name was Josh, and he and his family owned the resort, which had been operational for just under a year. I waited while Josh tried to get a few more people for his bungalows, watching the action on the street and keeping to the shade, away from the hot Thai sun. The island obviously had a strong Muslim influence – women in hijabs were zipping by on little scooters and most of the shopkeepers wore the same Muslim hats and shirts that I had seen the men wearing in KL. I asked Josh about

Islam on the island, and he informed me that the place was 99% Muslim, as was he.

"But – we are nice Muslims, man. We are mellow, yeah?" He smiled as he said this, and lowered his shades and winked at me. His eyes were blood red, and I noted that he probably had more in common with Bob than just the dreads.

"That's cool," I said, "I'm a mellow Muslim too."

"Right on man – Salaam Alaikum."

"Walaikum Salaam."

After fifteen minutes another boat came in and Josh was able to snag two couples and a single British girl to go along with me and we piled into his truck for the ride to his resort. The truck was a *songthaw*, covered in back with a metal shell and benches along both sides of the bed for us to sit on. We piled in and began the journey – Josh told us that Lanta Marine was on Kantiang Beach, which was a forty-five minute ride down to the south of the island. The road quickly turned from pavement to dirt, and the six of us in the back were continually thrown from side to side as Josh swerved to avoid the huge potholes that were ubiquitous on the road. We finally arrived, a bit harrowed and bruised, and I scored a bungalow with a beautiful view of the crystal blue bay, perched high on a hilltop.

The long journey had tired me out and I crashed for the rest of the day, only awakening when confronted with a full scale mosquito attack at dusk. I showered and went down to the resort's restaurant – a beautiful teakwood deck that was situated amongst the jungle on the hill, with flags fluttering in a cool breeze and sun-burnt patrons sipping tropical drinks and lounging on cushions and benches. I ordered some pad thai and tom yum soup and slowly chowed down, soaking up the breeze and the holiday atmosphere of the place. Next to the deck was the resort's watering hole – a small wood-carved sign announced it as the Shroom Bar. I spied Josh hanging there, with a mixed white and Thai crowd, and made my way over after my meal was done.

Josh was very accommodating, introducing me to the crowd and buying me a Lucky Stripe without asking. I settled down and struck up a conversation with a pretty girl named Christina from Germany – she had been island-hopping in Thailand for three months and regaled

me with tales of full moon X raves and giant waterfalls. The night
progressed quickly from there – Josh leading us down the hill to the
beach, where we came upon the Why Not Bar and watched fire dancers
perform to a huge sound system pumping eurotechno, slowly but
surely getting more and more buzzed and silly. At around 2 AM the
system was shut down and a guitar materialized, which Josh strummed
expertly, alternately singing Marley tunes and Thai rock songs. I was
able to commandeer it and played Peaceful Easy Feeling, for which the
Thai part of the crowd went nuts, as apparently the Eagles still ruled
there. We spent the rest of the night trading songs by the fire pit, losing
complete track of time and feeling as though there was not a problem
anywhere in the world.

The next morning I awoke to a rapping on my door – Josh had sent
one of the errand boys to let me know the boat for Koh Ngai was leaving
in thirty minutes. I showered quickly and put on my pack, all the while
feeling a bit guilty for my indulgences of the night before. What kind
of Muslim traveler was I, I thought, when I so easily succumbed to the
sauce whenever it was offered? Hadn't that got me into enough trouble
on Palolem?

The boat was packed with European tourists setting out for a
snorkeling trip to the four surrounding islands of Koh Lanta – Koh Ngai
was the first stop, and I would be dropped off there. Before leaving I
had asked Josh about accommodations on the small island, and he told
me not to worry – there was one family-owned bungalow operation
on the main beach and they almost always had open spots. We set out
on the aqua-marine water, the Euros crowded under the covered part
of the boat while I made my way to the back to sit with the captain and
first mate in the back. The captain's name was Anam – and he had been
part of our crew of revelers on the beach the night before. A quiet man,
he provided one word answers to any and all queries, and I soon just
settled into a nook on the back bow, content to soak up the sun and feel
the mist of the gentle ocean spray.

The ride took about half an hour, and I drifted off at the end until
Anam gently shook my leg and pointed to the beach we were nearing.
My jaw dropped – it was the single most beautiful place I had ever seen.
The sand was a fine, crystal white, sloping gradually down into the

bright blue-green water that gently lapped the shore. As we beached the boat and disembarked, I turned around to take in the view – directly in front of us were two gigantic granite outcroppings, sticking straight up out of the ocean and majestically dominating the horizon. Behind the beach was virgin jungle – coconut trees and tall palms climbing a small hilltop. The whole island seemed tiny – the beach we were on composed the whole northern shore, and it looked as though walking around the circumference of the whole island would not take more than thirty minutes.

I took a bit of time to take in the beauty before going to the open-air restaurant on the beach that also served as the front desk for the bungalow operation, named Koh Ngai Village. The young girl at the desk told me that only one room was open – it was in a dorm like hall they had built recently, and although no one was in it yet, they could not guarantee my privacy through the length of my stay. I took it, dropped my stuff off and changed immediately into my trunks. Swimming in that beautiful water was the only thing on my mind.

I passed the afternoon and evening on the beach, completely content to relax in such a beautiful scene. The resort was sparsely populated, and with a much different crowd than that of Lanta Marine the night before. This place was less touristy, with more Thai families on vacation than Euros freaking to techno. As twilight approached, I showered and went to the dining area to eat solo again. The server, a short wiry young guy with a ponytail, befriended me in broken English.

"Hello," he said hesitantly.

"Hi – can I see a menu?"

"Ah – menu. Yes yes," he said, slightly bowing his head as he backed up before turning and running to get a menu from the concierge desk.

"Menu," he said as he handed it to me.

The menu was surprisingly expansive for such a small island restaurant in the middle of nowhere – one could choose American, Italian, Chinese, Indian, and Thai dishes from the ten pages it covered. I was a bit overwhelmed, but my waiter did not detect this. He stood there, smiling at me and with pen at the ready.

"Um – can you recommend anything?"

He furrowed his brow and looked confused. "Me, no English good."

"Oh, okay. Um – What food good?" I asked, half pantomiming and shifting into basic communication mode.

He raised his hand in a shrug, smiling and bowing his head a bit all the while. Seeing that verbal communication would be tough, I fell to full miming, pointing to the menu, then to him, and then to my mouth. I finished with a shrug of my own to signify my question, and after a couple of run-throughs of this routine he finally understood, grabbing the menu and pointing out a seafood dish under the "Chef's Special Thai Food" section.

"Aw Mouk. Is good – I eat. Best. Best from us." This amount of English staggered him, and he stood back and smiled at his accomplishment.

"Okay," I said, warming up to his character, "What you name?"

"Noc. My name Noc. You?"

"Mo."

"Oh – Mo. Nice to meet you." Noc then hurried away to place my order, and when he came back fifteen minutes later I was not disappointed. The dish consisted of a bowl fashioned from banana plant leaves, with crabmeat steamed and seasoned with spices and herbs inside. I scarfed it down quick, much to the delight of Noc, who came by frequently to make sure I was enjoying myself.

I finished and left him a big tip before heading back to turn in. I was anxious to get to sleep and see if Khizr would come. But, my anticipation betrayed me, and I lay awake in my bed, unable to drift off. As I lay in the cot, tossing and turning, I thought of all the people and places I had been and I thought about the fallacy of absolutism – that we are good and they are evil, and that there is only the right way and the wrong way. If I had learned anything, it was that there were many ways, all valid and all entirely capable of bringing security and happiness. Eventually I did fall asleep, but not before the image of Cha Cha made an appearance in my head, looking at me with the kind of concern that people reserve for their brothers and making me feel a little guilty somewhere deep inside.

Chapter 21

Emerald Cave

The Green Man didn't come to me that night, or for the next week. But, it didn't faze me one bit – Koh Ngai was the most beautiful place I had ever been, and I spent my time relaxing, exploring every nook of the tiny island and making friends with the Koh Ngai Village staff.

Noc became my main man – he had only recently arrived from the mainland to work at the resort and earn money for his family back home. He was about eighteen with a starving mind – he asked me questions about everything and wanted to know all about the States and what it was like to live there. His main concern was learning English, and I wrote down the ABCs and started teaching him to read during long afternoons hanging in the shade out of the increasingly hot sun. In return for my help, Noc showed me how to play *takrow*, which was a huge sport in Thailand and played with religious fervor on the island.

Takrow is basically like volleyball, except you use your feet instead of your hands and have a lower net. It was a blast, and each morning I joined in the staff games towards the back of the resort. Some of the guys were incredible – they could even spike the ball by jumping high enough to kick the ball straight down over the net. I was nowhere near that level, but I became a respectable player (due to some transferable soccer skills) and a fixture on the court.

On my eighth day on the island, after many guests had come and gone, I had endeared myself to the staff enough where I was offered a free boat ride to Emerald Cave, which stood just inside the granite island that dominated our view from the beach. Noc offered to take me on the boat, as some other guests had rented it for the day and he was to be their guide.

The island's name was Koh Muk, and as we dropped anchor at the bottom of the sheer granite wall the place seemed even more impressive up close than it did from our view on the beach. A cave was at the bottom of the cliff, and we all strapped on life-vests and swam into it, Noc and the boat's driver sandwiching us to make sure no one got lost. Entering the cave was like entering a movie – it was hard to believe that the place was real. Somehow, light reflected into the cave and lit up the granite below the water, making the water come alive with a brilliant green color that almost blinded the eye. Emerald cave was the perfect name for it – swimming in it was like floating in emerald luminescence. We floated for a while, content to hang in the absurdly beautiful site, before continuing through the cave and into an opening on the other side. It brought us out onto a small beach, surrounded for 360 degrees by granite walls – it was like the center of the huge granite island had been hollowed out and replaced with a private tropical beach paradise. All of us oohed and ahhhed, and we were given an hour to lounge on the beach before swimming back to the boat and then heading back to Koh Ngai.

I thanked Noc profusely for letting me see such an amazing place before walking back to the dorm, my head truly swimming from the beauty that surrounded me. If God had intended a heaven on earth, I thought, then this had to be it.

It was in just such a state that I walked into my room and found someone in it, sitting quietly in my chair and smiling at me with that knowing smile.

"Yo Mo – wassup," said Khizr.

"G!" I fumbled. "How... I mean, what are you doing here man?"

"Whaddya mean? I told you I'd see you on Koh Ngai."

"Yeah, but I figured it would be in my dreams – you know, literally. I didn't know you'd come here for real."

"Even in your dreams I am there for real, but this time I've come in the waking state. My place isn't far from here and I figured that it would be nice to have our last meeting face to face. You know, so you'll remember it all better." He got up and came over to me, giving me a bear hug and then knocking fists with me.

"Where's your place?"

"It's not far – just scoot through the Straits of Malacca and you're almost there – it's near the Great Barrier Reef. I've got a Superman type set-up out there, only instead of an ice cave I've got a tropical paradise – a small island nobody knows about. Kinda like this place, I guess, but smaller."

"Sounds sweet man."

"Yup – when you've been around as long as me, you know where the good deals are, you know?" At this he scoffed and slapped his knee. "Like you – I knew you were a good deal the first time I talked to you."

"I don't know about that, man. I don't know if I'm that good a deal for you. I'm not pure, G – not pure at all. Meeting all these people, talking about all this Islamic stuff – I've felt like a hypocrite. I'm not a good Muslim, man. I don't know why you guys asked me to do this – I don't see how my trip has helped anything."

Khizr got up and took off his green robe – underneath he was wearing long bermuda shorts, flip-flops, and a t-shirt that gave the hand sign for hang loose. He smiled and said, "You'll think of something to make it all worth it. Wanna take a walk?"

I followed him out the door and we settled into a slow pace, ambling along for a bit without saying anything. I started telling him about Malaysia and the Islamic feminist I had met, and he listened with great interest and amusement. I talked for a while, but my stories ran out and we were silent. I waited for him to kick some knowledge – the suspense was killing me.

As we walked I looked at him, out of his robe and in the broad daylight. He had the body of a man in his fifties who kept himself in good shape – thick arms and legs and an iron gut. He reminded me of what guys look like at that age who have been surfing their whole life, or at least from behind. His face betrayed him – the lines were thick and numerous, and his emerald eyes sparkled with infinite wisdom. He must have known this, because he kept a bushy white beard that seemed incongruous with his body. When you saw him in his full green robe he looked much more the part of a 3,000 year old man than he did in t-shirts and shorts.

We had almost done the circumference of the island before he started. "Mo," he began, "being a good Muslim is an extremely subjective judgment. Good Muslims come in all shapes and sizes – some of the best Muslims I have ever known were actually Christians. Ha!" Khizr laughed at his joke and continued. "It's true. Being a Muslim has to do with what's in your heart, and the Big Man upstairs always knows the real deal – He specializes in the human heart. Tell me – what have you done on your trip?"

"Been a lot of places, talked to a bunch of people."

"No – be more specific. Tell me what you did, in order."

I thought back. "Well – the first mission was to the Kairouine in Morocco, where I was to give prayers, which I did. In fact, I re-learned them there."

"Yes – you re-learned the Islamic prayer there. Then what?"

"Right. And then the second mission was to Turkey, and I learned about the Mevlana and about the Sufis."

"Yup – you took a pilgrimage to Konya."

"And then it was on to Pakistan, where I had Ramadan in a Muslim country for the first time. And then I met the Wahabbis in India, and then on to here. You're the one that gave me the mission, right? You know where I went. Look, G – what's the point? You already know everything – why do you even need me? What am I to do with all this?" As I said this I gestured to everything around us – the powder blue sky and magnificent horizon spreading out before us. I still felt unworthy of it all.

Khizr smiled. "Ahh – the impatience of youth! You have it my friend. All the answers are within. What you seek will come, in good time. But I must warn you – it may not be realized for a long time, and it will take much work to cash it all in. I've got faith that you'll figure it out – you'll think of something I'm sure. You are embarked on a lifelong journey, which does not end here. Only my part ends here."

"What do you mean, G? This is it for us?"

"I'm afraid so, Mo. You see – the trip I've sent you on was designed for a reason. I wanted you to understand your religion, from every which way. I did not want you speaking about it from a position of ignorance, as this is one of the main problems of God's children today. People everywhere talk and represent like they know the truth, when in reality they have never even met the other side, or know at all what he's about. So, I sent you to Morocco to do your prayers, I sent you to Turkey to do a pilgrimage, I sent you to Pakistan for your fast and to India for your charity. And now, I have brought you here, a place that is unparalleled in its beauty, a shining example of the beauty and splendor of the one true power – God."

Khizr stopped and spread his green robe on the sand for us to sit on. From our position on the beach, the sun was setting just beyond Koh Muk and the clouds in the sky were being lit up with brilliant purples, oranges, and pinks.

"Do you know your *kalama*?" asked Khizr.

"Um, do you mean the saying 'there is no God but God, and Mohammed is His messenger?"

"Yes. Now, sitting here in this paradise, is there any way that you could tell me that this perfection all around you – the perfection you feel inside your own heart right now – is all by chance?"

"No – I guess not G. But I've always felt like I believed in God."

"Yes – you have. But I need to state this, as this is the last mission of your trip – the acceptance of one true power. You see - your trip signifies religion's most important traits – prayer, pilgrimage, fast, charity, and belief. How you perform all of these things can be up for debate – God has devised many religions, and they all were supposed to be tailored to certain peoples and certain cultures. But they all are built on these principles. In Islam's case, they have come to be known as the five pillars. And I have sent you on this trip to understand the five pillars from a Muslim's perspective, through Muslims from all over the world. And do you feel as though now you do?"

I thought about it – about the incredible spirituality of praying with thousands of people at the Kairouine, of the awe I felt at being in the presence of Rumi, at the cleanliness I felt during my fasts at YuMa's house, of how my charity to Cha Cha's family could potentially be a life changing event for their entire clan. I thought about all the people I had spoken with along the way, and how gentle and accommodating most of them had been.

"I think I'm starting to," I said. "But, I thought going to Mecca to perform hajj was one of the pillars?"

"Yes, it is. I substituted Rumi's tomb for this. The Muslim should go to Mecca when he has reconciled within himself his true beliefs, and you are not yet ready, so I sent you on an alternate pilgrimage instead. Mo – this trip has been your treasure – this is your gift. You have what very few people in the world have – you can communicate between East and West with confidence and clarity. That is why this gift was bestowed upon you. I am confident that you will use this gift wisely, my friend, because Lord knows we need all the help we can get."

We looked out into the setting sun together, watching it blip over the horizon before he sighed a contented sigh. I thought I detected a green flash when the sun vanished, and when I looked to Khizr his eyes flashed mischievously.

"I love sunsets, man. The planets and stars – they get my vote for God's greatest creation. We humans are just a little too mixed up for my tastes. The solar systems, though, those are perfect. But, that isn't what God thinks, and He's the only one that matters, you know? We've only got one of Him, so we've got to keep Him happy, right?" Khizr winked at me and got up, brushing off sand from his bermudas and robe.

He started off before I could say anything, whistling to his dolphins and riding off into the ocean. Later I had a million questions for him, but right at the moment of truth I had been tongue-tied.

I never saw the Green Man again. His abrupt departure made more sense to me later on – I'm sure he wanted to avoid the inevitable muddling of his point. His last words were what stayed with me on that beach, and I sat there for the rest of the evening, thinking about where I'd been and where I needed to go next. And as the stars appeared one by one in the night sky, I wrapped my treasure of a trip around me, lay back and thanked God for letting me be alive.

THE END